W. Dunn

Last Plane from Uli

LAST PLANE FROM ULI

Charles Kearey

Holt, Rinehart and Winston

NEW YORK · CHICAGO · SAN FRANCISCO

To the honourable members of The Mile High Club
who rightly prefer to make love in the Heavens
and not war

this book is dedicated

Library of Congress Catalog Card Number: 72-78116
ISBN: 0-03-001396-8

First published in the United States in 1972

Printed in the United States of America

ACKNOWLEDGMENT

Shortly after the end of World War II I met Bill Fortuin, an ex-Spitfire pilot, for the first time. Later I had the pleasure of meeting him on numerous other occasions as our flying paths crossed, operating around Africa. Over the years I learned to know him well and we became friends.

Later our paths clashed, as opposed to crossing, when Bill flew for General Mobutu's *Force Aérienne Congolaise* whilst I flew for the opposition, Moishe Tshombe's Katangese Air Force. Meeting in Zurich after the conclusion of that little fracas we decided to write a book based on our experiences, but, like most good intentions the resolution never got past the talking stage.

Recently, shortly after the Biafran-Nigerian shemozzle, I was at Salisbury Airport one wet and windy night. I watched a charter plane come in flown by Bill Fortuin.

We drank and talked long into the night and Bill told me he had recently been flying for the Nigerian Federal Military Government, operating Czech L29 Delfin jets against the Biafran forces. It was about 2 A.M. when we definitely decided that this time we would get down to it and do a novel based on the background of the Nigerian-Biafran conflict. *Last Plane from Uli* is the outcome of our meeting that rainy night at Salisbury Airport.

The publishers have put my name on the cover, but full credit as my co-author must be given to Bill who sweated equally with me to complete the manuscript.

I have been asked if the story is true. My answer is 'No comment'. The reader has the privilege of deciding for himself how much truth is intertwined with the fiction. I am only prepared to admit that such places as Lagos and Kano do exist and that Bill flew Delfins.

5

CHAPTER ONE

I w a s bored with London. Holed up in my bedsitter at Russell Square, I bleakly considered the situation. Three months had elapsed since my contract with the Congolese Air Force had expired, and I had no intention of renewing it. Two and a half years in that maelstrom of murder and chaos was enough. With seventeen thousand dollars still in my Swiss numbered account there was no pressing urgency about finding another job. But the restlessness was there, and I wanted to feel a control column between my hands and fly again. Preferably abroad. The past two months had been freezing and I wanted no part of another English winter.

I picked up the aviation magazine and read the advertisement again. 'An experienced versatile pilot required. Twin-engine experience essential. Knowledge of African flying conditions a recommendation. This is a position for a man with initiative who can make decisions on spot. Reply Box B 1234 T.P. Dallas, USA.' The room suddenly dimmed and I went to the window. It had clouded up and a light drizzle was soaking the dead leaves in the park across the way. The dirty brown brick buildings shone wet and cold. That was the clincher. So I wrote to Box B1234 T.P. Dallas, and told the renter that I was an experienced twin- and four-engined pilot, with 10,600 flying hours chalked up behind me, four thousand odd in Abyssinia, Kenya, North Africa, and Italy with the South African Air Force, and the balance postwar with charter companies operating in Angola, Rhodesia, and the Sudan. Culminating in two and a half years of flying operations in

7

the Congo, firstly for Tshombe, and later for Mobutu's
Force Aérienne Congolaise.

I gave my bankers as reference and concluded my application with the remark that were I not able to make decisions on spot, I would not be alive and in a position to
reply to their advertisement.

I sealed the letter, struggled into my old Burberry and,
braving the cold heavy drizzle, posted my envelope at the
little post office round the corner.

Two weeks later I received the reply. Enclosed was a
first-class return ticket to Dallas, and a money order for
two hundred dollars. The letter was brief. It read :

> Aloysius P. Kelly,
> Oil Associates Inc.,
> 1214 Barbon Towers,
> Main Street,
> Dallas

Dear Mr Gibson,
With reference to your application, I believe that you are
the pilot I require.

Enclosed herewith, your return ticket to Dallas and expenses
to cover the trip.

Please report for interview to the above address at your earliest
convenience.

> Yours faithfully,
> A. KELLY (President)

I cabled I was leaving immediately, and twenty-four hours
later, I was standing in Main Street, Dallas, craning my
neck, like any rubber-necking sightseer, at the twenty-
seven-storied office block rearing skywards before me. Kelly
Oil Associates occupied four floors with the executive offices
at the top.

I stepped into the lift. 'Twenty-seventh floor, please,' I told the operator. The office that I stepped into was straight out of a Hollywood set. The receptionist, a smart woman dressed in a severely tailored suit, with a trim figure, was somewhere in her early thirties. She smiled pleasantly. 'Mr Gibson?'

'That's right. Good afternoon.'

She held out her hand. 'Welcome to Dallas, we've been expecting you. I'm Mrs Hurst, Mr Kelly's secretary.' She pressed a button on the intercom. 'Mr Kelly, Mr Gibson is here.' The intercom crackled back tersely. 'Mr Kelly will see you, sir. This way, please.'

I followed her through to Kelly's office; a large room with a picture window, Dallas sprawled beneath us. It was simply furnished with a heavily-carved antique writing-table with a single phone. Opposite, grouped around a large marble coffee-table, were four leather club easy-chairs. Otherwise, the room was bare.

Large photographs were scattered around the walls. Two were of offshore drilling rigs, the others oil derricks in various stages of erection.

Kelly came across the room to meet me, hand out-stretched. 'Mr Gibson,' he said, 'I'm pleased to meet you. Thank you for your prompt response to my letter.'

I shook his hand, his grip was firm. 'On the contrary, Mr Kelly, I must thank you.'

He smiled and nodded towards his secretary. 'That will be all, thank you, Mrs Hurst.'

Kelly pointed to one of the easy-chairs. 'Take a seat, please, Mr Gibson.'

'Thank you.'

I ran a quick check over him as he walked across the room. He was tall, almost six foot, in the middle fifties, powerfully built, and carrying about twenty pounds of excess weight. He probably topped two hundred and twenty pounds. His nose had been broken sometime and badly set. He had a tough square jaw and bushy eyebrows. As I lowered myself into the chair, cold blue eyes watched me appraisingly.

Kelly wasted no time. 'Mr Gibson, I've seen your qualifications and I must admit I arranged for a Washington security risk clearance on you before I sent for you.'

I raised an eyebrow. 'Presumably your CIA have confirmed that I'm no Commie. They ought to know. I certainly saw enough of them in the Congo.'

He smiled briefly. 'Don't get me wrong, Gibson. Oil is of such strategic importance that these "I" guys are forever breathing down our necks, whether we like it or not. You'll be doing an important job for me. I'd be a fool to hire you without first putting you under the microscope. Got the idea?'

'That's your privilege, Mr Kelly. I'll assume you wouldn't have sent for me if you weren't reasonably satisfied I was the man you wanted.'

'The report was satisfactory. You've apparently been around quite a bit.' He waved a stubby hand, 'OK, Mr Gibson, we've cleared the air, let's get down to cases.'

He paused. 'I haven't always operated in the United States. I've wild-catted in Java and Sumatra, and have three producing wells in Arabia. I've a team at the moment prospecting in Alaska.' He leaned towards me, 'But there's one area where I've never operated, Mr Gibson, and that's Africa. That's why you are here.'

'In what specific part of Africa do you intend operating, Mr Kelly?' I asked curiously.

He frowned. 'You've never flown for an oil company, have you?'

'No, sir.'

He nodded. 'I know damn well you haven't, or you'd never have asked such a question. Remember, Gibson, in the oil business we eat, drink, and sleep security. Any time anyone asks you a question about your work, think about it three times before you reply, and then tell them a goddam lie anyway.'

He stood up abruptly. 'Come and look at this.' He walked round his desk, pulled out a map from a drawer, and unfolded it; it was a one in four million Mercator projection of Africa that extended east to cover the Persian Gulf.

He ran his stubby finger down the west coast of Africa, beginning with Nigeria. 'New fields are being opened up here,' he said. He ran his finger farther down the coast over Cabinda and Angola, 'And here.'

He lifted his hand and slammed it down on the southern tip of Africa. 'In South Africa they are drilling intensively. They struck a large field of gas offshore near Port Elizabeth and, believe me, if there's gas, there's probably oil. But there's more to it than that. Look at the distances involved. Now that the Suez Canal is closed, we're hauling oil all the way from Arabia, around the Cape, to Europe. Paying through the nose for it too, you ask the Greek millionaires.' His finger moved to the top of the map. 'The first break came when the oil companies opened up Algeria. From here, across the Mediterranean to Europe, is a short haul. Trouble is, there's not enough oil coming out of these fields at present to meet the insatiable demand.'

He dropped his finger down again to the extreme south of the map. 'There's no doubt that there's oil in South Africa, but it will take a few years to map it and establish a reasonable production. In any event South Africa's fast-expanding economy will absorb the production of their first wells. So where does that leave us?' he looked up at me.

'The west coast?' I ventured.

'Correct. North of Luanda, in Portuguese Angola, the oil has been coming in now for two years. Also at Onitsha in Nigeria, and likewise in the Portuguese Cabinda Enclave, north of the Congo. Production is rising every month.'

The stubby finger thumped the map. 'This is the area I'm interested in. The west coast of Africa, and Nigeria in particular. French and Italian oil interests are already established there, and the British have a finger in the pie. A few years ago I could have taken options over this area at twenty dollars an acre, but those days have gone. In Africa they're playing a game of poker, the Italians, Americans, French and British, with stakes running into thousands of millions of dollars. Remember, the supply of petroleum being produced right at this moment, is barely sufficient to keep ahead of world demands.'

He looked at me sharply. 'Any idea what it is?'

'I couldn't even guess, Mr Kelly.'

'Forty million barrels a day. Thirty per cent of it comes from the Middle East, and with the British pulling out, the Indian Ocean is fast becoming a Russian lake. The Western world can no longer safely rely on the output of those fields, with the rapid expansion of Red influence in that area.'

He tapped the map. 'So what's the answer?' He looked at me. 'Let's get back to Nigeria.' The thick finger traced a circle. 'There are vast areas of potential oil-rich tracts of land here that have not yet been allocated.' The cold blue eyes looked at me. 'I want some of those tracts, Gibson. That's why you're here.'

'I follow you,' I said thoughtfully. 'But how do I fit into the picture?'

'I intend spending a lot of time in the near future in Western Africa. I want my own aircraft there and my own pilot. A pilot who can think as well as fly.' He paused. 'Do you know anything about the Aero Commander?'

'Only that it's generally acknowledged to be an efficient twin-engined, six-seven seater, executive transport.'

'That's what my advisers told me. I've bought one. You will go to the plant at Oklahoma, take delivery, fly it to Rome and wait there for instructions. I've an office

there. A woman runs it, Gisela Griffin. Report as soon as
you arrive in Rome, I'll meet you there as soon as I've
tidied up some business in Alaska. OK?'

'OK, Mr Kelly.'

He paused. 'You haven't said anything about salary. You
happy at fifteen hundred dollars a month?' he asked
abruptly.

'I'm happy.'

He shook his head. 'You're no businessman. With your
qualifications you're worth much more to me. If I get the
concessions I'll look after you. Let me give it some thought.
I'll write you confirming what I'm prepared to offer.
Mrs Hurst will advance whatever cash you require for your
flight to Rome. Miss Griffin will handle any financial
matters that may crop up over the operation of the aircraft.
I'll relay my instructions through her. Got the idea?'

'Yes, Mr Kelly.'

He studied me. 'She's an efficient woman. Surprisingly,
she's quite a looker.' He made a shape with his stubby
hands and grinned. Aloysius P. Kelly, despite his millions,
was still human.

He pressed a button on the desk and that was the end
of the interview. The door opened and the secretary came
in. 'Mrs Hurst,' he said. 'Please arrange Mr Gibson's flight
to Oklahoma City, and notify the factory that he will be
collecting the aircraft. Inform Miss Griffin that she'll
handle the financial arrangements when the plane arrives
in Rome.'

'Yes, Mr Kelly.'

He held out his hand. 'Well, it's over to you, Mr Gibson.
Get the plane to Rome and await instructions.'

'Thank you, sir,' and so we parted.

I followed Mrs Hurst into her office. She turned to me.
'Would you mind waiting or would you prefer to come
back in an hour?'

'I'll wait,' I said. I watched Kelly's Oil Associates Inc.

move efficiently into action. Telegrams were sent to the Aero Commander factory advising them of my arrival. The local air ticket agency was phoned, and a messenger arrived with the tickets within half an hour. Simultaneously, cables were drafted to Miss Griffin in Rome, setting out the details. In less than an hour, I'd collected a bulky envelope with the necesary tickets, 1,000 dollars in travellers' cheques, said goodbye to Mrs Hurst, and was back at my hotel.

At Oklahoma City, headquarters of the Aero Commander factory, it took me four hours to do a thorough conversion course on the aircraft. I doubted if there'd be any engineers in the territories where I'd be operating with experience of the Aero Commander, so it was essential that I familiarize myself with the aircraft. I did just that.

I pulled out on the morning of the fifth day, flying the northern route via Montreal, Gander, Iceland, and Prestwick, and so on to London. There I stopped over for two days and sorted out my personal affairs, then took off from Gatwick in a heavy rain squall for Ciampino Airport on the outskirts of Rome. The weather was bad and I flew from beacon to beacon culminating in a blind let-down at Ciampino. At the airport I handed the aircraft over to Aero Flotto for servicing, and caught a cab to town.

'Hotel Excelsior,' I told the driver. I'd stayed there three years previously. It was expensive but good. Situated on the Via Vittorio Veneto it was central, and in reasonable walking distance of Harry's Bar and Giuseppe's Cellar. After lunch I phoned Kelly's secretary. I'd wondered about Miss Gisela Griffin. I had reservations about Kelly's description. She was probably in her early thirties, with a severe hair style, efficient, and a dedicated career girl. At best a smarter edition of Mrs Hurst back in the Dallas office. I heard the click of the receiver being lifted.

'Pronto.' The Italian word carried a slight American accent.

'Miss Griffin?' I ventured tentatively.

'Speaking.'

'Good afternoon, John Gibson. I believe Head Office notified you I'd be flying in.'

'That's right, Mr Gibson, glad to hear from you. I expected you a couple of days ago.'

'I stayed over in London for two days to sort out my private affairs. It appears it may be some time before I get back to the United Kingdom.'

'It's quite possible, Mr Gibson.' The voice was crisp, the American accent very slight. 'Where are you staying?'

'I've checked in at the Excelsior.'

'Oh!' There was a slight pause. 'I hope you're finding it comfortable.' Maybe it was imagination, but I seemed to pick up a slightly sarcastic inflection.

'The best is good enough,' I said easily. 'I'm quite sure Mr Kelly wouldn't expect his personal pilot to stay anywhere else.'

There was a short silence. Her voice was cool. 'When do I see you, Mr Gibson?'

'Whenever you like.'

'Let me see, it's now three o'clock. I have an appointment at five. Could you be here at four, Mr Gibson?'

'Sure.'

'Do you have my address?'

'Yes, Mrs Hurst in Dallas gave it to me.'

'That's fine. Please ring for me when you arrive.'

'I'll be there. Four o'clock, thank you.'

I allowed fifteen minutes for the cab and the timing was just right. At five minutes to four the taxi turned into a quiet cul-de-sac, closed off by a five-storied block of flats. There was a jungle of shrubs and rubber plants in the foyer, and the building had that expensive well-heeled look about it. A plain engraved card, at the top of the list in the foyer, read. 'No. 5. Miss Gisela Griffin, Kelly Oil Associates Inc.' I put my thumb on the number five button. Within seconds the indicator clicked on. A point in Miss Griffin's favour, she was punctual. I waited curiously. The lift stopped, the door opened, and she stepped out.

I'm six foot and this girl was well up to my shoulder, so she was five foot seven or eight. I saw soft full lips in a thin high-cheekboned face. The eyes were hazel, almost yellow, and widely spaced. Her nose was straight and finely chiselled. The body, with all the curves in the right places, fitted snugly into a white tailored suit, and the ankles and legs were perfect.

No youngster this, I registered, but a sophisticated and immaculately groomed woman, between twenty-five and thirty.

She held her hand out. 'Mr Gibson?'

'How do you do, Miss Griffin.'

I took her hand with its long tapering fingers. She shook hands like a man, with a firm pressure. 'You're punctual,' she said.

'I've had it beaten into me,' I told her. 'Flying around with air forces and air companies. It gets to be a habit.'

'It's a good one,' she smiled. 'I wish more people in Rome had it. Shall we go upstairs?'

She turned to the lift. The view from the rear was equally good. She slid her private key in the lock, we moved silently up to the fifth floor and stepped out of the lift straight into a large reception room, cum entrance hall. She spoke over her shoulder. 'We'll be more comfortable in my office. This way.'

The office was strictly functional. Grey metal furniture, a medium-sized desk, four filing cabinets, an Olivetti electric typewriter, and three metal chairs, gave an impression of bleak efficiency. Gisela swayed around and sat behind the desk. 'Sit down, please, Mr Gibson.'

'Thank you.'

'Tell me?' she asked. 'How did *you* meet Mr Kelly?'

'Simple. I saw an advertisement for a pilot, and answered it.'

I leaned back and pulled out a pack of Camels. 'Mind if I smoke?'

'Not at all.'

I offered the pack. 'Smoke?'

'No, thanks.'

I lit the cigarette, blew a puff ceiling-wards, and watched Miss Gisella Griffin, aloof and poised, behind her desk.

'And how did *you* come to be hired by Kelly?'

She flushed. 'I've been with Mr Kelly for several years,' she said stiffly.

'So.' I nodded approvingly. 'Mr Kelly told me that he'd pass on any further instructions for me through you.'

The gold-flecked eyes watched me coldly. 'Did Mr Kelly give any indication what your duties would be?'

'Only that he's interested in obtaining oil concessions in West Africa, and needs his own aircraft to fly him around.'

She nodded. 'That about sums it up, Mr Gibson. He has been negotiating now for several months for oil concessions in West Africa.'

'West Africa's rather a large area,' I said. 'Where specifically?'

She shook her head. 'I'm sorry, I don't feel I could tell you that. Mr Kelly will tell you when he arrives. If he wishes.' The snub registered.

I shrugged my shoulders. 'It's all the same to me,' I said indifferently.

She was suddenly serious. 'Mr Gibson, security is all-important in this oil business. Italian and French oil interests are also competing in West Africa for oil concessions, with the full backing of their governments. It's quite a struggle for an independent operator to try and break in.'

I thought of Aloysius Kelly back there in Dallas. 'Well, if anybody can break in,' I said, 'I'd be inclined to put my money on Mr Kelly.'

She smiled faintly, showing small, perfect teeth. 'You're quite right there.'

That about seemed to cover it. I stubbed out my cigarette. 'Well, Miss Griffin, is there anything I can do here?'

She shook her head. 'Nothing at the moment. Is the aeroplane serviceable?'

'Yes,' I said. 'I handed it over to a company at the airport called Aero Flotto for a routine service. They have a good reputation. It should be ready day after tomorrow.'

'Good,' she said. 'Tell them to send the account here. Head Office told me to advance you such sums of money as you reasonably require. Please send your hotel bills to this office.'

'Right.' I relaxed in the chair.

'That's all,' she said. 'The moment I have my instructions from Head Office I'll contact you. Meanwhile you can get in some sight-seeing around Rome.'

'Sight-seeing on your own is not much fun, Miss Griffin,' I said tentatively. 'Would you care to show me around? In your spare time, of course?'

She shook her head. 'I'm sorry, but I don't believe in associating with people in the same company, out of office hours.'

'It's a good rule if you can stick to it,' I said easily. 'Do I call you sir, or do you prefer ma'am, Miss Griffin?'

She flushed. 'Miss Griffin will do. I just happen to believe that in a company relationships should be on a business and not a personal footing.'

'Fine,' I said. 'So I'll take myself off and await your orders, ma'am.'

I stood up, walked to the lift, and waited for her to unlock the door and let me out.

"Bye, ma'am,' I said. She flushed, and I grinned at her as the door closed noisily behind me.

Five days dragged past before I heard from her. I was having a Martell at the bar and reading the *New York Herald*, when a page handed me a message. It was brief and to the point.

'Please pick me up at my apartment tomorrow morning at 7 A.M. We have orders from Mr Kelly to proceed immediately to Lagos. Will you make all the necessary arrangements regarding the aircraft? Thanks. Gisela Griffin.'

I looked sourly at the 'Thanks, Gisela Griffin,' went up to my room, grabbed the phone, and told the engineer at Aero Flotto to have the aircraft on the tarmac and ready for an 8 A.M. take off the next morning.

Next morning the clouds were low and dreary, trailing against the tops of the higher buildings, as I drove round to Gisela's apartment.

She was waiting in the foyer, smart in a grey costume, with a small snugly-fitting matching beret. She smiled brightly. 'Good morning, Mr Gibson. I suppose you're glad to be leaving Rome?'

I recalled the brush-off at our last interview and shrugged noncommittally. 'I do what I'm told, Miss Griffin,' I said, and watched her flush as she stepped into the taxi. I slammed the door and walked round to the other side.

'Ciampino,' I snapped at the driver.

He nodded dutifully and slid away in typical Italian style, accelerating frantically up through his gears as he headed out of town.

CHAPTER TWO

WE drove along the Via Appia through a heavy soaking drizzle to Ciampino Airport, and Gisela spoke only once, 'Where's the first stop?'

I was equally terse, 'Malta.'

The aloof, flawless profile, as she looked out the cab at the miserable wet surroundings, irritated me. As the porters collected our baggage, I told her, 'I have to report to the flight-planning centre. Wait for me in the airport lounge. I shouldn't be longer than ten minutes.'

She nodded distantly and swayed off towards a bookstall.

The Italians took their time that morning, as only they can. Rome control enjoyed the dubious distinction of owning the thickest file of air traffic violations at the International Airline Pilots Association Headquarters. It was thirty minutes before I finished my flight planning and rejoined Gisela.

She glanced at her watch as I arrived. 'It was a long ten minutes,' she said. 'I thought you'd decided to flight-plan for Mars, not Malta.'

I smiled pleasantly. 'One of the advantages of space flight is that, to-date, the Yanks have been able to avoid lugging women along. Let's go.'

We cleared with Customs and Immigration. I draped my raincoat across my shoulders and cheerfully watched her struggle to open her umbrella and simultaneously cope with her hand baggage. She needed at least four hands, as she ran across the tarmac, and I was damned if I was prepared to help. Mr Aloysius Kelly's super-secretary needed taming.

At the Aero Commander I stood under the wing, taking my time about opening the cabin door and the luggage boot behind it. Raindrops streaked her face like tears, momentarily softening the aloof expression. As she climbed into the cabin I packed the cases into the boot and locked the door.

She settled herself in one of the centre seats. 'I'm sorry,' I told her. 'You'll have to work this trip. Come forward and read the check list for me.' She sighed as she moved up forward and settled herself sulkily in the co-pilot's seat.

I passed the plastic-covered check list to her.

'What do I do?' she asked.

'Read it to me slowly,' I said. 'Call out each item as soon as I've checked the previous one. Begin from "Before starting engines".'

She read each item with interest, watching me as I performed the necessary actions. I started the engines and turned to her. 'Right, now let's do the "Before taxi-ing check". Begin here.' I pointed.

'Pressurization?' she asked.

'Selected for 1,000 feet above Malta Luqua altitude. Cruising level set. Pressure checked and okay.'

'Fuel?'

'On mains. Boosters low. Quantities checked.'

'Flaps?'

'Ten degrees. Cowl flaps one-third open.'

'Gyros?'

'Checked and set. Suction fine. Selector on slave.'

As we checked systematically through all the systems, so my unlicensed unofficial co-pilot relaxed, and the sulky expression vanished. Then we'd finished the check and were ready for taxi-ing clearance from the control tower. The outside temperature had dropped to $+2°C$, and the visibility was less than a mile.

'Ciampino Tower,' I called. 'This is November Charlie 24. Taxi clearance. Over.'

'November 24. Ciampino. You are cleared to runway one

nine right. Quebec November Hotel, one zero one four decimal seven millibars. Stand by for ATC* Clearance.'

'Roger. November Charlie cleared to one nine right. Altimeter one zero one four decimal seven. Standing by.'

I opened the throttles smoothly, setting the barometric pressure on two altimeters as we moved through the murk. I flipped the wing de-icing switch on to single cycle and watched the rubber boots built into the leading edge of the wing began to pulsate, then switched on the Pitot heating and checked the increase in the alternators' charging rate, as they stepped up the output of current to cope with the increased electrical loading.

Ciampino was once the principal airport of Rome. Now it was a very poor second to Rome Fumancino, situated thirty miles away on the coast. The airlines operating from Ciampino were spared the usual delay taking off, but, operating from here we had the inconvenience of flying a complicated clearance to join the airway traffic route west of Fumancino leading to Malta, our first stop.

On cue, the tower called : 'November Charlie 24, I have your ATC Clearance. Are you ready to copy?'

'Go ahead.'

'Roger. Roma Control clears you to Malta Luqua via Airway Amber One. Right turn out after takeoff to intercept Fumancino VOR† on a radial of zero six six degrees, and thereafter join Amber One at a point five nautical miles out to sea. Pass over Fumancino at not less than ten thousand feet or as cleared otherwise en route. Confirm.'

'Roger.' I read out my clearance from the scribbled notes.

'Clearance correct,' the tower confirmed. 'Cleared on

* ATC. Air Traffic Control.

† VOR. Visual OMNI Range—a VHF direction finding device.

and off runway one nine right. Call Roma Control when airborne.'

'Roger Dee,' I said, lining up. *'Arrividerci, Roma.'*

'Grazie,' the voice brightened. *'Bon voyage.'*

We had barely left the runway and the wheels retracted, when we nosed into a dense overcast, with moderate to severe turbulence. The rain beat savagely, and the windscreen rattled as though pelted by fine granite, then ice formed rapidly, creating a characteristic hiss in the radio speakers. I checked the Pitot heat, and watched the leading edge of the wings, waiting until a sufficiently heavy layer of ice had formed before applying the de-icing boot switch.

The speakers crackled into life. 'November Charlie 24, this is Roma.'

'Go ahead, Roma.'

'Roger. What are your present flight conditions?'

We were still in cloud, completely blind. In aviation parlance this was known as instrument meteorological conditions or IMC. 'I'm India Mike Charlie, passing through six five. Request clearance to flight level one nine zero.'

'Negative, November Charlie. Not approved. You are cleared to climb to and maintain flight level nine zero until passing over Rome Fumancino. Request flight level change after that. Copied OK?'

'November Charlie checks. Will call you top of initial climb nine zero.'

The Aero Commander shuddered momentarily in heavy turbulence, and the fuselage thudded as chunks of ice broke away from the propeller tips. I activated the wing de-icing boots and watched the ice break away. At eight thousand feet we emerged from the overcast, breaking through into bright sunshine.

Gisela was staring pensively out of the co-pilot's window. I intercepted the VOR radial as cleared by control, and

engaged the automatic pilot. It was an H14 Honeywall
that flew better than any pilot. A thousand feet beneath
us the overcast extended as far as I could see.

Gisella leaned back, opened a pack of cigarettes, and
pulled out a lighter. I grabbed her wrist. 'No naked flames,'
I said. 'Hold on a moment.' I pushed in the dash lighter,
waited for it to heat up and jump out, and handed it to
her.

'Thanks,' she said. 'I'm sorry about the lighter, I should
have remembered.' She smiled apologetically.

I picked up the microphone. 'Roma Control, this is
November Charlie 24.'

'Go ahead 24.'

'Roger. Two four is established on radial zero six six
flight level nine zero Victor Mike Charlie* on top. DME†
reads two nautical miles to go for intercepting airway
amber one. Go ahead.'

'Roger. Roma copies. You are now cleared to climb to,
and maintain, flight level one nine zero. Report top of
climb and establish on Amber One. What is your estimate
for abeam Palermo?'

I gave him the estimate and applied climb power, ad-
justing the nose upwards with the auto-pilot trim wheel.

Gisela looked at me. 'I'm sorry I was so bitchy at the
airport. There's a lot more to this flying business than
I thought.'

'Forget it,' I said. 'I should have only been ten minutes,
that's the normal time, but there was a queue and the
Italians were particularly slow this morning.'

I made the necessary air traffic control calls, and
adjusted the cabin temperature to a comfortable seventy
degrees. I was flying in short sleeves despite the minus
18°C. outside air temperature. The pressurized Aero Commander was a pleasure to fly. Aloysius Kelly's advisers

* VMC. Visual Meteorological Conditions.
† DME. Distance Measuring Equipment.

had done well in selecting this aircraft. As the ship droned steadily along, I relaxed and sat back.

'Tell me,' I asked, 'how long have you been with Kelly?'

'Four years,' she said. 'He's a hard man, but I like working with him. He can be very generous.'

'Must say he gave me a pretty square deal. Do you like Rome? Wouldn't you rather be back in the States?'

She shrugged. 'Not really. My parents are dead and there's nothing there to draw me back. I have no relations. I was the only child.'

'What, no boy-friend?' I joked.

She looked away. 'There was. I made the age-old mistake. I fell for a married man. It lasted two years. I was a fool and believed everything he told me. Finally I got wise. I was in the Dallas office shortly after Kelly offered me the job in Rome, so I took it.'

'Oh well,' I said. 'It happens all the time, you'll survive. Have you got him out of your system?'

'Completely, but it took quite a while.' She grinned. 'Now I'm man-proof.'

'Famous last words,' I said easily. 'I'd better call Malta.'

I flicked on the mike button. 'Malta Centre, this is November Charlie two-four on eighty eight twenty. Do you read?' There was plenty of static on the high frequency band.

'November two four. Go ahead.'

'Roger. Request latest Malta weather. Over.'

'Stand by one.' I studied the written forecast for the route that I'd collected in Rome. It predicted showers at Malta, with a cloud base of 500 feet and visibility two nautical miles.

Malta centre called. 'November Charlie two four, the latest Malta weather. Cloud base two hundred feet, lowering. Light to heavy rain. Visibility one half to one nautical mile. Weather deteriorating. Copied okay?'

I cursed mentally. 'Thank you, Malta. November Charlie

checks.' The weather was already at airline minima and deteriorating.

I checked the fuel gauges. I had plenty of fuel for holding and then diverting to Benina Airport or Tripoli. However, having flown in and out of Israel a number of times in the past few years, I wanted to avoid landing in an Arab state. My Israeli flying was probably known. I didn't fancy a spell in an Arab jail.

Gisela frowned. 'The weather sounds terrible. Will you be able to land?'

'We'll see. No matter how bad it is I don't mind going in if their Ground Controlled Approach radar is operating. The Malta controllers are good.'

Ten minutes out from the Malta Gozo Beacon I called Malta Approach. Beneath us the weather was a solid dirty grey-white sheet. 'Malta Approach, November Charlie two four.'

'Two four, Malta. Our weather below accepted minima. Cloud base less than fifty feet, visibility one to two hundred metres, less in heavy precipitation. Surface wind two six zero degrees, gusting twenty-five to forty knots. What are your intentions? Over.'

'Roger Malta. Is your GCA operative?'

'Affirmative but weather below talk-down minima. If you wish, call Malta Talk-down now, on frequency one one nine decimal seven. Go ahead.'

'Roger, changing frequency.' I twirled the knobs on the VHF set, selecting the appropriate frequency in the slitted windows.

'Malta Talk-down. This is November Charlie two four.'

'Roger two four, this is Talk-down. For your information the weather is below my legal minima. Prepared to give you Talk-down approach below this minima at captain's discretion and responsibility only. Advise, over.'

'November Charlie checks. This is the captain speaking. Request Talk-down to touch down. Go ahead.'

Every word was now being recorded on a tape, so, if I spread the aircraft over a wide area of the white limestone island, the controller was in the clear.

GCA controllers were a select breed. The training was savage, and if they made the grade, they were in a class of their own. Their calm reassuring voices never panicked, and any competent pilot would fly to their instructions. I reckoned, in a landing under the conditions such as existed below, they shared the credit equally with the pilot.

'Roger,' the GCA controller was saying. 'Understand you have copied the latest Malta weather. Stand by to turn right for positive radar identification. You are cleared to descend immediately to five thousand feet, on altimeter setting one zero one six decimal three millibars. Report leaving flight level one nine zero.'

'Roger Dee.' I repeated my clearance, reduced power and commenced a rapid descent. 'The landing approach might be a rough ride,' I told Gisela. 'Tighten your lap strap.'

She smiled. 'I'm holding thumbs.'

'November Charlie, this is Talk-down. Turn right now through ninety degrees for identification.'

I turned and watched the cloud layer swim towards us as we lost height.

'Roger, November Charlie. I have you positively on radar. Your position ten nautical miles north west of Malta. Turn left on to one five zero degrees.'

'November Charlie turning left on to one five zero degrees.'

I operated the turn module on the auto-pilot, and we banked left. I rolled out on to the required heading.

'November Charlie steering one five zero degrees.'

'Roger, November Charlie. You are now on a long right hand base for runway two four. Expedite your descent to five thousand feet. Talk-down standing by.'

'Roger.' I reduced power, lowering the landing gear, and

slapped on quarter flap. Before we entered cloud I applied
the Pitot heaters to prevent the airspeed icing up. As we
hit the top of the overcast the Aero Commander shuddered
and twisted. I fought the turbulence, watching for icing on
the wings. So far there was no indication, but the temperature was climbing from minus six degrees and I knew that
icing would come, as we passed through the critical temperature zone between.

'November Charlie from Talk-down. Don't acknowledge
any further instructions. Stand by to turn right on to
two four zero degrees. If you lose radio contact, overshoot
on a heading of two seven zero degrees, and call Malta
approach on frequency one one nine decimal one. Maintain your present heading.'

The Aero Commander protested violently against the
turbulence as I concentrated on maintaining our heading.
I visualized the final approach, when accuracy of heading
and height would be all important. The gusting cross-
wind from the right, would make landing even more difficult in the bad visibility. I began to sweat.

'November Charlie, this is Talk-down. Turn right on to
two four zero. Maintain your present altitude.'

Rain splashed and formed a thick speckled layer of ice
on the windscreen. Without taking my eyes off the blind
flying panel, I felt for the wing de-icer switch, applied a
single pulse, and rolled out on to the correct heading.

'November Charlie, you are now eight nautical miles
from touch down. You are above the glide path. Your heading is correct.'

I reduced power and increased the rate of descent. I
watched the panel, checking the artificial horizon and bank
and turn against the direction indicator. Then I glanced
across to the altimeter and vertical speed indicator. The
airspeed needle jumped in the turbulence, flickering between a hundred and ten and a hundred and twenty knots.

'November Charlie. You are now only one hundred feet

above the glide path. Alter course right on to two five zero degrees. You are six nautical miles from touch down.'

The wind was drifting us to the left and the correct allowance for this would be vitally important as we approached touch down. 'November Charlie. You are now fifty feet above the glide slope. Turn right on to two six zero degrees. You are five nautical miles from touch down.'

Christ, I thought, the cross-wind must have increased. We were already crabbing at an angle of twenty degrees towards the runway. Ice pelted us, the static registering a frenzy of noise as it hissed loudly in the speaker above my head. I was sweating a lot more now, I battled to keep the aircraft on the glide path.

The controller's voice was reassuring. 'Very nice approach, November Charlie. You are on the glide path, you are on the runway centre line, you are three nautical miles from touch down.'

Ice clumps, thrown off the propeller tips, thudded against the fuselage. 'November Charlie, you are left of the centre line. Turn right right on to two six five degrees. You are thirty feet below the glide path.' I increased power slightly and raised the nose a fraction, turning on to the new heading as I did so.

The Controller's voice speeded up, still calm and reassuring.

'November Charlie, you are on the centre line. You are on the glide path. One nautical mile from touch down. Continue.'

I glanced at the altimeter. Three hundred feet. We were in a rain-lashed greyness, with ice sliding off the windscreen and the approach lighting not yet in sight.

'November Charlie, you are eight hundred yards from touch down. Your heading is good. Very nice approach. Turn right on to two six eight degrees. You are four hundred yards from touch down, on the glide path, on the centre line. Now two hundred yards from touch down. Maintain approach.'

The words were streaming fast now. 'You are near the runway threshold . . . Approach very good . . . You are now at touch down . . . Look up and land.' I jerked my head up, and, at an angle of at least twenty degrees to our left, the white dotted runway centre line disappeared into the rain lashed mist. I dropped the right wing to counter the drift and kicked the nose to the left. Banked steeply, the Aero Commander landed gently, touching down first on the right wheel, then the nose wheel. I held it that way, until the air speed dropped, and the left wing fell slowly until the wheel made contact.

The dotted lines grew longer, our speed decreased, and I applied gentle braking action.

'November Charlie from Talk-down. Nothing further. Call Luqua Tower on one one eight one. Good day, sir.'

'Good day to you, sir,' I said fervently.

As I turned down the taxiway I was conscious of Gisela watching me. I pulled out my handkerchief and wiped the sweat off my forehead.

'I think the boss got himself a good pilot,' she said. 'Congratulations. I never saw the runway until the wheels touched.'

'Thanks,' I said. 'I don't know about you, but I could use a drink.'

She nodded. 'Makes two of us.'

As we taxied in I looked over the white stone wall of the airport boundary. Several disconsolate grey and white seagulls were parked in the field. I pointed to them. 'Look at those birds,' I said to Gisela. 'They've got brains.'

The marshal flagged us into the parking lot, and a big mobile refuelling tanker pulled up in front of the Aero Commander.

'Fill it up,' I said and left them to it.

We ran across to the airport terminal through the rain. 'Order something for me at the restaurant,' I said. 'While I book in and file a flight plan.'

In the tower I studied the met reports. Strong north westerlies, up to sixty knots, were forecast over the Sahara. Although this would create a port drift problem, the resulting increased ground speed should enable me to make Kano, in Northern Nigeria, non-stop. Maybe. Met reports are a guide not a gospel. However, if the winds were wrong, I could make a refuelling stop at Fort Lamy, in Chad.

I filed the flight plan, and joined Gisela in the restaurant. We had a hasty meal. The steak was tough and the eggs yellow and rubbery. I washed them down with a beer. It was a long haul to Kano and there was no time to waste.

I settled the account and we hurried back to the aircraft. I quickly checked through the desert survival kit. The Maltese were notorious for their skill in snatching anything valuable from under your nose. Water supplies, signalling strips, metal mirror, emergency rations, were all there. The first aid kit and portable radio transceiver were still in position. There was nothing missing.

We took off and climbed away on our first heading. Malta approach cleared us to flight level two zero, zero, 20,000 feet. Below us the overcast was dense but ahead it was breaking up over the North African coastline into scatter blocks of cumulus. We hit the coast line, west of El Adem, ten minutes ahead of my ETA, the white line of breakers clearly visible through the broken cloud. I took a bearing on the El Adem NDB and calculated our ground speed, then checked it carefully. The upper winds were certainly pushing the Aero Commander along. I showed Gisella my calculations. 'Our ground speed, so far, is two hundred and sixty knots and we haven't hit the forecasted high altitude jetstream yet. If met's correct, we ought to pick up another twenty knots within half an hour.'

'Wonderful,' She settled back. 'I'm enjoying this.' Her smile was warm and friendly.

I checked my calculations again. With these upper winds, I'd have to watch our drift carefully. It was all very well gaining a hell of a lot of extra speed, but there was no point in finishing up in Timbuktu, miles off course.

Now the Sahara, spreading ahead of us, was completely clear of cloud. I had no drift sight on the Aero Commander and the VOR station that we were heading for, well south of Tripoli, wasn't due to come up for another hour.

I took visual sight of two desert peaks in the distance, and watched them carefully. A few minutes later they were on our starboard side. 'We've a hell of a drift to port,' I told Gisela. I slapped on another ten degrees to starboard and re-set the auto pilot.

Gisela groped under the seat and produced a small Thermos flask. 'I had this filled while you were flight-planning, John,' she said. 'Would you like some coffee?'

So, it was John now. My lady was thawing.

'Thanks,' I said. 'I've got a stewardess as well as a co-pilot, that's great.'

While she got busy, I selected the VOR frequency and set the bearing selector on our course to the next station. Once within range, the position of the needle would indicate the direction of the station, and I could ascertain our drift.

Gisela handed me a cup. 'I'm enjoying this trip,' she said. 'Especially after being tied to a desk in Rome. I've often flown on big airliners, but it's more fun this way.' She looked happy and contented for the first time since we'd met.

I nodded. 'It's not always fun, but I wouldn't swop it for any other job.' I took the cup of coffee. 'Thank you.'

Below, the Sahara stretched ahead like a giant moon-scape with its craters and outcrops. In less than an hour, fifty-five minutes to be exact, we passed the VOR station, situated beside a lonely oilwell. I established our drift as a staggering twenty-six degrees to port, and our speed at two hundred and ninety knots. The jetstream was certainly pushing us along.

I checked the map. The next available check-point was Zonder, six hundred nautical miles to the south. I hoped the wind direction would stay constant and the drift correction would bring us close enough to establish radio contact with Zonder beacon. With the desert sliding away beneath us, the sun went down, resting for a minute on the horizon, a fiery red ball that looked as if we were peering at it through a filter. Suddenly it was gone. Darkness closed in on the desert beneath and the light in the upper sky began to fade.

Gisela leaned towards me. I was conscious of her perfume, faint and fragrant. 'May I sleep for a while in the rear seat? I feel tired.'

'Sure,' I said. 'Be my guest.'

She placed her hand on my shoulder as she went past and hesitated momentarily. Her eyes were mischievous. 'Are you sure you can make it without me?'

I squeezed her hand. 'Don't worry, I'll ask for your co-operation some other time.' She smiled and went back to the rear seat. Maybe it was my imagination but I thought I felt a faint increase of pressure on my shoulder before she removed her hand.

I settled back, and watched a satellite drift lazily across the starlit sky. It flashed occasionally as it tumbled, catching the invisible sunlight at that altitude and reflecting the sun rays. Thirty minutes before ETA I switched on the radio and the beacon signal from Zonder pulsed through clearly.

The flight to date, I thought, had gone like clockwork. I altered course five degrees to starboard, and as we passed over Zonder I re-checked the ground speed and fuel. We were still making good speed, two hundred and ninety knots, and there was ample gas to enable us to carry on to Kano, without landing at Zonder.

Gisela slept peacefully across the rear cabin seats, until two hours later the lights of Kano glowed faintly ahead, a yellow smear at the edge of the distant darkness.

I called the tower and received landing clearance, adjusted the cabin pressurization for landing, and called Gisela. She came forward sleepily, rubbing her eyes. I pointed to the glow on the horizon. 'Kano. Do you mind getting out the check list?' As we ran through it, the tower cleared us for a direct approach, I dropped the wheels and flaps and went straight in losing altitude fast.

I touched down and taxied off the end of the runway, heading towards No. 8 parking bay, the figure 8 illuminated in a large bright square of glowing light.

As I cut the motors, a Nigerian in long flowing robes, mounted on a camel, blew a salute on a long horn, the traditional Nigerian welcome for aircraft. I gave the refuelling agent his instructions, and saw a large number of soldiers patrolling the tarmac and the entrance to the terminal building. I took Gisela by the arm. 'Welcome to Nigeria,' I said. 'They've laid on a guard of honour. Are you hungry?'

'Not really,' she smiled. 'What about you?'

'It's a long haul to Lagos, maybe we'd better find something to eat.'

At the airport building the officials were very polite and correct. Too polite and correct. I could sense the tension around us. Several soldiers had crowded in and were watching us closely.

'Are you night-stopping, sir?' the Immigration Chief asked curiously.

'No. I'm taking off for Lagos as soon as the refuelling's finished. Is the restaurant open?'

He shook his head. 'No, sir, it's been closed for the last two days.' He broke off abruptly. A Nigerian captain came up and stood beside us, making no attempt to disguise his interest in the conversation. I can smell trouble as fast as the next man, and you could have cut the tension at the moment with a knife.

'It doesn't matter,' I said casually. 'I'll file my flight plan and we will be on our way as soon as the refuelling squad have finished.'

He nodded. 'Perhaps it is best,' the immigration chief said softly.

I left it at that. 'Come,' I said. I took Gisela by the arm. The soldiers watched us in silence as we headed towards the flying control office. 'Something funny is going on here,' I said. 'The restaurant has been closed for two days and there are a hell of a lot of soldiers patrolling. I don't like the smell of it.'

'I think I know why,' she said quietly. 'I'll tell you in the aircraft.'

I hurried the flight planning along, and fifteen minutes later the wheels of the Aero Commander lifted off the runway, and the willing ship began to knife its way up through the darkness to our assigned flight level. At cruise level, I adjusted the power, trimmed the aircraft, set the automatic pilot, and turned to Gisela. 'What the hell's going on down there? What do you know?'

'I'm sure it's political,' she said. 'Kelly mentioned in his last letter that, whatever we intended to do in Nigeria, would have to be tackled fairly soon as there is liable to be a change in government. He didn't seem to think the trouble would be very serious, though.' She slackened her seatbelt. 'I'll find out tonight in Lagos, Kelly has contacts there with one of the top Government officials. Now I'm going back to catch up with the rest of my sleep.'

She squeezed past and curled up again on the rear seat. As we droned through the night towards Lagos I wondered what the hell I was letting myself in for. I'd seen enough fighting in Mobutu's Congo Air Force to know that a full company of heavily armed soldiers at an airport usually meant trouble was brewing. Maybe they were waiting to arrest some local VIP passenger off an incoming plane. I shrugged my shoulders. I decided that whatever was going on I'd keep my nose clean and out of it. Upheavals in African states were liable to be tough, explosive and dangerous for interfering outsiders, and I'd had my full share the past few years.

I settled back and waited for the lights of Lagos.

Two hours later they blinked into view. I woke Gisela, we ran through the check list and fifteen minutes later, I greased the Commander down on Runway 19 at Ikeja Airport.

CHAPTER THREE

C O M P A R E D to Kano, the atmosphere at Ikeja Airport, eight miles outside Lagos was even tenser. The aerodrome swarmed with soldiers and the customs official went courteously but thoroughly through our baggage.

The immigration official was equally curious. 'May I ask what your business is in Lagos, sir?' he asked curtly.

Gisela broke in. 'I have business with Mr Gobi, special financial adviser to the Federal Military Government,' she said abruptly.

The immigration officer's attitude changed immediately. He stamped my passport, smiled, and handed it back. 'Everything's in order, sir,' he said. He called a porter. 'This man will take your case and find a taxi for you.'

'Thank you.' We climbed into the taxi.

'What the hell is brewing?' I asked Gisela. Ahead a line of cars were parked, with soldiers peering into the boots, checking on the passengers and their identification papers. Our driver drummed his fingers impatiently on the steering wheel.

'What are they doing?' I asked. 'What's it all about?'

He turned his head. 'The soldiers are looking for weapons, sir. We are expecting trouble with the Ibos from the east.' He spat out the window to express his disgust.

'Who are the Ibos?' I asked innocently.

Gisela answered me. 'A large tribe. They comprise eight million of the total Nigerian populuation of fifty million. They're a very intelligent race, probably the most advanced group in Nigeria.'

The taxi driver chimed in. 'I think the Ibos want to make trouble, mister.'

'I hope not,' I said. 'There's been enough trouble in

Africa lately without the Ibos starting up in these parts.'

'General Gowon will sort it out,' said Gisela confidently. 'He's Sandhurst trained and head of the army.'

'Christ,' I said. 'A war's all we're short of.'

The taxi driver shook his head. 'General Gowon and Colonel Ojukwu of the Ibos have already met many times. They can't agree. Now blood will flow.'

'What's the fuss about?' I asked Gisela.

'The Federal Military Government has decided to cut up Nigeria into twelve states, instead of the present four. The three main tribes, Hausas in the north, Yorubas to the west and the Ibos in the east, are really sub-divided into twelve tribes. The snag, as far as the Ibos are concerned, is that under this arrangement, they lose the oil-wells at Onitsha on the Niger River. Ojukwu refuses to accept this.'

As the troops came up our driver climbed out and opened the boot.

A heavily armed thick-set sergeant stopped beside the taxi. He was very polite. 'Would you and the lady please open your suitcases, sir. I have orders to search.'

'Certainly,' I said. 'No guns this trip, though,' I got out and joined the driver at the back of the taxi.

The sergeant rifled through the suitcases. 'Very good, sir, you may go.'

Forty-five minutes later we pulled up in front of the hotel, signed the register, and collected the keys of our rooms. 'Come on, Gisela,' I said. 'I need a drink and a bath and a sleep, in that order.'

'I could use a drink,' she said wearily.

We moved across to the lounge and sat at a semi-circular bar in the corner. The occupants were solemnly staring at a television set flickering in the corner and I recognized General Gowon on the screen. I ordered two scotches, and when they came I raised my glass. 'Here's to success,' I said. 'Provided this scenario doesn't erupt into a full-scale shooting scene.' I tossed back my drink. 'Well, Gisela, what are your plans?'

'I'm going to bath and change, then make a couple of phone calls.'

'Tonight? Why not call it a day and get some rest. It's after nine.'

'No. I must make the calls. Remember, I slept most of the way between here and Kano. You must be about all in.'

'I am,' I confessed. 'I'm having another drink, then off to bed.'

Gisela looked at me critically. 'You look as if you need it. I think it would be a good idea.' She put her hand on my wrist. 'Thanks for the drink, John. I'll see you in the morning.' She stood up, and I watched her walk gracefully out of the room. I shouted to the waiter to bring another scotch and sat back to take a look at the surrounding scene.

On the wall was a large picture of General Gowon. Underneath was a slogan, 'Get On With One Nigeria.' The first letter of each word was underlined and spelt his name 'G O W O N'. Very clever, I thought appraisingly. A Madison Avenue touch.

In the corner, on the television, an announcer kept intoning after every message in heavily accented English. 'To keep Nigeria *one,* is a task that *must* be done.' It seemed that the possibility of the Ibos seceding didn't appeal particularly to the Lagos Nigerians. Wherever the colonial powers pulled out, tribal differences and jealousies invariably seemed to erupt in a wave of savagery and violence. The Nigerians in the bar were in a sombre, serious frame of mind. They seemed to be aware of some vague disaster approaching, without knowing how to avoid it.

I sipped my scotch and thought about the secession of Katanga from the Congo and the bloodshed that followed.

I knew it only too well, I'd flown for Tshombe in Katanga against the Central Congolese forces, and later, when the Congo was re-united under Mobutu, for the Congo Air Force against the Communist-led rebel Simbas in the Eastern Provinces. If this Ibo secession developed into another Congo, the Nigerians had my sympathy.

I finished my scotch and went to my room. I showered, but the cold water was lukewarm and did little to cool me off. I threw myself down on the bed and fell asleep almost immediately.

I woke to the shrilling phone beside me. I cursed, rolled over, and grabbed it, my hands wet and clammy with perspiration. The room was hot and airless and the temperature well up in the nineties.

'John,' it was Gisela's voice. 'Hello there. I'm sorry, did I wake you?'

'Yes, but don't apologize. What's the time?'

'After midnight, John. I'm sorry.'

'That's quite all right. What's the score?'

Her voice dropped slightly. 'I'm downstairs in the bar with Mr Gobi.' Her voice dropped to a murmur. 'He's financial adviser to the Ministry of Economic Development. I'd like you to meet him.'

'Give me ten minutes.'

Gisela was in the corner of the bar farthest from the television screen as I came in. Her companion was a light skinned, well-dressed Negro over six foot tall. He wore a light-weight tropical suit with pointed alligator brown and white shoes. A lizard skin belt held up the smartly cut slacks, cutting into the expansive paunch. The over-all impression was expensive and flashy. He had the shifty manner of a successful used car dealer. The blood-shot dark eyes behind horn-rimmed glasses, were alert and intelligent. He stood up as I approached the table.

'John,' Gisela introduced us. 'This is Mr Gobi.' We shook hands.

The clasp was firm. 'Pleased to know you, Mr Gibson.'

There was no trace of the sing-song intonation so often heard in the English speech of the Nigerians. 'Will you have a drink?'

'Thank you.'

Gisela looked good. She was wearing a white sharkskin sleeveless dress, with white shoes and her hair tied back with a white ribbon. She was crisp and businesslike and wasted no time.

'This is the situation, John, Mr Gobi tells me he has information that the day after tomorrow Colonel Ojukwu will announce that the entire Eastern Region of Nigeria will secede from the Federation. It will call itself Biafra. When this happens, says Mr Gobi, General Gowon will immediately declare war in order to bring Ojukwu's rebel regime to order.' She paused.

'How's this going to affect Kelly's business?' I asked.

Gisela glanced across at Gobi. 'Mr Gobi tells me that the revolt will be crushed in a few weeks. I don't think it will make any real difference.'

'That's what the Central Congolese Government said about Katanga when it seceded,' I said drily. 'Yet the war went on for several years.'

Gobi shook his head. 'There's no danger of that, Mr Gibson. The vast majority of army officers support General Gowon.'

'I hope you're right,' I said. 'He's going to need them.'

Gisela looked at me. Her left eyelid drooped a fraction. 'John, in view of the possible troubles here, I suggested to Mr Gobi, that he might find it convenient to have the use of the Aero Commander for the next few weeks. I have offered him the aircraft and he has accepted.'

Gobi glanced at me. 'It could be very useful, Captain Gibson. I hope you have no objections.'

'It's all right with me,' I said. 'But what does the boss back in Texas say? After all, he pays me.'

'I sent him a cable this evening,' said Gisela, 'setting out the proposition. I'm quite certain he will agree.'

I shrugged my shoulders. 'In that case,' I said to Gobi, 'I'm at your service, sir.'

Gobi smiled. 'Thank you very much, Mr Gibson, I appreciate your attitude and co-operation.'

Gisela groped around in her handbag. 'Here's a letter for you, John. It was waiting for you care of Mr Gobi. He gave it to me this evening in his office.'

I tore it open. It was short and to the point and typed on Kelly's letterhead, dated April 15, 1967, it read:

'This is to confirm that John Gibson, employed by this Corporation, will be entitled to the payment of one million US dollars, or alternatively, one quarter percent of the net profits, should the above Company succeed in obtaining the oil concessions in Nigeria in which it is interested. The above offer is dependent upon Mr Gibson's full co-operation in all matters appertaining to the securing of the above mentioned leases.

ALOYSIUS P. KELLY
President

Gisela was watching me curiously.

'Any idea what's in this letter?' I asked.

She shook her head. 'No.'

I passed it across and she read it carefully. 'Very nice,' she said. 'It should help reconcile you to your stay in Lagos, particularly after the fleshpots of Rome that you've been sampling for the past three weeks.'

'What fleshpots of Rome?'

'Don't argue with me, John Gibson,' she said. 'I've seen all those accounts for dinners for two passing through the office. Who do you think you're fooling?'

'Did you expect me to sit at the hotel every night?' I

asked. 'After all, I did ask you out but all I got was a brush-off.'

Gisela looked down demurely. 'Women should never go out with men immediately they meet them,' she said. 'Don't you agree, Mr Gobi?'

Gobi shook his head. 'I'm out of my depth, Miss Griffin. No comment.'

'Well,' Gisela said. 'That's settled. Mr Gobi will keep in touch with you, John. He carries a lot of weight in these parts. He's an old friend of Mr Kelly's and he'll do his best to obtain the concessions that Mr Kelly wants.'

'You've known Mr Kelly long?' I asked Gobi casually.

'Yes,' he said. 'Just over a year. I last saw him a few months ago when I spent a week as his guest in Texas.'

'I read you loud and clear,' I said. 'Now that you're practically one of the family, let me buy you a drink to clinch the relationship.'

'That,' said Gobi, 'is an excellent idea, Mr Gibson.'

'What do you think of the possibilities of war, Mr Gobi?' I asked.

He sighed. 'I don't think anything can stop it. Ojukwu refuses to co-operate with the Federal Government. If war comes, we will have to crush him swiftly to keep destruction and bloodshed to a minimum. We have tried to obtain fighter and bomber aircraft from Britain and America, but they refuse to supply us. These would help us to achieve a quick victory. Without a sizeable air arm, the conflict could go on for several months.'

'Mr Kelly has a lot of influence,' Gisela said. 'Should I discuss the matter of arms with him?'

'By all means,' said Gobi. 'But I doubt if he, or anyone else, can change British and American policy. We are negotiating with them at high level, but I'm pessimistic. However, irrespective of what Britain or America decide, we shall still procure arms. If not from the West, then from the East.' He stood up. 'Miss Griffin, Mr Gibson, please excuse me. I have another meeting scheduled for tonight.' He held out his hand. 'I shall be contacting you, Mr Gibson.'

'Sure, any time,' I said. He went off. Gisela sipped her scotch thoughtfully. 'Give,' I said. 'Tell me all about him.'

'He's a very clever cooky, John, and he's very close to the boss. Although Kelly's not the only oil man he's friendly with.'

'Who else?'

She shrugged. 'There's a deputation of Italians here at the moment, and also the representative of one of the biggest French combines. Both British and American oil companies have permanent representatives in Lagos. Handle him carefully.'

'Any suggestions?'

Gisela shook her head. 'No. You'll have to play it off the cuff, John. Try and find out who his associates are. He'll ask you to fly ministers and generals around, cultivate them. Let it be known that Mr Kelly is a multimillionaire, interested in oil concessions, and would not be ungrateful for any assistance rendered. That sort of thing. Kelly's clever, planting you here with the aircraft. It gives you an in. You'll also be flying senior government officials around. Work on them. You've an open expense account.' She rummaged in her handbag and pulled out an envelope. 'Here are travellers' cheques to the value of five thousand dollars. Spend them as you think fit. Don't stint, Kelly's playing for big stakes. Regard yourself as his ambassador in Lagos. Get to know everyone, and find out what they do. I'll come over every fortnight or third week at the latest.' She finished her drink and stood up. 'Please excuse me, John, I've had a long day. Would you like to collect me at eight and take me to breakfast?'

'It will be a pleasure,' I said. 'And I mean it.'

She put her hand on my shoulder. 'Don't get up. Enjoy yourself, I'll see you at eight.'

After she left I went up to the bar counter. Everyone seemed to be discussing the Biafran Ojukwu, General Gowon, and the possibility of war. Many of the men were dressed in the traditional Nigerian long flowing robes, trying to prove their nationalism maybe.

Oscar, the hotel proprietor, joined me at the bar. 'Have a drink, Mr Gibson.'

'Thanks.' Over the drinks he tried to pump me as to where I came from and what I did. What the hell, I thought. Let everybody know who I am, they'll find out soon enough. So I told him. 'I'm personal pilot to a multi-millionaire American oilman. I'm waiting for him to arrive.'

I left it at that, and settled down to a little serious drinking. It was almost daybreak when I staggered wearily off to bed, my head pounding with the whisky. I slept until midday and woke to the regular throbbing of a tom-tom in my skull. Outside, the street was noisy with voices. Nigerians are an uninhibited race, and the shouting and laughter that fell naturally on their ears jarred me in my present sensitive condition. I saw a note on the dressing-table, propped up against the mirror. Walking gently, to avoid any unnecessary jarring of my throbbing temples, I moved across the room and picked it up. It read :

8 A.M.

'Dear John,

I hope you're not feeling too bad this morning. I looked in to say farewell, but you were sleeping so soundly it seemed a pity to wake you.

Thank you for the wonderful flight from Rome. Be seeing you.

Best of luck,
GISELA

I crawled in under the shower and let the tepid water run, hoping it would cool off. It didn't. I shaved gingerly, and as I put my razor down there was a knock. 'Come in.'

Gobi walked in. 'Good morning, Mr Gibson,' he grinned. 'I hear you had a late night. How do you feel?'

I ran my hands through my hair. 'Terrible.'

'You need a Chapman's.'

'What the hell's that?'

'Our special drink in Lagos. Lemonade with a dash of bitters, fresh lemon, and plenty of ice.'

I pointed to the phone. 'Order two while I get dressed. What's the news?'

He replaced the receiver on the hook. 'The news,' he said slowly, 'is as bad as it could be, Mr Gibson. Colonel Ojukwu has formally seceded from the Federation and christened his break-away state Biafra. War has been declared.'

I sat down on the edge of the bed. 'War!' I said unbelievingly.

'Yes, Mr Gibson.'

'Okay,' I said. 'Since war's been declared, where do we go from here?'

'That's why I'm here to see you,' he said. 'We'd like you to do an urgent flight for us.'

'When?'

'Probably tomorrow. I'm awaiting further details.'

'I'll go anywhere within reason, Mr Gobi. See you in the morning.'

I watched him leave hurriedly, then strolled down to the bar. People were clustered round a blaring radio, faces grim, and their eyes bright with anxiety.

I ordered a Chapman's and half listened to the news. This latest African war was one for the locals to sort out. This one I'd make sure I kept my nose out of. My optimism, could I have known, was as ill-based and unbalanced as the Chapman's I was drinking. I switched to Spey Royal.

CHAPTER FOUR

T H E following morning, after breakfast, I moved out to the verandah. Although it was only nine o'clock, the day was warming up and little wisps of steam were beginning to rise from the puddles of dirty water in the gutters. As I settled down in one of the old creaky wicker chairs, the receptionist came to the door. 'Telephone for you, Mr Gibson.'

It was Gobi. Fast and excited the words came tumbling over each other. 'I must see you at once, Mr Gibson. It is very important.'

'I'll wait for you on the verandah.'

Ten minutes later he arrived in a large black chauffeur-driven Buick.

'Good morning, Gibson.' He pointed to two chairs in the far corner of the verandah. 'Shall we sit over there?'

'Sure.' I followed him along. He wiped his face continually with a large yellow silk handkerchief.

We sat down. 'Mr Gibson, there is much I shall have to explain. Please give me your full attention.'

'Go ahead.' Gobi was certainly in a sweat about something and it wasn't altogether due to the climate.

He leaned forward. 'This morning, an hour ago, we learned that the rebels have occupied an area close to Onitsha. You know that many of the oil-rich areas are situated around there. A French oil company has concessions over a large portion of that area. They have been granted an exclusive exploration permit. We have reason to believe that they are supporting the rebels, but we have no proof.' He wiped his face and crumpled the handkerchief excitedly between his hands. 'They have been flying over the area and carrying out intensive magnetometer surveys for the past year. The French geologist

47

in charge is called Marcel le Clarry. He has his headquarters
at a small village called Wakki, twenty miles southwest
of Enugu. The rebels have declared Enugu as their capital.
We know that these survey maps show the key geological
areas where oil may be found. It is vital we recover them
immediately. If they reveal favourable indications of oil,
then Colonel Ojukwu's clique will succeed in arranging
loans or military supplies from France or other European
countries interested in oil concessions. If they obtain funds
they will be able to buy armaments. If they do, this war
may go on for a long time before we subdue the rebellion.'

'Or possibly lose the war?'

Gobi mopped his head again. 'Possibly,' he conceded,
'but it's not likely. Yet you can appreciate how vital it is
that we recover these surveys immediately.'

The picture was clear. If the French backed Biafra,
and they came out top in the dogfight, they would be
sitting in the pound seats, oil-wise. Being French, they'd
probably play their cards cannily. Any help afforded the
Biafrans would not be direct, but funnelled through arms
dealers, or even their own agents, posing as arms dealers.
Shades of Katanga, I thought.

'What about the other oil companies?' I asked curiously.
'How do they fit into the picture? Are they pro or against?'

Gobi shrugged. 'Who can tell? We will go on getting
revenue from Gulf Oil as their wells are off-shore and it
would be impossible for the rebels to attack them. Okan
Field is seven miles off-shore. It produces 65,000 barrels
of oil a day. Shell BP send their oil by pipe-line to Bonny
terminal on the coast. It's possible the rebels may destroy
these facilities. The Italians are busy at Mbede and
Ebocha, sixty miles north of Port Harcourt. We may lose
those fields to the rebels. Phillips Oil Company is drilling
at Gilli-Gilli, ten miles west of Benin City. Tennessee
Gas Transmission and Sinclair Oil are at Brass River, twenty
miles south of Ughelli. All are in the danger area.'

'With all the other international companies involved, why are you so worried about the French?'

Gobi thumped the table softly. 'Because, at the moment, we believe the others will remain neutral, or officially neutral, in the conflict. But we feel sure the French will back the rebels. There are reports of arms waiting at Libreville in Gabon ready to be flown in. You must realize how vital it is that we recover these maps?'

I beckoned a waiter. 'Calm down, what are you drinking?'

'A Chapman's.'

I shuddered. 'Bring me Spey Royal on the rocks and a Chapman's.'

The waiter went off and I thought over what Gobi had told me. I'd learned the hard way that whenever someone tried to rush me into a deal it was usually to his benefit and my detriment. I held my right hand up in front of his face, fingers widespread, then slowly opened and closed them a few times. 'Excuse me, Mr Gobi, it's time for my five-finger exercise.'

He looked at me blankly. 'I don't understand.'

'Let me show you.' I closed my fingers slowly and deliberately, one by one. 'Listen carefully,' I said, 'to what the fingers are conveying. The five finger exercise. WHERE . . . DO . . . I . . . COME . . . IN. Alternatively, WHAT'S . . . IN . . . IT . . . FOR . . . ME?'

'Fly me to Wakki to secure these oil maps. Mr Kelly will be pleased you did.'

There was some sharp angle to this deal. I probed gently. 'Why not commandeer an air force plane?'

He shook his head. 'We do not want the French to know that the Nigerian Federal Government has taken official military action against their company at this stage. We fly as civilians and could blame a few hot-headed soldiers if there's shooting for acting without orders. We can't afford to make enemies unnecessarily. My Government would not be ungrateful Mr Gibson and it would be in Mr Kelly's interests if you co-operated with us to help recover these maps.'

I shook my head. 'You'll have to do better than that, Mr Gobi. If I'm going to help you pull the chestnuts out of the fire, I want to finish up with a few of them. Here's my proposition. Mr Kelly wants oil concessions, that's why I'm here. You agree to furnish me with copies of all the survey maps, plus an undertaking in writing on behalf of your government that Kelly will be given first option to take over such areas of the French concessions he selects, should the Federal Government cancel the French leases.'

Gobi shook his head protestingly. 'You don't trust me, Captain. I give you my word.'

'Don't be naïve. There's millions of dollars' worth of oil concessions at stake.'

He was silent for a few seconds, then tried again. 'Your orders were to put your aircraft at my disposal, Mr Gibson.'

'Putting myself at your disposal and flying an aircraft into rebel territory is quite a different issue. I'm certain Mr Kelly never had that in mind when he offered his aircraft.'

'There will be no danger,' he said. 'There's a small dirt air-strip beside the bungalow at Wakki. The tribal chief there, the Aku Uka, is a supporter of the Federal Government. How many passengers can your plane take?'

'Six.'

'Then we will take four soldiers as an escort.'

'Did I hear you say there'd be no danger?'

'We take them as insurance only,' he said blandly. 'We will land at Wakki, the bungalows are beside the strip, demand the papers from the French, and return immediately.'

The aeromagnetic charts, I realized, would be invaluable to Kelly. Abruptly I stood up. 'Give me that in writing and we'll go.' I went across to the reception desk, took a sheet of paper from the clerk, dated it Lagos, May 1st, 1967 and wrote.

'I, Yousef Gobi, in my capacity as Economic Adviser to the Federal Nigerian Government, do hereby certify that in return for Mr John Gibson's flying me to Wakki in order to recover certain oil maps, I agree to the following:

1. He is to be furnished with duplicates of all documents collected.

2. His employer, Mr Aloysius Kelly, of Dallas, USA, shall be entitled to first claim on oil drilling concessions that may become available and which the Federal Government will make available for leasing after the conclusion of the current hostilities.

Signed

I pushed it under his nose. 'Sign,' I said.

Reluctantly he took a pen from his pocket. 'I assure you, Captain,' he said. 'My word is good enough.'

'I believe you,' I said drily, 'but Mr Kelly would prefer a signature. Even if your Government repudiated the agreement, it would help to dissuade anyone else jumping in too hastily and risking an expensive law-suit.'

I folded the document and placed it carefully in my wallet.

Gobi stood up, 'There are arrangements I must make. I'll meet you at the airport in an hour. My driver will take you there immediately to prepare your plane. I'll take a taxi to headquarters.' He hurried off.

I went up to my room, collected my briefcase and maps, and Gobi's driver drove swiftly out to the airport. When Gobi arrived forty minutes later, I had the Aero Commander fuelled, warmed up, and waiting on the tarmac. Two cars came speeding round the international terminal

and drove on to the tarmac beside the plane. As Gobi and
three Nigerian civilians climbed out, four heavily-armed
Nigerian soldiers jumped out of the other car, one of
them a lieutenant. They all carried Sten guns, and grenades
dangled from the harness of their uniforms. Spare maga-
zines of Sten ammunition were clipped round their belts.

Gobi held a hurried final conference with the officials
around him, then scurried across to the aircraft. 'I have
arranged everything, Captain. Can we leave at once?'

'Sure.'

Five minutes later our wheels cleared the tarmac and
I hauled out the map to check the course for Wakki. Gobi,
in the co-pilot's seat, leaned towards me. 'What route
are you flying, Mr Gibson? Small villages in the jungle like
Wakki are difficult to locate after a long flight.'

'I'll head for Enugu first. It should be easy enough to
pinpoint Wakki twenty miles south-west. If we try and
hit Wakki direct we're liable to miss it.'

He shook his head. 'It's best not to fly over Enugu,
Captain. They may see us turn towards Wakki and send
soldiers to investigate.'

'You have a point there,' I conceded, 'We'll keep well
away from the town. We'll set course for Wakki from a
few miles south of Enugu.'

He nodded his agreement. 'I think it would be wiser.'

The land was a pattern of yellow and green with strips
of silver indicating water. There were a lot of silver strips.
From 15,000 feet a range of mountains were barely discernible in the haze. I checked them against the map. We
were on course. There were no fires, no smoke, no indication in the peaceful landscape beneath of the hordes
of blacks fighting a war over oil.

An hour and a half later Gobi pointed, 'There it is.'

Ahead lay a small, red-coloured, earth strip, heading
north-east, south-west into the prevailing winds, and barely
six hundred yards in length. In the north-east corner was

a large bungalow and scattered around it were several corrugated iron sheds. A new roof of one of the sheds caught the sun and flashed as we flew over. Drums of petrol were stacked around it. Two miles to the south was the village of Wakki, comprising a few dozen huts clustered around a single main street of small shops. The jungle crowded thick and dense around it.

'I'll make a low pass over the strip and have a look at the surface,' I told Gobi.

'No,' he was emphatic. 'It's best that we go straight in. Avoid coming in to land over Wakki. The rebels may have soldiers in the village and they'll come out to the airstrip to investigate.'

I pulled back the throttles. 'And if they do, what do you propose to tell them?'

'That I have orders to pick up the papers and fly them to Port Harcourt. That's in the centre of Ibo territory. It may induce them to let us go.'

'I hope you're right,' I said. I checked the wind against smoke streaming from a small clearing where someone was burning bush, dropped the wheels and flap and headed straight in to land. It had been raining and as I touched down, showers of red mud splashed up over the clean polished fuselage of the Aero Commander. I stood heavily on the brakes, pulled up short, spun round and taxied rapidly back towards the bungalow at the north-east end. I turned the aircraft round into the wind ready for a quick take-off and cut the motors. 'Come on,' I told Gobi. 'Now we're here let's move fast and get to hell out of it.' We slipped hastily out of the cockpit, I opened the door, Gobi jumped down and we headed towards the bungalow, the Nigerian soldiers following close behind.

As we approached the bungalow, a thick-set sallow European walked out of the house and down the path towards us. Dressed in khaki shirt and slacks, he wore a grubby blue beret. He was forty or so years of age and running into fat around the waist and jowls.

He looked at us enquiringly as we approached. '*Bonjour, messieurs,*' he said. 'My name is Marcel le Clarry. Can I be of any assistance?' He looked at me enquiringly.

I held out my hand. 'Gibson. I'm only the pilot,' I said. 'Mr Gobi here is running the show.' He shook my hand and turned to Gobi.

Gobi was abrupt. 'Good morning, Mr Le Clarry. My name is Gobi. I am an adviser to the Ministry of Economic Development. I have orders to collect all your company's survey documents and take them to Lagos for safe-keeping. My department regards it as vital that these geological surveys do not fall into the hands of the Ibos.'

Le Clarry frowned. 'I'm not sure that I can agree with you, Mr Gobi,' he said. 'The documents are the property of my company. Without authority from headquarters in Paris, I cannot hand over our surveys. They are highly confidential.' He spread his hands. 'You understand my position. We have spent a lot of money on these aerial investigations and their interpretation. The information they reveal would be worth millions of francs to any rival company interested in potential oilfields in the Onitsha area,' he paused, 'or to any individuals. I am sure you appreciate my position, Mr Gobi. I must refuse.'

Gobi turned to the lieutenant and spoke briefly in some local dialect. The lieutenant raised his Sten gun and pointed it at Le Clarry. 'Mr Le Clarry,' said Gobi, 'I have my orders and these soldiers are here to see that they are enforced. The maps, please.'

Le Clarry froze. I watched his fists clench as he turned white with rage. 'I refuse,' he said furiously. 'The papers are the property of my company.'

Gobi spoke quietly to the lieutenant. Swinging his sten gun in a short vicious arc, he smashed it across the side of Le Clarry's face. The Frenchman reeled back and collapsed. 'Pick him up,' said Gobi. Two of the soldiers stepped forward and hauled him half-dazed to his feet.

Gobi caught him by the hair and jerked his head back. 'We have no time to waste, Le Clarry. The papers at once please, or I'll give orders to shoot you in the legs.'

Le Clarry looked at him shakily. 'Very well,' he said, 'but somebody's going to pay for this.'

Gobi ignored the remark. 'The papers, please.' He nodded and the soldiers released Le Clarry—who led us back to the house, through the living-room, into a large office. There he pointed to two large wooden tables, covered with geological maps. 'There are the maps.' Two padlocks secured a massive cupboard that filled most of the opposite wall.

Gobi held out his hand. 'The keys, please.'

Reluctantly Le Clarry reached into his pocket and threw a key-ring with two keys on to the table. Snatching them up, Gobi moved across and opened the padlocks. Bundles of files filled the cupboard, packed neatly away.

Gobi pointed. 'Take them to the plane.' The lieutenant beckoned to two of the soldiers, who collected the files and headed for the aircraft, as Gobi and the lieutenant began to roll up the maps on the table. Moving across to the window, I saw the two soldiers open the cabin door and climb into the aircraft with their files. As I turned away, I saw a young man in khaki run across the corner of the strip and disappear into the bush in the direction of the village.

I told Gobi. 'I've just seen a man running towards Wakki. I've got a hunch that alarm bells are about to start ringing.'

He nodded. 'We'll be leaving in a few minutes.'

Le Clarry, slumped in a chair, watched us bitterly. 'This robbery will be reported to my government,' he said.

Gobi whirled on him. 'If you speak again,' he shouted,

'I'll have you shot. International oil companies such as yours are responsible for this Ibo rebellion.'

The lieutenant finished rolling up the maps. 'Come,' said Gobi. 'Let's go.' He opened the last two drawers of the desk, collected several files there, and clutching them under his arm, ran from the room. As we jumped down the steps of the verandah on to the path, the soldiers running back from the aircraft joined us. I heard a truck motor grinding down the road that ran past the rear of the building.

Gobi swung round to the lieutenant. 'Take your men,' he said, 'and guard the back of the house while we start the aircraft. If they are Ibos, open fire immediately, hold them back until you hear the engines, then join us.'

'Yes, sir.' Beckoning to his soldiers, the lieutenant ran up the steps into the house.

'Come,' said Gobi. The noise of the truck grew louder, then it died down and I heard the squeal of brakes as it pulled up.

As we ran to the plane, Gobi jumped into the cabin and dumped the files on the rear seat. 'Quick! Start the engines. I'll wait at the door for the soldiers.'

I'd left the petrol on and the trim tabs set for a quick take-off. I dropped into the seat and hit the port starter button. The engine coughed twice, then fired. As I jammed my thumb down on the starter, I heard a rapid burst of firing from the house. Several soldiers, wearing pale jungle-spotted uniforms darted round the side of the bungalow and ran up the steps on to the verandah.

I felt the thud of compressed air against my ears and knew that Gobi had slammed the door shut. As the starboard motor caught and spluttered into action, he dropped into the seat beside me.

'Take off,' he shouted. 'We can't help them. They're surrounded. Get away before the rebels start shooting at us.'

I slammed the throttles forward, and as the Aero Commander commenced to roll, I glanced back at the bungalow. One of the Ibos, crouching before a window, was firing into the house. He turned towards us and just before he passed out of sight behind the starboard motor, I saw him swing around and face the aircraft. I waited helplessly, my back muscles tensed, all set to feel bullets smacking into them while the plane slowly gathered speed and pulled away, but for some reason known only to himself and Allah he never opened fire! Maybe one of Gobi's Nigerians shot him a second later or possibly he'd emptied his magazine. A seemingly interminable period lapsed before we began to pick up speed and hurtle down the runway, the motors screaming under full emergency power. I hauled the Aero Commander off the ground just on the stall and slammed up the undercarriage lever as we gathered speed and climbed away. I checked the wings carefully. There was no sign of bullet damage.

Gobi was smiling. 'We made it,' he said.

'By about five seconds,' I told him. 'I only hope the papers are the right ones.'

'They must be,' he said confidently, 'I cleared everything out of the office.'

I nodded. 'I hope you're right. What about the lieutenant and his soldiers?'

Gobi shrugged. 'They're soldiers in a country at war. They're expendable. My government would be prepared to sacrifice an entire battalion to prevent these documents falling into rebel hands. What are four men to a country at war?'

'Nothing,' I told him. 'Unless of course you happen to be one of them.'

One hour twenty minutes later we touched down at Ikeja Airport. As I taxied up, Gobi left the cockpit and, darting back to the cabin, began assembling the files the soldiers had dumped.

I cut the motors and moved swiftly back to the cabin. 'Just a moment. Remember the deal. I get copies of all the files and maps.'

Gobi looked at me reproachfully. 'Of course, Mr Gibson,' he said. 'I will see that you get them.'

I picked up one of the files and glanced through it. It was technical, in French, and to me quite meaningless. I'd have to go along with Gobi. I had no facilities for having photostats made. 'Where are we having my copies made?' I asked. To emphasize the point I deliberately picked up several of the files and tucked them under my arm.

'I'll have them Xeroxed at headquarters,' he said. 'We have a machine there.'

'Good,' I said casually. 'I'll come along with you and see it done.'

I watched every sheet xeroxed and collected a copy of each of them as it came off the machine. When I left the Ministry of Economic Affairs' Building it was after midnight, but I had a duplicate of every file we had collected. For whatever they were worth, they would have to be sent to Kelly immediately for evaluation.

Stopping the taxi at the cable office I drafted a message to Gisela. 'Come immediately collect important documents stop Too valuable to post stop Most urgent. John.' Back in my room at the hotel, I put them in the wardrobe, locked it and hid the key under the carpet.

I wedged a chair under the door handle, and poured myself a shot of Spey Royal; diluted with warm water, it still tasted good. The documents in the wardrobe might be the key to a new oil field.

The chair was a poor substitute for a safe deposit but it would have to serve as a bodyguard.

I fell into bed, and even the heat and angry buzzing of mosquitoes couldn't stop me falling asleep.

CHAPTER FIVE

D R E A M I N G , I heard again the intermittent stutter of
the Sten guns at Wakki. I woke with a start and sat up.
The intermittent shrilling of the telephone had roused
me. I reached for the phone. Outside it was broad day-
light and the sun poured a hot-flamed beam through the
windows. Flies buzzed round my head, attracted by the
salty sweat, and tried to settle on my face. Wearily I answered. 'Yes?'

'One moment, Mr Gibson.' The receptionist's smooth
voice. Someone else came on to the line. The English was
fluent with a heavy foreign accent. 'Good morning, Mr
Gibson. My name is George Dakis. I am sorry to disturb
you, but I should like to meet you. There are urgent
matters I wish to discuss to our mutual benefit.'

I shook myself awake. 'Give me ten minutes,' I said.
'I'll see you on the verandah.'

Dakis was standing by the entrance as I came down the
stairs.

Dark and sallow with black darting eyes, he was wearing
green shorts and stockings. A green shirt matched the shorts.
I assessed his nationality as either Lebanese or Greek.

I was right about the Greek. He introduced himself :
'George Dakis, Mr Gibson, formerly of Athens and now of
Lagos.' He sighed, 'I regret to say.'

'Good morning. Why?' I asked abruptly.

He glanced around and lowered his voice, 'Lagos! You
think any Greek in his right senses would voluntarily
live here when Athens has so much to offer?' He shrugged.
'Unfortunately it is necessary to earn a living.'

A black polished Cadillac with a chauffeur was parked
in front of the hotel. I nodded towards it. 'That yours?'

59

'Yes, Mr Gibson.'

'You don't seem to be doing so badly,' I said drily. 'Shall we sit down?' I studied Dakis as we walked out to the verandah. He must have been a good-looking man in his youth, but now, at forty plus, the jaw-line was obscured by layers of fat and his jowls sagged. His hair receded well back from his temples. A soft life and plenty of drink had put its stamp on the face watching me, but the brown blood-shot eyes were bright with intelligence.

The verandah was almost deserted. A few tables away, two Nigerians were drinking a long, coloured, sickly-looking brew and talking in French with a European. As we sat down they lowered their voices and leaned closer together, glancing occasionally in our direction as they obviously discussed us.

A three-stripe BOAC pilot and a radio officer were drinking beer at the table beside the entrance. They had it easy, I thought. All they had to do was fly their aeroplane, do what they were told, keep out of trouble, and wait for their pensions. But even as I watched them I knew that the soul-destroying life of flying scheduled services wasn't for me. I could never change places. I glanced at Dakis, watching me steadily.

'Well, Mr Dakis, what do you want to tell me?'

He called a waiter. 'A drink first, Captain, or is it too early?'

'It's too early until I have a drink.'

With a flourish he produced a card. Expensively engraved, it read, 'Monsieur George Dakis. Sales Manager, Central European Arms Distributors, Rue Vende, Liechtenstein.'

I tucked it in my pocket. 'I'm not a buyer, Mr Dakis, I'm a civilian pilot for an oil company.'

'It's your flying abilities that I'm interested in, Mr Gibson.' The brown eyes watched me steadily. He lowered his voice. 'I know a little about you, Mr Gibson. You flew in Katanga for Moishe Tshombe and later for General Mobutu in the Congo Air Force. I am told that you are a competent and reliable pilot who gives good value for money received.' He smiled and sat back as the waiter came up with the drinks. He picked up his whisky and sipped it delicately. Then, putting the glass gently down on the table, he studied it for a moment. I took a slug of my Spey Royal and waited for Dakis to get round to whatever he had in mind.

'Mr Gibson,' he said, 'I know of your company and what brings you to Lagos. You're flying an aircraft that is on loan to the Ministry of Economic Affairs, owned by Mr Kelly of Texas, an oil millionaire. He is interested in obtaining oil concessions, possibly in the area where a French company has been prospecting. However, that is none of my business and does not concern me. On behalf of my company I have been responsible for selling certain arms to the Nigerian Federal Government. Unfortunately, due to the refusal of Western countries to supply aircraft, we have been forced to buy Russian MIG 17s and Czechoslovakian Delfin jets. The MIGs and Delfins will be assembled at Kano. I would have preferred to deal with the West, but they refused to supply, so we had no alternative. I'm sure you will agree with me, Mr Gibson.'

'You're in business,' I said noncommittally. 'Where you get the goods is your concern.'

Dakis smiled. 'I think we can speak frankly.'

'What's the proposition?' I asked abruptly.

Dakis leaned across the table. 'My contract with the Federal Government states that I must guarantee the aircraft are airworthy and fully operational before they are handed over to the Nigerian Air Force. These aircraft are not new. The Federal Government, who are aware of your past experience, would accept your signature confirming that the aeroplanes I am selling them are airworthy. My proposition will not clash with your duties to Mr Kelly,

on the contrary. It is possible that you will have time to
spare whilst in Nigeria. If you could assist me, Mr Gibson,
I am prepared to make it well worth your while. I'll
be frank. My company is making a considerable profit on
these aircraft and can afford to pay you well.'

I toyed with my glass, watching the condensation run
down the outside and make small rings on the table. 'What's
your idea of paying well?' I asked curiously.

Dakis pushed away his glass. 'As my technical adviser,
you are to be available whenever I require you, provided
you are not flying Mr Kelly's plane, and give me your
full technical co-operation. For that I would be prepared
to pay you the sum of five hundred pounds a month. I
think it's a generous offer, Captain Gibson.'

'For advice only, without flying, it's a fair offer,' I
admitted. 'What about the flying angle? The aircraft will
have to be test flown.'

Dakis ran his fingers through his thick greying hair.
'That is difficult for me to evaluate. What would you
suggest?'

'Let me think that one over.' I poured the rest of my
whisky down my neck, savouring the coldness as it slid
down. I sat back and closed my eyes. 'The aircraft weren't
new,' he had said. That meant the MIG 17s were probably
ex-Egyptian Air Force jobs that had been replaced by
MIG 21s. God knows where the Delfins had come from, all
I knew was that they were light single-engined Czechoslovakian jet trainers. A Jewish pilot told me: 'When I
don't eat kosher it must be extra good.'

Test-flying old beaten-up surplus Gyppo MIG 17 aircraft
was certainly not eating kosher, so the price had better be
good. I opened my eyes and smiled at Dakis. 'It will cost
you fifty pounds an hour.'

He never hesitated. 'It's a deal.' He'd agreed too easily.

I held up my hand. 'Not so fast. That's for the fighters.
The Delfin trainers are more expensive—£75 an hour.'

He nodded sadly. 'You drive a hard bargain.'

'Maybe, but I'm good and I don't break aircraft. Whatever you pay me is cheaper than having one of them smeared across the runway.'

He nodded again. 'That makes sense, Captain.' He held out his hand. 'Fifty pounds an hour for the MIGs, £75 for the Delfins. I agree. It's a deal.'

We shook hands.

He beckoned to the African waiter at the door. 'This,' he said, 'calls for another drink.' The bastard seemed too cheerful. I should have doubled the Delfin rate. Over the second drink he told me that Russian transport aircraft would be flying the MIGs and Delfins into Kano within the next few days. Russian and Czech technicians would accompany the aircraft and assemble them there.

Now I knew the reason for the tension at Kano Airport when I'd landed with Gisela.

Over further drinks Dakis opened up. He told me his company had supplied a considerable proportion of the arms used in the Congo, and he had seen me several times in Kinshasa. 'We want pilots,' he said. 'What's happened to those who flew with you in the Congo? Do you think you could persuade any of them to join the Federal Forces?'

'Yes, provided the money is right.' Tubby Sanders, I knew, was flying for an air charter company in Rhodesia. Karel Olivier was probably on his farm near White River in the Eastern Transvaal. Once I put the word out on the grapevine they'd come homing in on Lagos like homesick pigeons. Perhaps vultures was a better description.

'They'll cost you a thousand pounds a month each,' I told Dakis. 'For that I can guarantee you good efficient professionals.'

He nodded thoughtfully. 'I'll have to confirm the salaries, but I think it will be in order. In the meantime would you try to locate them?'

'Will do,' I said. 'Is there anything else?' I'd suddenly

remembered the survey maps and Xerox file copies in the wardrobe.

'Yes, excuse me, but do you hold any definite political feelings about this Nigerian dispute?'

'None whatsoever,' I said. 'Nigerians, Hausas, Yorubas or Ibos, they're all the same to me. I'm a professional, I'm paid to fly. Period.'

Dakis nodded thoughtfully. 'That's very interesting,' he said. 'Very interesting indeed.' The brown eyes watched me consideringly. 'You are no doubt aware, Captain, that the Ibos are also in the market for aircraft.'

'I should imagine so,' I said easily. 'Are you supplying them as well?'

Dakis grinned. 'No comment, but I'm going to ask you a straight question. If you don't agree, I have your promise that the matter is forgotten?'

'You have my word,' I said, 'and that's a promise.'

Dakis said seriously, 'I'm putting my neck on a block, but sometimes in business it is necessary. Captain, would you be prepared, at a later stage, to defect to the Ibos with one of the Delfin jet fighters?'

I'd heard a few propositions in my time but this took some beating. I considered the implications. It would mean abandoning Kelly's $200,000 Aero Commander at Ikeja Airport, and put paid to his hopes of oil concessions. I'd cut a few corners in my time but this proposition . . . I whistled gently. I asked Dakis curiously, 'What's it worth?'

'One hundred thousand pounds paid into your Swiss bank account.'

It was a lot of money. Regretfully I shook my head. 'That's one hell of a lot of money, George,' I said, 'but I'm sorry, it's out. Too many complications. I couldn't ruin Kelly's chances of tying up the oil concessions he's after.'

He stood up. 'Don't condemn the idea entirely, Mr Gibson, maybe one day you will change your mind. In the meantime we agree that further discussion is postponed and the proposition forgotten.'

'Fair enough. I'll give you the names of a couple of good pilots I know.' On his cigarette packet I scribbled down the addresses of Jerry van Ginkel and Karel Olivier.

Dakis drained his glass and stood up. 'Thank you, Mr Gibson. I will arrange that your salary as technical adviser starts as from today. Now I must go.'

I watched the short stocky figure weave his way through the tables and climb into the Cadillac. The driver closed the door gently behind him and he waved as they pulled away. George Dakis, I thought, was quite an operator. Then I remembered the survey maps in my room and headed rapidly for the hotel entrance.

CHAPTER SIX

M y rubber-soled shoes made no sound as I moved down the passage towards my room. As I turned the door handle I heard the door of my wardrobe slam shut. I kicked the door open and moved in fast.

Standing with his back to the wardrobe, and several files in his hands was the Frenchman from Wakki, Marcel le Clarry, dressed in a grey sweat shirt and old blue denims. He dropped the files and, pulling a knife from his pocket, flicked it open. The blade sprang out and he moved towards me.

'I've come for my files, you'd better stand back.'

'You're wasting your time. When your Government decided to back Biafra you lost your title. Get out. And leave the files.'

He moved slowly towards me, the knife held flat and level. 'I'm going to kill you,' he said. Moving fast he closed in. He feinted and tried for my groin with a fast upward slash. I swayed sideways and jumped at him. I struck his arm, the one holding the knife, and at the same time hit him with the edge of my hand across his neck as he drove past. He staggered, turned, came back fast and kicked viciously at the pit of my stomach. I grabbed his leg and, swinging with the kick, gave it a tug. He fell on the bed.

'You son of a bitch,' I said, and moved in. As I bent to grab him he slashed at my leg. I dropped my left hand and felt the knife rip against my palm. I grabbed his wrist, fell on him and butted him in the face as he tried to pull out from beneath me. I felt the bone in his nose crunch as I slammed my head down.

There was still plenty of fight left in him. He squirmed from underneath me and pulled away. Desperately holding on to my wrist we slid off the bed on to the floor. I grabbed a handful of long black greasy hair and, lifting his head, slammed it down on to the concrete floor. I felt him go limp beneath me. Shakily I stood up. A long shallow cut across the palm of my hand, was bleeding profusely. I rolled my handkerchief into a wad and placing it over the wound, tensed my fingers around it to stop the bleeding. The cut didn't appear deep enough to justify stitches, the handkerchief would do until I could get some plaster over it. I picked up the files, put them back into the cupboard, and locked it. Then, picking up the flick knife, I took the water urn that stood beside my bed and poured it slowly over the Frenchman's face.

He shook his head groggily. I hauled him up and threw him into the armchair, and pushed the blade against his throat at the base of his ear. I don't like knives, they've never been my line of territory, but they spoke a language Le Clarry understood. I waited for him to come round completely, then pricked him gently. He flinched. 'Tell me,' I said, 'who are you working for?' He glared at me. I pushed the point in a little farther, and a small drop of blood broke the skin. 'Talk,' I said, 'or I'll cut you to ribbons, I'll tell the police that I caught you in my room and was forced to defend myself. Talk, you bastard!'

'You stole the papers,' he said. 'You stole them from my company at Wakki. You have no right to them.'

'As much right as you,' I said. 'The papers are the property of the Federal Government.'

'Then why did you have copies made?' he snarled.

'I don't need to tell you,' I said, 'but you might say, for services rendered helping the Federal Government to get them before your company did a deal with the Biafrans.'

He tried to sit up. I pressed him back into the chair. 'You forget, there's a knife under your ear. You really shouldn't jump about.' I pressed the knife a fraction harder.

He flinched, 'You won't get away with it. My company provided the capital for the surveys. French enterprise has succeeded in locating the oilfields, and the maps are ours. I know that you represent American oil interests.'

'Correct,' I told him. 'But they pay me and I'm not here to make the French Government happy. You French are playing a dirty game. Your company is encouraging the Biafran secession, hoping to grab the oil concessions that have been granted to other nations by the Federal Government. As a reward for services rendered. You couldn't care less how many thousands are killed or suffer as long as you can obtain the concessions. Now get out.'

I stood back, the blade of the knife pointed at his groin. 'Turn round and walk out slowly.' I followed him, knife against his back, as he went. At the door he paused and turned his head. 'You'll regret this,' he said. His hand, moving in a blur of speed, snatched the knife from me. I sprang back as he came towards me, hands thrust out low in front of him. I recalled once seeing Judo experts at a demonstration adopt a similar stance. I moved forward and slammed into him, simultaneously bringing my knee up into his crotch as I grabbed him by the neck. I held on grimly to his knife arm, and threw him against the iron end of the bed. The knife clattered noisily to the floor. As we staggered back, he jabbed me in the solar plexus with the stiffened fingers of his right hand. I felt them drive in and hung on grimly while I rode out a wave of pure agony. His other hand swung back and chopped me savagely at the bottom of my rib cage. I felt as if he'd slammed me with a club. He was having the best of the deal.

Again the edge of his hand slashed me across the back, the blow landing on my kidneys and now the pain was indescribable. My left fist, jabbing at his body, seemed to be doing no damage. My face was jammed against his as I clung to him. I gasped for air and his ear was beside my mouth. I clamped my teeth down and bit, grinding my teeth down, and at the same time pulling away with every muscle in my mouth and neck strained to the limit, as I tore at it.

He screamed and his hands came up under my chin in a desperate effort to lever back my head. Behind us was the open window. With a last desperate effort, as he chopped me again across the kidneys, I pushed him backwards towards it. His knees struck the sill, and releasing my grip around his neck, I placed both hands against his chest and shoved. Too late he tried to grab my shoulders.

He fell backwards and out of the window, screamed once, then there was silence. I leaned out. Two storeys below he lay still and crumpled on the cement sidewalk. I knew he was dead.

I staggered to the washbasin and looked into the mirror above it. My mouth, chin and throat were scarlet with the blood from his ear. I turned on both taps and vomited into the basin as I washed it off.

Beneath the window there was a lot of shouting, I staggered across the room, sat on the bed, and grabbed the phone. 'Get me Mr Gobi,' I told the operator, 'Ministry of Economic Affairs. Tell him to come here at once. Then call the police. I caught a man stealing and he jumped out of the window.' Wearily, my ribs aching like hell, I started to prepare my story for the police.

They arrived about fifteen minutes later, an inspector smart and trim in khaki, accompanied by a sergeant. Fortunately Gobi arrived a few seconds after they walked in. It was an hour before we got rid of them. If it hadn't been for Gobi I'd have been hauled off to the local station for interrogation. I kept my story simple. I had come into the room, found the man standing at the wardrobe and he attacked me. I had grabbed him to prevent his escaping but he had torn himself free and, in his panic, forgetting he was two storeys up, jumped out of the window in a des-

perate effort to escape. I showed my cut hand to sub-
stantiate the story as the inspector looked sceptical. 'No,' I
told him, 'I have no idea what he was after, probably
money.' I pointed to my open suitcase.

The inspector shook his head. 'I doubt it, Mr Gibson.
We found over three hundred pounds in the dead man's
pockets. However, you will be here if we wish to ask you
any further questions.' Politely phrased it was clearly an
order : 'Don't attempt to leave.' There was an awkward
silence. The sergeant wrapped up the flick knife in a towel.
'I'll vouch for Mr Gibson, Inspector,' said Gobi smoothly.

They finally went off and the inspector gave me a wooden
look as he closed the door.

'What happened?' asked Gobi. I told him what I'd seen
as I opened the door.

'Somebody in my department must be in the pay of the
French,' he said.

I tenderly rubbed my aching diaphragm. 'You're not
kidding,' I told him.

'Those papers,' Gobi said innocently. 'I have a safe in
my office. Would you like me to put them into safe keeping
for you? It would be a serious blow to the Federal Government if your copies were stolen.'

'And to me,' I said drily. 'No, thanks, I'll keep them.
Believe me, no one else will have an opportunity of stealing
them.' I stressed the 'no one' and he looked pained.

'As you wish, Captain.'

I opened my briefcase tipped my airmaps on to the
bed, packed the files carefully into the case, and snapped it
shut and locked it. 'From now on,' I told Gobi, 'this case
stays with me.'

He got up and walked across to the window. 'They've
taken our friend away,' he said casually. He glanced at
his watch. 'Captain, I must go.'

'I'll see you to the car,' I said.

He went off in his big Buick. I bought a copy of *Time*

and settled down on the verandah, the case tucked between my leg and the side of the chair.

Ordering a double Spey Royal and water I began to page through *Time*. I found an item which stated briefly that certain oil companies had paid eighty million dollars in oil royalties to Colonel Ojukwu's Biafran Government. It also said that the Biafrans were claiming territory covering nearly thirty thousand square miles which included some of Nigeria's richest oil land.

Civil wars were the dirtiest wars,. I thought, and now, with the help of the oil royalties, it looked as if Biafra would be able to find the necessary finance to give its army a punch. The teams were beginning to shape up. Great Britain, anxious to combat Soviet influence and safeguard its own oil interests, would certainly continue to supply weapons other than aircraft to the Federal Government.

France with De Gaulle and his anti-U.S.-British politics, would back the Biafrans, gambling on a victory that would enable France to control the incredibly rich oil reserves of the Niger Delta. I wondered where the Yanks fitted in on this little deal. Kelly, from whatever sources of information he relied upon, had decided that the winning team would be the Federal Government, so he was backing them. Hence my presence in Lagos. Still, Kelly was only a wildcat operator. I wondered what the official U.S. policy was; probably what the CIA thought was best for Uncle Sam.

I mentally shrugged and called for another drink. What the hell! I was a paid employee. A minute pawn in a colossal game of chess played at top government level. Whatever the outcome, I'd guarantee that a hell of a lot of black Nigerian pawns would be chopped before the game ended. I'd be prepared to underwrite that one. I thought about the scene some more. Finally I came to the conclusion that it was a privilege to live in these times. There was seldom time to be bored. The best of Irish

luck to the lot of the bastards; I decided I'd look after
Kelly and Gibson and let the chips fall as they would.
It was hot, and the coolness of the swimming pool beckoned,
but swimming around clutching my case in one hand would
appear peculiar. Regretfully I rejected the idea.

I decided to go back to my room and write a few overdue letters. Somewhere in my suitcase was one from Tubby
Sanders. Gisela had given it to me in Rome, and I hadn't
yet got around to replying. Back in the room I dug out
the airmail pad and read briefly through Tubby's letter.

> Rhodesian Air Freighters,
> Salisbury Airport,
> Rhodesia
> 21.4.67

Dear John,
How goes it, you old sinner? If you're tired of loafing around
London, I can get you a job out here. We're operating 3 old
ex-KLM DC7C Freighters and managing to keep well out of
the red. We fly in a lot of meat from outlying areas, plus
various unmentionable items that are in short supply due to
sanctions. The 7C's have a decent range, plus minus 5000
miles. So we can cover most of Africa. Not all the African
states are interested in boycotts. When it comes to choice
between ideology or business, believe me, business wins every
time! The day they lift sanctions I go into mourning! So
we keep flying! Salary is reasonable. £8,000 a year, plus
bonus. Let me know if you are interested.

> Best regards,
> Yours sincerely,
> TUBBY

P.S. There are also some very nice pickings. Tax free!

> TUBBY

I folded up the letter and slipped it back into my suitcase. It might be an idea to join Tubby in Rhodesia one day. I wondered what he meant by 'pickings'. I began to write :

Dear Tubby,

I'm flying an Aero-Commander around these parts for an American oil millionaire. You're no doubt aware that a Civil War has broken out in Nigeria. There may be a few 'pickings' going here as well, but it's still early to say and I'm keeping my fingers crossed. The local air force are getting Russian MIG 17s and some Czechoslovakian Delfins. I've a deal on as technical adviser to check them out for service ability etc. It's worth £500 a month, plus fifty pounds an hour for test flying the MIGs and seventy-five pounds per Delfin. Snag, I don't know how long this show will last, so I may be taking up your offer of a job in Rhodesia.

Salaams,

All the best,

JOHN

I attended to some other routine correspondence, grabbed my case with the files, and, taking the letters, strolled out into the hot streets and posted them at the local post office.

Arriving back at the hotel, the clerk handed me a cable. It was from Gisela.

'Arriving BOAC Ikeja. 2100 hours Thursday. Congratulations. Gisela.'

'Mr Gibson.' I turned, Gobi was standing behind me. 'Good morning.' He nodded at my case. 'So you were serious about your papers, Mr Gibson.'

'Yes,' I said. 'Let's go into the bar, it's cooler with the air conditioning.' He mopped his forehead as we sat down. 'You needn't bother to carry that case around, Mr Gibson. It wouldn't have mattered had the Frenchman succeeded in stealing the charts.'

'Why?' An icy finger traced a path down my spine.

The brown eyes watched me sadly. 'Because,' he sighed, 'they are valueless.'

'What!' A hovering waiter approached. 'Two whiskies,' I said. The waiter went away. 'What do you mean, Gobi?'

'Just that. Our experts have been going through them carefully. They are all purely routine correspondence, and the survey we collected can be obtained from any map office overseas. Our Intelligence has discovered that all the evaluated magnetometer surveys and confidential material were handed over to Ojukwu's representative in Benin City. We know the people who have them, and our agents there have been instructed to concentrate on their recovery.'

I was suspicious. Maybe he was telling the truth, maybe not.

'Well,' I said slowly, 'be that as it may, Le Clarry was certainly interested in recovering them. Come hell or high water, I'm still hanging on to my copies.'

He shrugged. 'You're welcome, but believe me, they are valueless.'

Something about his delivery and manner convinced me that he was speaking the truth. 'It doesn't make sense. What else could Le Clarry have been after? Christ,' I said, 'all that effort and those four poor bloody soldiers lost, for nothing.'

Gobi nodded. 'That's war, Mr Gibson,' he said. 'It's how it goes. Perhaps Le Clarry was investigating you, and was taking the files as a blind. Who knows. Meanwhile our agents are busy in Benin City. They may be successful.' He stopped speaking and waited as the waiter placed the drinks on the table. I paid for them.

'Meanwhile,' he said, 'the position is extremely serious. The rebels are advancing and are now only ninety miles from Lagos. The Federal army is struggling to stem its advance. Our field commanders have been instructed that

Benin City must be recaptured at all costs in order to furnish us with an airfield. Then air strikes, to protect and recapture the oil wells at Onitsha, can be made.' Picking up the glass of whisky, he downed half of it in a gulp. 'That is why I am here,' he concluded. He gulped down another mouthful of scotch and continued. 'Our air force has hired several of your former associates, pilots you flew with in the Congo. They will be arriving in Lagos tomorrow. I want you please to give me a report on each of these men and their capabilities.'

'If I know them, I will.' I put my glass down with a thump on the table. 'White mercenaries. Now the game really begins to hot up.'

Gobi finished his drink. 'Regretfully, yes, Mr Gibson. But the government feels the sooner this rebellion is quelled the better for all.'

He hesitated, then looked at me directly. 'I have been requested,' he said, 'by Air Headquarters, who know of your record in the Congo, to ask you to assume command of this group of pilots.'

I pushed my chair away from the table. 'Nothing doing, Gobi! I'm employed by Mr Kelly to fly his personal aircraft and place it at your disposal. I also agreed with Mr Dakis, and provided it did not interfere with my duties to Mr Kelly, to flight check and advise him on the serviceability states of the MIGs and Delfins supplied by him to the Federal Government. That's where it ends. Period. I'm not getting involved in any shooting war.'

Gobi shook his head. 'You'll forgive me if I say so, Mr Gibson, but you are taking a very short-sighted view. Ask yourself : "Why did Mr Kelly place his personal aircraft and pilot at the disposal of the Ministry of Economic Affairs and the Federal Government?" He tapped the table emphatically. 'I'll answer it. To obtain sympathetic consideration when applying for a lease when new oil-bearing areas are offered. I am quite sure, knowing his objectives, that he would wish you to collaborate with and assist the Federal Government.'

I finished my drink thoughtfully. Gobi was right. He had me over a barrel. He snapped his fingers at the waiter. 'The same again,' he said. He smiled. 'Do you agree, Captain Gibson?'

'You have a point,' I said gloomily. The smile broadened. 'You are a sensible man,' he said. 'Believe me, the Government requires your technical expertise. Naturally it is prepared to pay for it.'

'Naturally,' I cheered up somewhat. 'How much?'

'What sum,' he asked delicately, 'do you feel will ensure your wholehearted, I repeat, wholehearted, co-operation.'

The wholehearted, repeated, rang a small warning bell. Checking out the aircraft and test-flying them was one thing. Machine-gunning and rocketing people I had no personal grievance against, was another. A small voice inside said softly, 'Don't be a hypocrite, Gibson, it's only a matter of degree, not of principle. If you check the aircraft out you are as guilty as the pilot who presses the firing buttons in the cockpit, and sends the rockets swishing off.' 'Be quiet,' I answered firmly. 'This will be my last African war. When it ends, I'll settle down to a clean boring airline job. Besides, the money is too good to afford the luxury of a conscience.' So I said to Gobi, 'To placate my conscience and ensure my wholehearted co-operation, you'll have to double my salary and double my flying pay. One thousand pounds a month and one hundred pounds an hour flying time, for MIGs and one-fifty for Delfins. For that I'll include operational as well as test-flying. And may the Lord have mercy on my soul.'

'It's a deal,' he said simply. 'You will receive official confirmation of your appointment, in writing, this afternoon.'

He stood up, 'The new pilots,' he said, 'will be arriving

by Nigerian Airways at Ikeja tomorrow morning ten
o'clock. I will arrange transport for you to meet them.
Good morning.'

'Be seeing you.'

As he went out of the door I ordered a double scotch
to wash out the dirty taste the interview had left in my
mouth and thought about my new appointment. Hatchet
man to the Federal Government. I had a few more scotches
but the dirty taste was still there. After dinner I took
a taxi to Ikeja Airport to meet the VC10 bringing Gisela.
It was windy and palm trees were shaking their heads
disapprovingly as I drove past. A light rain was falling
and the windscreen wipers clicked monotonously. Sourly
I watched the VC10's red anti-collision lights flashing as
it came straight in, jets whining as it taxied up. The aircraft was full. From the balcony I caught a glimpse of
Gisela in a white raincoat amongst the passengers. I waited
outside the customs hall for her. She was one of the first
out, and as she walked towards me, carrying a small
suitcase, my spirits lifted.

'It's good to see you,' I said. 'Where's the rest of your
luggage?' She took my arm. 'That's all,' she said. 'I've
booked out for Rome on tomorrow's flight. I'm expecting
Mr Kelly to arrive any day.'

I'd kept the taxi waiting. As we pulled away, I told
her, 'I'm afraid I may have brought you here on a wild-
goose chase. I'll give you the details at the hotel.' I booked
her in and, as she went off to her room with the porter,
I told her, 'I'll give you fifteen minutes to get settled, then
I'll be along.'

She smiled over her shoulder, 'I'll be ready, John,' and
followed the porter off down the passage.

It was, I thought cheerfully, a different Gisela to the
cold efficient business woman I had met in Rome weeks
ago. Her arrival and presence brightened the whole dreary
Nigerian scene. Checking my watch, I wandered into the

bar to watch the news on television for the next fifteen
minutes. The programme seemed to consist of various
cabinet ministers who invariably urged the public to
insist on one nation and one people. It made sense, but
unfortunately Colonel Ojukwu and his eight to twelve
million Ibos had other ideas.

When the fifteen minutes had passed, I headed up
the stairs for Gisela's room and knocked.

'Come in, John.' She was standing against the window,
long legged and graceful. Her breasts, thrust against the thin
silk of her dress in profile against the glare outside, curved
in a line of sheer beauty. She held out her hands as she
came towards me. Ignoring them, I placed my hands on
her waist. 'Gisela, you're beautiful.' The corners of her
mouth quirked in a slight smile. 'I'm glad.'

I drew her to me. She put her arms round my neck and
kissed me, the kiss was soft and lingering. Her breathing
was rapid when I finally released her.

She stepped back and smoothed her hair. 'You surprise
me, Mr Gibson!' As I moved to grab her, she side-stepped
me smoothly and pointed to the chair. 'That's enough. Now
sit down, please, and tell me all about these documents.'

She sat on the bed out of reach. I'd learned long ago
not to rush my fences. I flopped into the armchair. 'This
is the situation to date . . .' I told her of Gobi and the flight
to Wakki, how I had obtained copies of the maps and
papers, and the attempt to steal them, culminating in the
death of the Frenchman. Finally, I told her of Gobi's
remarks about the value of the documents. I held up
the case. 'Here they are, I'm inclined to believe Gobi, but
I'm not certain. They haven't left my possession since Le
Clarry tried to take them. They're your responsibility
now.' I shoved the case under the bed. Gisela nodded
thoughtfully. 'I'll have them translated in Rome,' she
said. 'Whether they have any value or not, I'm certain

Mr Kelly will appreciate the way you've tried to handle his interests.'

She lay back, one elbow propping her up. 'Anything else happened since I left?'

I told her of Gobi's air force proposition and concluded with, 'What do you think Kelly will think of the deal?'

She shrugged. 'He'll probably approve of it. He's pretty ruthless. He wants those French concessions and the fact that you'll kill a few Ibos helping him get them, won't keep him awake at night. I've seen him in action before, I think you're a good pair.' Her voice was cold.

'Damn it,' I said. 'He pays us to work for him. That includes you.' She looked at me thoughtfully.

'Including shooting up the Ibos. You've already killed the Frenchman.'

'It was him or me, and the way they swindle tourists in Paris a lot more of them should be put down. What should I have done? Let him carve his initials on me?' I moved across and took her into my arms.

Gisela shook her head. 'John, you're hopeless, and past redemption. I refuse to argue with you. I want to forget business. Are you going to take me to one of the noisy night-clubs tonight?'

*

It was just after midnight when we returned to the hotel, the nightwatchman sleeping soundly against the wall. There was no war scare a hundred miles away for him.

I opened the door of Gisela's room. It was dark and I groped my way across to the window and threw the shutters open. The moonlight flooded in and Gisela was in my arms, her face a pale blur in the darkness as she lifted it to me.

Later, much later, I fell asleep. When I woke the dim

light of early morning was creeping through the shutters. Gisela was sleeping, her hair spread across the pillow. No artist could have improved on the heavy dark lashes contrasting with the pale matt of her skin. I bent over and kissed her and her arms came up round my neck. 'Hold it,' I said, 'I'll be back in a minute.'

When I padded in from the bathroom she was lying back, the smoke from a cigarette curling lazily in a spiral in the still air. I took her head in my hands. 'You look good, even at 5:00 A.M. You have a good bone structure and an excellently shaped frame.'

Lazily an arm circled my neck. 'Thank you, sir. Would you like to see my pedigree?'

I licked the cold cream off her nose. 'Not necessary, I'll take a rain check on that. You know, I think I'm beginning to feel sexy again.'

She pushed my hand away. 'What makes you assume I feel the same? I don't feel a thing.'

I took her in my arms. 'Don't worry, darling,' I said confidently. 'It's only temporary. The old biological urge will return.' I took her cigarette and stubbed it out. 'This,' I said, 'is no time for smoking.' I ripped the sheet away.

Later, with the sun flaring scarlet through the early morning mist, throwing a rosy glow against the wall, Gisela, her head against my shoulder, asked: 'John, do you think I could have my cigarette now?' I stretched for the pack and matches. As we lay there, smoking in silence, I thought about Gobi's proposition, and decided it had its merits.

Then Gisela snuggled into the curve of my body, her mouth against my ear.

'You remember those biological urges you mentioned . . .' she whispered.

I nodded: 'I've never forgotten them.'

CHAPTER SEVEN

I N Rhodesia the poinsettias were red splashes of flame beneath the wings of the Douglas, brightening the neat squares of the town centred around the central park, as Tubby circled Salisbury. He picked up the mike. 'Control. Tango Lima on left hand downwind for runway zero six.'

'You are number one to land, Tango Lima, runway zero six. Wind zero two zero degrees 5 to 10 knots.'

'Roger.'

Tubby turned the heavy DC4 in a gentle turn, and slid down the glide path towards the runway. Touching down smoothly, he taxied up to dispersal and cut the motors.

The chief mechanic met him at the foot of the steps. 'Any snags, Captain?'

'Negative, she's running like a clock.'

'That's fine.' He nodded in the direction of the office block. 'The manager wants to see you at once. He says it's urgent.'

'Thanks.' Tubby went across the tarmac towards the long low Nissen hut that served as offices for Rhodesian Air Freighters. Life in Rhodesia, he thought, after the recent unpleasantness of the Congo, was pleasant. He fingered Gibson's letter in his pocket. After the Congo deal John must be crazy to get himself mixed up in another African war. I'll write him tonight and tell him to turn it up and come out here. I'll ask Fletcher now about fixing him up with a job.

He walked into Fletcher's office. "Morning, Bob. Chiefie said you wanted to see me.'

'Yes. How did the trip go?'

'Fine.'

'Aircraft OK? Any snags?'

'Nothing at all. No complaints.'

'Well, seeing it's just had its annual C. of A. and complete overhaul, it should be able to keep going for a while.' Fletcher leaned across the desk. 'You're probably aware there's a small war starting up in Nigeria?'

Tubby eyed him warily. 'Something seems to be cooking. I haven't paid much attention to the newspaper reports. After the Congo, I'm allergic to that type of operation. No future at all.'

Fletcher said casually, 'After all, in the Congo you were flying a twin and there wasn't much maintenance. A four-engined ship is another proposition.' He pushed a cigar box at Tubby. 'Have one.'

'Thanks. You wouldn't by any chance be referring to a newly overhauled DC4 that's just completed its annual certificate of airworthiness?'

Fletcher looked at him innocently. 'How clever of you. How did you guess? You know, Tubby, that's one of your characteristics that I most admire. The ability to anticipate a question and come up with the right answer before it's posed.'

Tubby lit the cigar and sat back. 'Go ahead, let's hear your proposition. But before you start, it's only fair to warn you that the answer is going to be "No".'

Fletcher shook his head. 'Wait until you've heard this one. A portion of Nigeria has broken away. It calls itself Biafra, and has declared its independence. Most of the oil wells are situated in the territory it claims. That means it has revenue.'

'Not if the Nigerians blow up the wells.'

Fletcher waved his hand. 'Anyway, there's enough of the folding stuff guaranteed to pay for the hire of the DC4 and yourself.'

Tubby pushed his chair back. 'Thanks for the cigar, it's been nice knowing you. I suppose the usual month's notice will suffice?'

Fletcher slammed his fist on the table. 'If you don't want

to go, the DC4 will carry on as usual, with you flying it. But I thought you still had a hard streak, and the idea of real money, not the chicken feed you're drawing for flying around here . . .' he corrected himself hastily, 'not that it isn't a good salary for what you're doing but Biafra might appeal to you.'

Tubby puffed the cigar meditatively. 'I'll listen, but I'm promising nothing.'

'This is it,' said Fletcher. 'I've had an offer from a French contact in Libreville whom I've done business with before on a couple of sanctions-busting deals. He's completely reliable and pays. They want to hire the DC4 to fly in and out of Biafra. You'll operate from Libreville and Sao Tomé into Biafra.'

'Flying what?'

Fletcher closed his eyes. 'It is not for me to ask impertinent questions of my customers.'

Tubby snorted. 'Where's Sao Tomé, for God's sake?'

'It's a Portuguese controlled island almost on the Equator and south of Nigeria. It will be purely routine flying. Nothing operational. The Nigerians have got no air force to reckon with.'

'Is that so?' Tubby patted his breast pocket. 'I've a letter here from a friend up there at this moment, that says he's been hired to set up an organization there to check out some surplus MIGs and Czech Delfin jets. I was in the Congo with him and the bastard can fly. He'll probably work a few of his old Congo pals into flying them. His name's Gibson. All I'm short of is for my old mate to come up behind me when I'm cruising along at a steady 200 mph in the DC4 and give me a squirt up the arse with a couple of rockets or a burst of 12.7.'

'Drop him a line,' grinned Fletcher. 'Ask him to lay off. Offer to pay him if necessary.'

'Very funny.' Tubby drew hard on the cigar. 'This is no sort of deal.'

'Let me finish. In view of the slight risk you've told me you may incur, I've decided to increase the offer I was making you.'

'I'm listening,' said Tubby wearily. 'Talk.' He blew a cloud of smoke ceilingwards.

'I was going to offer you £1000 a month. I'm going to up it to £1500. How's that sound?' He sat back in his chair.

Tubby held his hand to his ear. 'I'm a little hard of hearing. Your noisy aeroplanes. Did I hear you say plus a bonus of £100 a trip?' He inspected the end of his cigar and gently flicked the ash on to Fletcher's expensive carpet.

Fletcher swallowed. 'You're a hard man to deal with, Tubby.'

'Yes,' said Tubby drily. 'That hard streak you accused me of losing, I feel it coming back.'

Fletcher threw up his hands in disgust. 'You win,' he said sourly. 'You leave midnight for Sao Tomé.'

He snapped the lid of the cigar box closed as Tubby stretched towards it. 'You can have the rest of the day off. I'll brief you at five.'

Tubby stood up. 'And you called me hard! See you at five o'clock.' He flicked some more ash on the floor as he went off.

*

The rain was cascading down from the low black storm clouds, as Tubby greased the DC4 on to the runway at Port Harcourt. The ground crews ran out as he taxied in and cut the motors. Strange aircraft were a novelty in Biafra.

As he clambered stiffly out of the cockpit Tubby saw the warlike preparations and the twin .5 machine-guns pointing steadily at the DC4 and wondered how it would all end. He refused to accept, despite evidence around him, that what he saw really concerned him. It all seemed curiously unreal. Over the years he had seen several of his fellow pilots killed in mercenary operations as a result of enemy action and errors of judgment. Tubby firmly believed that he was incapable of an error of judgment. So, armoured with complete confidence in his own ability, he waited until the engineer had dropped the cabin steps and strolled nonchalantly across the tarmac to the terminal building. He blandly ignored the armed and trigger-happy soldiers that swarmed around him.

To Tubby, Port Harcourt was just another airport and the war between Biafra and Nigeria merely an impersonal background to the local scene.

A smartly-uniformed Biafran approached him. He was wearing the insignia of a full colonel, on his shoulders the Biafran national emblem, a rising sun. The colonel halted, saluted smartly and held out his hand. 'Captain Sanders? I am Colonel Christopher, the air liaison officer, I'm pleased to meet you. We have been expecting you. Welcome to Biafra.'

Pushing his old battered flight cap back on his head, Tubby took his hand. 'Pleased to meet you, Colonel.' Then, gesturing towards the DC4 he asked: 'Can you send somebody along to give the engineer a hand? The ship needs refuelling.'

Christopher smiled, white teeth in vivid contrast to the dark ebony complexion. 'I have already done so, Captain. There is an office here where we can have a drink and talk in peace whilst they are servicing your aircraft. Will you come with me, please?' Christopher led Tubby to a small room off the main concourse. He mopped his forehead. 'It's always hot here. I hope the heat doesn't trouble you, Captain.'

Tubby shrugged. 'I can take it or leave it,' he said indifferently, 'I got used to it in the Congo last year.'

Pulling open a drawer, Christopher produced a bottle of gin and a couple of glasses. 'Sorry, Captain, it's all I can offer you. Would you care for a drink?'

'Thanks,' said Tubby. 'It's been a long haul from Luanda.'

He watched Christopher splash two generous tots into the grubby tumblers and fill the glasses with water from the plastic bottle on the window sill.

Christopher raised his glass. 'Cheers, Captain—God Bless.'

Tubby took a swig of the raw gin and choked. 'This local gin's got quite a bite. No doubt I'll get used to it.' He put his glass down. 'Colonel, I set off here on very short notice. Perhaps you'd care to fill me in on the local background.'

Christopher smiled. 'It'll be a pleasure.' His English, Tubby noticed, was almost perfect. Probably one of the Sandhurst-trained Ibos who had been the backbone of the regular Nigerian army. He stood up. 'If you'd care to come across and look at the map, I'll explain the present situation.' A long slender finger stabbed at the map. 'We hold, at present, Port Harcourt, Benin City, Enugu and all the country to the north and west of this line.' Christopher traced it out. 'At present, we are driving towards Lagos.'

Tubby nodded. 'Where do I come in with the DC4 operation?' he asked curiously.

'For a start, Captain Sanders, your DC4 will be used to fly food and supplies from the Island of Sao Tomé to Port Harcourt.'

Tubby studied the map thoughtfully. 'The Nigerians; what have they got in the way of aircraft?'

Christopher frowned. 'A few DC3s and small transports, but we have recently had some disturbing reports from our intelligence. We understand the Russians are supplying them with MIG fighters and Delfin jets. They are presently assembling them in Kano.'

'I see,' said Tubby. He strolled back, sitting down in

front of Christopher's desk, and poured himself another gin. 'What are you doing about it?' he asked.

'We only received the news yesterday,' said Christopher defensively. 'We are hoping to train one of our pilots to fly the B26 bomber we recently acquired.'

'Where is it?'

'Here, at Port Harcourt,' said Christopher. 'It's under camouflage nets at the end of the runway.' He looked at Tubby hopefully. 'Do you know anything about a B26, Captain?'

'Yes,' said Tubby. 'I flew them in North Africa in 1943. They're underwinged and overpowered and land fast, but they're not bad ships if you treat them with respect.'

Christopher hesitated, then spoke slowly, almost diffidently. 'Captain, the pilot we were going to train is young and inexperienced. He has had no flying experience on heavy twin-engined aircraft such as the B26. The pilot who delivered it, returned to France the next day. He left no flight or maintenance manuals.' He took a long swig at his gin and slapped the glass down on the desk. 'Captain Sanders,' the words came with a rush, 'would you be prepared to fly the B26 and bomb the Russian aircraft at Kano?'

'And let somebody else fly my DC4? No, thank you, Colonel.'

Christopher was insistent. 'Don't you see, Captain, it would be in your own interests. Wipe out these Russian aircraft while they are still on the ground and they'll cease to be a danger when you are flying around in your DC4.'

Tubby grinned. 'They won't present any danger to me, Colonel, because when I fly in and out of here, it will be at night, and those babies don't operate at night. The Federal Government has imposed a blanket ban on all night flying.'

'I see.' Dispiritedly Christopher picked up his glass.

'Then, would you perhaps be prepared to give our pilot instructions on how to fly this B26 bomber?'

'Sure,' said Tubby easily. 'That I can do.' He finished the gin, shuddered and held out the glass. 'Your gin's terrible, Colonel, I'll have another.'

He thoughtfully watched Christopher splash the gin and fill the glass with tepid water. 'Assuming Colonel, just assuming, that I flew a few raids for you on this B26, what would it be worth?'

Christopher smiled over his glass. 'I don't know, Captain, I've never hired a bomber pilot by the raid before. What fee would you require for your services?'

Tubby leaned across the table. 'Tell you what, Colonel, it's an old aeroplane, plus bad flying country, and tricky weather. Pay me a thousand dollars a raid plus a bonus of five thousand dollars for each jet aircraft destroyed.'

Christopher thrust out his hand. 'I have sufficient authority to accept your offer. It's a deal, Captain. I'll formally confirm with Colonel Ojukwu's Ministerial Council, but I can assure you they'll accept your terms.' He grinned wryly. 'We have no option. Now, Captain Sanders, accommodation has been arranged for you. Let me take you to your room. I will have your engineer sent for as soon as he's ready. Come with me please.'

Tubby followed him out to the staff car waiting in front of the airport terminal. Christopher opened the door and waited for Tubby to get into the baking interior of the vehicle.

Beside the road a seated blind beggar, his eyes opaque with trachoma and covered in flies, raised his hands skywards in supplication.

Feeling in his pocket, Tubby thrust a coin into the beggar's hand, 'For luck,' he said succinctly. 'I'm going to need it.'

CHAPTER EIGHT

AFTER leaving Gisela, I had a quick shave and headed for the dining-room. The manager behind the reception desk, was excessively polite. 'Good morning, Mr Gibson, there's a message for you from Mr Gobi.' Gobi seemed to carry weight locally. I tore open the envelope and studied the note. It was brief and to the point.

Dear Mr Gibson,
I have arranged a military pass for you. You have been granted the rank of Major. Please collect it at the Defence Ministry Headquarters, Room 412.

> Regards,
> GOBI

I wandered out into the street to look for a taxi. Lagos, I thought, was an odd mixture of the old and new. Rows of modern buildings which, standing aloof like rich relations, kept their distance from the mud huts, roofed with everything from old rusted tin to palm thatch.

Stagnant pools of slimy blue-green water gave off a sickly stench. Vendors displayed neat pyramids of tomatoes, onions, dried fish, and green coffee nuts, arguing excitedly over prices with bare-footed women whose long robes looked as if they had been washed in the adjacent pools. An elderly Ford taxi suddenly materialized, summoned by the doorman's piercing whistle.

'Defence Ministry Headquarters,' I told him.

As we took off, I glanced back. A green Consul pulled out from the parking lot in front of the hotel, slipped into place fifty yards behind and stayed there. We turned left at an intersection and the Consul followed discreetly.

There was a large café on the next corner. I leaned towards the driver. 'Stop here a minute. I want some cigarettes.' I went in and made the purchase. When I came out the Consul was parked twenty yards behind the taxi. There were two men in it. Ignoring them, I watched in the rear-view mirror as we pulled away. Sure enough, it trailed along, keeping a steady fifty yards behind us. As the driver braked at the waterfront parking square in front of the eight-storied mustard-coloured Defence Ministry building, the Consul swung over to the left and parked in the far corner of the lot.

'Wait,' I told the driver, and strolled over to the tail. The driver was a Nigerian but the passenger beside him was a European. Thin faced and dark, he could have been Italian or French, a typical swarthy Mediterranean type. I poked my head through the open window beside him. 'I'll save you the trouble of following me. I'm going in there,' I pointed. 'I'll give Defence Headquarters your number. If they've sent you, it won't matter.'

I left him to mull that over, and dodged my way through the speeding traffic into the green-painted interior of the Ministry. A sergeant behind a desk, dressed in a dirty olive green battledress, was lazily surveying the scene. 'Room 412 please.'

He straightened and looked at me curiously. 'Certainly, sir.'

He called a private who took me up in the lift and along a long passage to a room marked: 'Permanent Secretary for Defence.'

He knocked, opened the door and stood back, closing the door behind me as I entered.

A medium-sized smiling Nigerian, wearing an expensive charcoal suit that said Savile Row, came across the room to greet me. Through the large window behind him, I glimpsed a United Arab Airline Comet IVB whining past, heading for a touch-down on Runway Zero One at Ikeja

Airport. He held out his hand. 'Captain Gibson. I'm pleased to meet you. I'm Peter Wanja. Mr Gobi asked me to arrange a military pass for you. I understand you are assisting him in his efforts to get the Air Force established. When these unfortunate troubles are over I can assure you that my Government will remember those people who came to its assistance.'

I slipped in a plug for Kelly Oil Associates Inc. 'Mr Kelly's instructions to me were to co-operate with your Government. He was very definite.'

Wanja smiled blandly. 'I am in possession of all the facts. Rest assured, Mr Gibson, his assistance is appreciated. Let me give you your permit.' It was lying on the desk and he picked it up. 'You are officially a "technical adviser" and carry the rank and status of a major.' The permit was in a small leather folder with a plastic viewer.

'Thank you.'

The phone rang. He took the message and replaced the receiver. 'That was Mr Dakis. He is at the airport and requests you join him there at once. Several of the new mercenary pilots will be arriving in an hour.'

'Thank you.' He handed me the permit. 'I'll go out there right away. By the way, I was followed here by two men when I left the hotel. Here's their car number. If they're yours, it doesn't matter. If not, you may care to check.'

'I certainly will, Major Gibson.' He scribbled the number on his immaculate blotter and I left him looking at it thoughtfully as I went out. When I reached the taxi, the Consul had gone; across the road a screaming newspaper placard read, REBELS USE AMERICAN BOMBER.

I bought a copy. 'Ikeja Airport,' I told the driver and settled back to read the tabloid, written in the flamboyant journalese peculiar to the Nigerian press. 'At sunset last night, an American B26 bomber, acquired by the treacherous rebels, swooped low over Makurdi, raining terror and death on the innocent population. It carefully avoided military targets and confined its attack to the civilian market place. Many women and children were killed. This wilful act of murder will not be unpunished. The fanatic Ojukwu will soon experience the full wrath of the Federal Military Forces.'

At the airport I flashed my new permit at the security guards and passed into the international lounge. There was no sign of Dakis. I passed the time inspecting the ebony carvings and camel leather work at the curio counters, and the variety of tribal markings sported by the various characters around the place. They ranged from diagonal strips running from nose to cheekbone to more ambitious jobs incorporating vertical lines over the cheeks and forehead. The cuts were so deeply engraved that I doubted whether the best plastic surgery could put them right. Not that the Nigerians, steeped in tribalism, would ever want it that way.

I ordered a beer. It slid down and simultaneously turned to sweat and ran down my neck. Where the hell is Dakis? I thought irritably. A breeze had sprung up, the shrubs in front of the building swaying gently to its hot caress. Above, small clouds formed over the sea, drifted inland, and then vanished in the blue haze overhead, burned up by the blazing sun.

I saw Dakis walking across the tarmac and ambled out of the sweltering lounge to join him. A couple of soldiers manning a sandbagged machine-gun emplacement eyed me thoughtfully as I went past. I tapped Dakis on the shoulder. 'Good morning, you arms-peddling racketeer.'

He grinned. 'Ah, John, good morning. You got your permit?'

'Yes. But remember : I'm here to further Kelly's interests, and not to get involved in your local war. Keep it in mind.'

Dakis' grin widened. 'You forget, I am also interested in

Kelly's welfare.' He pointed. 'Five mercenaries are in that Nigerian Airways VC10.' We watched the marshaller waving his orange day-glo bats as he signalled it into the parking lot. The whistle of the jets died, the turbines sighed to a slow-down, and there was a burst of activity as the ground staff went into action. The stairs were towed into position, the first passenger through the door I recognized as Boozy Brown, an ex-Congo pilot. He was wearing a bright scarlet baseball cap.

Following him were four others. I knew two of them. One was Jerry van Ginkel, a tall Hollander who always wore a homburg, and was perhaps the most sober and reliable of the Congo set, and the other Karel Olivier, a baby-faced character who looked much younger than his thirty-five years.

'Well,' said Dakis. 'You know any of them?'

'Three,' I told him. 'They can fly anything. Fighters, bombers, transport. Pay them well and regularly, and you'll have no trouble. I don't know the other two, but I'll check their track record with the others.'

'Good. Please wait in the VIP lounge, I'll get them cleared and bring them there.' He bustled off.

The VIP lounge was an air-conditioned haven. I ordered a scotch and settled back to enjoy it. As I ordered a second the boys arrived, Dakis fluttering around them like a hen with chickens. While Dakis ordered drinks, I was brought up to date on the Congo scene they had just left by van Ginkel.

'Who are the other two?' I asked.

'Belgians, ex-Belgian Air Force. They've flown Nord Atlas transports, but only as co-pilots. Not a great deal of experience.'

They'd do for the Dakotas, I thought. Through the window I watched a black Mercedes pull up. Yusef Gobi, now dressed in white flowing robes, and followed by a Nigerian Air Force Colonel, came into the room.

Dakis introduced the pilots. 'Gentlemen, Minister Gobi and Colonel Bello.'

Gobi wasted no time. 'I'm pleased to see you and welcome you to Nigeria. Our present position is serious. We have three DC3s and MIG15s and seventeen fighters are arriving at Kano. Also, eight Czech L29 Delfin jets are being assembled there by our Russian and Czech allies. The oil wells at Onitsha are in danger, and, in order to protect them, Benin City must be recaptured immediately. We must have the use of its airfield to extend our air striking range. If the rebels capture the Onitsha oil wells and destroy the installations, the Nigerian economy will have been struck a crippling blow.'

He looked at me meaningfully. 'You will appreciate the seriousness of the situation, Major Gibson.' He was telling me there would be no oil concessions for Kelly if that happened, and it was up to me to get the pilots moving.

'Sure,' I told him, 'but I'm only a technical adviser. Once I get them started, then it's over to these boys. When do we fly up to Kano and get moving?'

The colonel pointed to the tarmac. 'That Nigerian Airways Fokker Friendship has been commandeered for the purpose. You will leave in an hour. Gentlemen, please order whatever you require in the interval in the way of food and drink. Major Gibson, I'll take you back to the hotel to collect your baggage.'

I followed the colonel and Gobi back to the Mercedes. We drove into town in silence. Gobi spoke only once. 'It will be in your employer's interest if you help to get these aircraft operating efficiently, Mr Gibson.'

'I realize that. Leave it to me.' I hoped I sounded more confident than I felt.

At the hotel I looked for Gisela. The reception clerk told me she'd gone out and would be back in an hour. I left a note for her at the desk.

Darling,

The Mercenary pilots have arrived and I have to leave immediately for Kano to supervise training. Will keep in touch. *Bon voyage,* honey, and thank you!

Love,

JOHN

I collected my kit and the colonel drove us back to Ikeja.

*

There was a distinct atmosphere of good cheer when the turbaned Indian pilot rotated the Fokker smoothly off Runway one nine an hour later. The whisky in the VIP lounge had been severely punished, that was obvious.

Heading for Kaduna, our first stop, the pilot turned on to course and I watched Lagos sprawling below. To port, the shimmering grey-brown river split the city with the two connecting bridges joining it. To the east was the affluent portion of the city, and the swimming pool of the Federal Palace Hotel flashed momentarily as the Fokker passed over. To the south, the wooded coastline veered away, ending in a white lacy fringe where the Atlantic rollers tumbled against the shore line.

Red mud roads threaded their way through the jungle, occasionally straddled by clusters of huts. A few solid-brick, red-roofed mission stations or trading stores, stood out like sentinels amongst the villages. Then, as the Fokker gained altitude, the detail faded. Ahead the Niger came into view, twisting southwards to become the Niger Delta, with its hundreds of small silver river capillaries running through the green body of tropical bush and mangrove swamp. The mercenaries dozed peacefully until the Indian reduced power and the nose dropped.

Kaduna was a cluster of white and grey-brown buildings sprawling amongst the green and yellow of the countryside. I watched the wheels drop and strain against the opposing airflow as the hydraulic pumps locked them into position. Over the field, a flock of vultures circled contemptuously as we slid down through a hot bumpy thermal and on to the runway. Camouflaged single-engined Dornier and Macchi aircraft were dispersed in the long grass; some, between the taxi-ways and runway, were covered with netting and branches. To the west were rows of neat identical apartment blocks, looking as if the architect had run out of ideas. Gun crews, stripped to the waist, manned Bofors and heavy machine-guns, their bodies shining black and metallic in the blazing sun.

As we followed Gobi into the glare and heat, a white Volkswagen Combi was waiting on the tarmac. A Nigerian Air Force major stood beside it.

'Major John,' Gobi introduced us. He indicated the open door. 'Will you please get in. Your baggage will follow as soon as it is offloaded.'

As I bent to enter the Combi I paused. The unmistakable drone of a powerful twin-engined aircraft beat through the hot air. Major John held up his hand as I looked enquiringly at him. 'One moment please, gentlemen.'

'You expecting an aircraft?' I asked curiously.

'No.' The engine beat, throbbing in waves, was getting close. Whoever was flying it was pushing the motors close to the limit, pulling 90% power. No civilian pilot would be flying that way. The mercenaries stopped talking and were looking uneasily around, trying to locate the aircraft. Suddenly van Ginkel pointed: 'There she comes!' Simultaneously the Nigerian major shouted: 'It's the bloody B26,' and dived for shelter behind a small wall.

I saw the gun crews jerk into action as the aircraft bored in at tree top level, its front guns spraying lead at the parked aircraft. I followed the major and made for the wall, the others piling in behind me. Thunder boomed overhead as the B26, only feet above the field, spewed a stream of canisters that dropped amongst the parked aircraft beyond the Fokker, then piled on full power and went screaming up in a steep climbing turn. The air became highly metallized. The boom-boom-boom of the Bofors and crackle of automatic weapons was amplified by the explosions of the canisters as they struck. Flattened behind the wall, I heard jagged particles of metal whistle overhead. Then, as suddenly as it started, all was silent. We scrambled to our feet. Several aircraft were leaning at crazy angles, and three were burning furiously. We watched as Major John ran off, and the fire squad swarmed to extinguish the flames.

John returned, 'He flew right over us, yet we couldn't get him.' He displayed a jagged piece of tin. 'The bombs are made of paint tins packed with incendiary material and scrap iron, yet look at the damage the bastard's caused.'

'Kano will be next,' I told him cheerfully. 'If he learns the Delfins and MIGs are there, he'll go after them whilst they're being assembled. He won't worry about the small transport types you've got here at Kaduna.'

He nodded glumly. 'I'll notify Lagos and Kano immediately and warn them to expect an attack.'

'You do just that,' I told him, 'or you'll lose your Air Force before it gets off the ground.'

'You're right,' he said dejectedly. 'I'll drive you to your quarters.'

Then, as we approached the Combi, I again heard the beat of the hard-driven B26's motors, John screamed at the Bofors crew beside the building. 'Here he comes again! Get him, for Christ's sake, men, get him!'

We dived for the safety of the wall. I heard the B26's four front guns in action as it screamed in low from the north and the pilot sprayed the still undamaged aircraft parked beside the burning transports. He fired, then banked in a tight vertical turn to port directly above us, and headed south-west.

I caught a glimpse of the pilot's face, a white blur in the cockpit as he screamed overhead fifty feet above us, before the aircraft levelled out, waggled its wings in a friendly farewell greeting, and streaked away.

'How do you like that,' I said admiringly. 'The son-of-a-bitch has the cheek to wave his wings in farewell on his way home. That's no flying club pilot. The sooner we knock that B26 out of the air, the better.'

John stood up wearily, looking downcast. 'Come on, gentlemen, let's go. I think he's gone, for the time being anyway.'

We climbed into the van and he drove glumly towards the mess. There was the wail of a siren, and John pulled over to let an ambulance pass.

Bright green tropical trees, exuberant with explosions of orange and red blossoms, lined the road. Outside the rows of apartments, the families of air force personnel had gathered in groups. The women screamed to one another across the roads in high-pitched voices. The bombing had scared hell out of them. I wondered how the Lagos dailies would report this affair.

'That B26 must be destroyed,' Major John kept repeating. 'If it isn't done soon, it will destroy our air force before we ever get the jets into the air.'

'Don't let it bother you,' I told him. 'Once we get the MIGs airborne, that'll be the end of him. These boys are quite capable of handling that B26. A five-second burst of 26 mm. up its arse will solve that problem.'

John laughed. By the time we pulled up at the mess, he was quite cheerful. I was overcome by a fit of nostalgia as we entered. It was built on typical RAF lines, with an entrance hall and a small signing-in cubicle on the left with an open register on a pedestal desk. On the right were rows of hooks for the airmen to park their caps. Beside them was the inevitable mailbox, with pigeon holes marked from A to Z.

John led us into a large ante-room with white-decked coffee tables plastered against the walls. To the left was a small lounge with a bar running the length of one wall, bedecked with pin-ups from *Playboy, Rogue* and *Playmen International*. In true RAF tradition, the dining-room was tucked away somewhere beyond the main lounge and the bar room. Flights of stairs led to the upstairs rooms and bathrooms. Shades of Grantham, Peterborough and Mildenhall, I thought, and wished back the twenty years the locusts had eaten since I last graced their portals.

Leaving the others congregated at the end of the bar, John led me to one of the small coffee-tables, 'Well, Major Gibson, what do you think of the situation?'

'The B26's got me worried,' I said. 'Apart from the raid on the small transports, do you realize what it can achieve, flown daringly as it is, against the oil wells at Onitsha. Operating from Enugu, Calabar or Port Harcourt, or any dirt strip with a minimum length of 1500 yards, it could hit Onitsha without difficulty.'

Major John nodded glumly. 'You're right.'

'What are your plans for us?' I asked.

'The pilots who are going to fly the DC3s with Boozy Brown will remain here.'

'That will be the two Belgians.'

'You and the other pilots who will fly the MIG and Delfin jets must leave at first light for Kano. I have laid on an Aztec to fly you there. The Fokker Friendship will return to Lagos immediately. It is too valuable to risk it being destroyed up here. Now we'll join your friends at the bar. Tonight, if you wish, I'll be happy to collect you after dinner and show you what Kaduna can offer.'

'Thank you.' We joined the others.

After dinner he rounded us up at the bar. 'Now I'll show you the local night life.'

Two hours passed at the night club when it happened. The drink had been disappearing at a prodigious rate. The

atmosphere in the Royal Empire was basically the same
as in any dive in Tokyo or Hamburg. The band in the
corner made up in rhythm and volume what it lacked
in tune, and the smoke-filled interior was completely up
to standard. A bevy of black belles, bewigged in the latest
Afro bee-hive fashion, invited themselves to our tables,
to belt down as much expensive imported Chablis as
they could persuade John to buy. Fortunately the attempt
took place reasonably early in the proceedings, when my
reactions were still functioning. An hour later, I doubt if
I'd have reacted soon enough.

Leaning across the table to grab a bottle of Chablis
from one of the thirsty hostesses, I felt something thud
against the leg of my chair. A heavy and solid thump, like
that of a shoe or boot. Instinct, or a suspicious nature
developed through several hectic years in the Congo,
made me stoop to investigate. The moment I felt the
little black cast-iron object, I registered. Black and dully
metallic with grooves like those of a small pineapple.

I grabbed the grenade and threw it violently upwards,
almost toppling in my chair, as the grenade arced in a
high trajectory towards the nearest window. As I threw
myself on to the floor, I felt, seconds later, the shock-wave
of the explosion followed by the terrified screaming of
the women. Plaster rained down from the ceiling filling
the room with white dust.

There was a crash of tables being knocked over and the
clatter of broken glassware, as the band and dancers
scrambled for the door. Frantically, they kicked, butted and
clawed their way out. Slowly we stood up as several police,
who'd been on duty outside, charged into the room. It
was an hour before they let us go, and then not until
Major John had called the police captain aside, and told
him confidentially that we were on top secret mission for
the commander-in-chief and needed sleep before first light.

John drove us back to the mess.

'We'll have to watch our step from now on,' I told the mercenaries. 'Both sides in this war are playing for big stakes, also the international oil companies. Several of them operating this side of the fence would be happy to see us out of the way.'

Said Karel slowly, 'But how the hell did anyone know we'd be in the night club tonight?'

'That's easy,' I told him. 'John collected us in the mess and there were a dozen Nigerians at the bar who saw us leave. Anyone of them could be in the pay of the Ibos or their sympathisers. This is a civil war, and the divisions are apt to be elastic. Now we know we trust nobody, not even members of the Federal Nigerian forces. And, in future, we keep away from public places like night clubs.'

CHAPTER NINE

D A W N, next morning, came far too soon as I struggled out of bed. The air had not yet heated up, and the light was clear gold as the clouds to the east began to catch fire. The wind was gusting, slapping the windsock around the old rusty iron pole beside the terminal building. The Aztec pilot was a cheerful British lad in his early twenties. I watched his cockpit check carefully. I needn't have bothered. He was systematic and precise, so I relaxed and left him to it as he taxied out and took off.

Kaduna lay on the southern side of the encroaching desert which farther north changed to the awesome Sahara. The terrain began to alter rapidly as we droned northeast. Pastures of green gave way to grey and then brown. Clumps of small shrubs nestled in the folds of the dark dunes like blackheads in a giant furrowed forehead.

At the back of the aircraft, Karel and Jerry had tilted their seats back and were sleeping happily, Karel snoring gently against the contented throb of the Lycoming motors. There was nothing below, I thought, to indicate that Africa's most populous nation was in a state of violent turmoil. The land looked peaceful enough but I didn't let it fool me. The thick green jungle of the Congo used to look the same way. I knew there was all hell lurking under that flat green carpet of trees. The sun was a large trembling fireball on our right, dancing on a black horizon bar with blue light reflected faintly above it. I closed my eyes and dozed until I was awoken by the pilot calling Kano on the VHF.

'Bloody fools,' he said. 'They didn't want to let me land. They state they have no notification of our arrival, and I could be an enemy aircraft. Do they think an enemy aircraft would bother to call them up before clobbering them?'

'You never know,' I grinned. 'That crafty bastard flying the B26 is liable to do anything.'

He twirled the turn control module of the auto pilot and I glanced out. Ahead, Kano swam into view, the pitch black runways making an X on the brown desert. He brought the Aztec in slowly, wallowing gently on the approach, just above the stall. Then the wheels brushed the tar lightly, and we were down, taxi-ing towards the numbered parking bays. I noticed that the tribesman on the camel, who had blown the welcoming horn for the benefit of Gisela and me on our Southbound trip, was no longer in evidence. I wondered idly if he'd been conscripted and was now perhaps an army bugler.

Scattered around the airport were MIG 15s and 17s in various stages of assembly, parked between the hangars at the south and extending in a curve to the north-west past the terminal buildings. Four blue-nosed, completely assembled, Czech L29 Delfins stood apart from the MIGs, as if unwilling to fraternize with their Russian comrades.

At the terminal, two giant khaki-coloured Aeroflot Turboprops were parked nose to tail, their internal power units throbbing quietly as they were unloaded. I watched a 20,000-litre tanker being driven out of the nearer Aeroflot and swarms of khaki-clad Russian technicians offloading a complete mobile flying control unit from the other. The pale faces of the Russians were in startling contrast to the black Nigerians.

A defaulter undergoing punishment drill ran past, holding a rifle above his head, double-timing to the orders of a stocky Nigerian drill sergeant with a back stiff and erect as any Guards Officer.

A Nigerian major, with a leg in plaster and leaning heavily on a stick, came up and saluted. 'Major Gibson? Morning, sir, I am Major Alfa. These are the pilots you have brought to fly the MIGs and Delfins?'

'Yes, Major.'

A Russian approached and stood beside Alfa. He introduced him. 'This is Mr Boris, Major Gibson, your inter-
preter.' Boris nodded stiffly.

I held out my hand and he took it awkwardly. 'Pleased
to know you, Boris.'

'And I also.' He smiled pleasantly enough. 'Would you
like to inspect the aircraft now, or later after you've eaten?'

I glanced at Jerry and Karel, Jerry nodded. 'No time
like the present. We'll look them over now.'

'The MIGs or the Delfins?'

'I've been hearing about MIGs ever since the Korean
War. Let's have a look at your MIG 17s.'

'Certainly, sir. Major Nusi is your instructor. He is also
in charge of the assembly contingent. Please follow me.'

We trailed him to a partly assembled MIG, still lacking
ailerons and elevators. A stocky, fair-skinned, blue-eyed man,
in a grey shirt with beige corduroy slacks, was standing
beside the wing.

Boris saluted. 'Major Nusi, the British pilots.' Nusi
nodded sourly. 'They wish to start instruction at once.' Cold
blue eyes surveyed us. Then Nusi shrugged, spoke briefly
to Boris, and climbed into the cockpit.

'He says he will give you the pilot's notes later, and I
will translate them. Now he will show you the cockpit.
Please stand on the ladders leading to the cockpit.'

We scrambled up and I stood beside Boris with Jerry
and Karel perched on the other side. Nusi wasted no time.
Starting from left to right, he explained the layout, naming
each control and waiting for Boris to translate.

The MIG interior was like that of any other jet, cramped
and austere and smelling of a mixture of kerosene, oil
and hydraulic fluid. I noticed that Nusi kept his fingers
well clear of the armament firing buttons on the control
column.

Completing the dashboard layout, he explained the ejection firing mechanism. Lifting his feet from the rudder pedals, he placed them on the footrests above, pointed to his knees and then the windshield rim. He spoke at some length to Boris. For the first time he smiled, as Boris translated.

'The Major says if you fail to raise your feet when you eject, you will smash your knee-caps against the windshield rim and never walk or fly again.' The Major's grin broadened as Boris translated.

'Tell him,' I told Boris politely, 'that we prefer our knee-caps where they are, and will do our best to keep them there.'

As Boris finished translating, Nusi laughed, and the tension eased appreciably.

Nusi carried on to explain the remedial action should an engine develop a 'rumble,' and ran through the starting and stopping procedures twice again, answering the questions we fired at him by nodding vigorously with a series of *Da-da-da*s or shaking his head to a string of impatient *Nyets*.

Finally he'd had enough. As he stood up in the cockpit, Boris told us : 'The Major says he will give you the books and I will translate them for you. Tomorrow he will instruct you again. He asks what do you think of the MIG 17 which is sought by many countries?'

'He'll have my opinion after I've flown it tomorrow. I know the Egyptians were seeking more after the Israeli Mirages had shot down all their MIGs in the six-day war.'

Nusi scowled. 'Egyptians!' He spat out the word, climbed down the cockpit steps and walked off.

'You have annoyed him,' Boris looked upset.

'Terrible thing,' said Jerry. 'Let's go.'

Alfa was waiting patiently beside the wing. 'Let me take you to the mess. Mr Boris will join us there.'

The mess was crowded with Russians, Czechs and

Nigerians, each group practising strict apartheid. Nusi was in the centre of the Russian group.

Boris joined us several minutes later, a thick blue manual under his arm. We moved across to a secluded table and he opened the manual with a flourish.

'I have already made many of the translations,' he said proudly.

His English was good, but his command of technical terms left a lot to the imagination.

'Get a load of this lot,' I read aloud. 'If the required velocity is excessive, it may be trimmed off by the dive brake actuating control switch in order to achieve optimum requirement factors.' I found another gem: 'When the up-down switch is not, do not activate for fear of reprisals.'

I turned to Jerry and Karel. 'Now you South African Dutchmen tell me what the hell that means!'

'Please,' Boris interrupted. 'Translation no good?'

I patted his shoulder. 'Don't worry, we'll sort it out later. Let's have a drink.'

Boris brightened perceptibly. 'I'll fetch beer. OK?' He brought the drinks and we settled down.

Several drinks later, Boris asked. 'Major Gibson, you are English?'

'Yes.'

'Your friends, I heard you say. "You South African Dutchmen". What are they? Not English?'

'No, Karel is South African, and Jerry came from Holland after the war. He is now a naturalized South African. He flew in the Dutch Air Force. Karel flew in the SAAF and I flew in the RAF.'

'I understand.' Shortly after that he left us.

We slept that afternoon and later read the manual. At dinner, I told Alfa. 'Tomorrow, we fly the MIGs.'

'Good,' he beamed. 'I'll fetch you at 8:30. Breakfast is at eight.'

Next morning he was waiting as we entered the mess

hall. 'There's trouble, Major.'

'There always is,' I said wearily. 'Let's have it.'

'Major Nusi! The bloody Russian has been questioning me about your nationalities. It seems that, although my Government bought the MIGs from arms dealers, the Russians can forbid us flying them if the pilots nationalities are not acceptable. He does not want South Africans to fly them as their country is hostile to Russia. Since you are with them, you are included. He has sent a letter to the Russian ambassador in Lagos, requesting instructions. Until then, you may not fly the MIGs.'

I shrugged. 'Well, let's go out to the airport anyway.'

We climbed aboard his Combi and watched unhappily as the driver drove recklessly to the field. By the way he handled it, it seemed as if he hated the Combi.

I climbed out thankfully. 'What about the Delfin jets?' I asked. 'Is there any such condition with the Czech Government?'

'I'll check with Lagos,' he said bitterly. He hobbled into the Administration Building. Christ! I thought, at this rate it will be weeks before I can get after the oil concessions.

Compared with Kaduna, Kano, with all its jets, was practically undefended. A lone Bofors poked its muzzle tentatively into the dry desert air as if to frighten the hundreds of idly circling hawks. This was a cockeyed war run in a crazy manner. No wonder the Biafrans were already closing in on Lagos.

'I don't get it,' Karel started to say, but the sentence ended there. The shouting of the soldiers combined with the noise of vehicles coming and going, had drowned out the approaching sound.

Its engine thundering, the now familiar Biafran B26 roared towards us, booming in over the top of the southernmost hangar, heading for the numerous jets. We raced for the protection of the Administration building.

Sprinting for the doorway, I watched the B26 bearing down. From its belly, a brown cylindrical object, like a forty-four gallon drum, tumbled lazily in a curve towards the nearest MIGs. I was still ten yards from the doorway when it smacked the tar with a dull thud and burst open, spewing a black oily liquid in all directions as it bounced and tumbled towards us. There was a grinding screech of metal each time it struck the tarmac. The drum flattened itself on the wall twenty feet to the left as we dived into the doorway, and I heard the unforgettable 'woosh' of flaming napalm.

Men streaked past, shouting and cursing, waving automatic weapons.

I poked my head out cautiously, flames blazed in patches on the tarmac; streaking two of the aircraft. On the wall alongside, flames flowed in rivulets to the tar below.

Once again the Biafrans had carried out another vicious strike on the Nigerian's Air Force. Once the jets were operational, the B26 would have to be priority target number one.

Alfa stood silently next to me, his face drawn and haggard from the physical and mental pain he was enduring. He dejectedly watched the fire-fighting squad spraying the burning aircraft.

'You'd better chase up Lagos,' I said. 'If there are any more attacks like this, there won't be much of your jet squadron left.' I imagined the smile of satisfaction on George Dakis's face when the Federal Government approached him to supply a squadron replacement. Alfa gripped his stick tightly. 'To hell with Lagos,' he said grimly. 'Can you and your pilots fly the Delfins without training from the Russian instructor?'

'Sure,' I said confidently. 'All we'll need is a few circuits and landings to get the feel of them. To hell with Nusi.'

'The Delfins are all yours,' he said. 'I'll take a chance

on Lagos' confirmation. But get that bastard B26—that's all I ask.'

He shook my hand fervently and I watched him leave. He was walking a lot straighter now. Even his limp had a breezy spring to it.

*

The Czech L29 Delfin was the standard jet trainer for the Warsaw Pact forces. It wasn't designed with a lot of range, as a trainer it didn't need it. As an operational attack machine, the limited range was a serious problem.

Three hours later I sat in the Kano Station Commander's office, measuring distances carefully on a small-scale map. With the aid of the Czech mechanics we completed an hour's familiarization, and carried out three landings apiece. Karel and Jerry were due to leave for Lagos immediately. The Russians had watched us sourly as we took off after the Czech technicians had explained the cockpit drill.

I put down the ruler, 'Keep an eye on the fuel gauge,' I told Karel and Jerry. 'You can't strike Benin City from Makurdi. It's a one way ride. The Delfin wasn't built for distance.' I spread a pair of dividers from Lagos to Benin. 'A hundred and forty nautical miles exactly,' I continued. 'You can make it back to Lagos provided you only do one dive and fire all your rockets in pairs. Before take off at Lagos, switch off your primus stoves at the runway threshold and top up. The fifty litres you'll consume taxiing might well be your undoing. Any questions?'

Karel groaned. 'It's a hell of an operation. If the weather's duff on return we can't stack in the holding pattern for even five minutes. If we miss the runway the first try, we can't even overshoot for a low level circuit. It's crazy!'

'You're right,' I said. 'But you're paid to take risks, so you'll strike at Benin City from Lagos. You'll have to climb straight on course to 5000 metres, stay up there until you're on target and then allow yourself only one dive. No dawdling on the way back; come straight home, like good little boys.'

'OK, OK,' Jerry grumbled. 'We get the picture. We'd better press on to Lagos before the B26 returns.'

'Once Benin is captured, and you can operate from there, your range problems are over. You can stop worrying about fuel and concentrate on what the Ibos will do if they catch you.'

We shook hands. As they left hurriedly, Alfa came in. 'Lagos confirms my action regarding the Delfins,' he said. 'Mr Gobi's orders are that the B26 must be destroyed at all costs. There is a £20,000 bonus for its destruction.'

'Leave it to me,' I promised him. A cash register began to ring in my mind. Considering friend Gobi was the man on whom I was relying for the oil concessions, I was going to get the B26 if it took me a month. The Delfin's sole armament comprised two rocket rails holding four Polish 1½-inch rockets apiece. I'd have preferred two heavy calibre machine-guns, but nevertheless the rockets were highly lethal.

After Karel and Jerry took off, I studied the map carefully. The B26 could operate from any number of airstrips in Biafran territory. It could strike anywhere in Federal-held country and return to its base at full throttle without giving range problems a thought.

I decided to station myself at Kaduna. It was close to rebel territory. I'd get airborne early each day and patrol the countryside. Refuelling periods aside, I'd spend all and every day in the air, until I saw the B26. That, I promised myself, would be the end of both it and the bastard who flew it.

I told Alfa of my plans and he nodded approvingly. 'When are you leaving for Kaduna?'

'Right away,' I said. 'I'll collect my bag and be off.

Please check the Delfin is fully armed. I'd hate to pass
the B26 on the way and be unable to do anything about
it.'

He nodded again and rushed off, his stick beating time
to his limp.

I was airborne in twenty minutes. I pushed the Delfin
up in a fast climb to 5000 metres. The airspeed indicator
was also metric and I did little mental conversion sums
from knots to miles an hour, and feet to metres. The Delfin
flew like a bird, with a pleasant positive feel to the controls,
and a quiet reassuring purr from the engine behind.

Lengthy shadows formed by the setting sun obscured
large tracts of ground. The visible ground was a dirty
speckled red. It would be difficult to spot the camouflaged
B26 against such a background. As the sun dipped, Kaduna
lay before me, the runways miniaturized by height, like
black strips of liquorice laid out across the semi-desert.

As I applied dive brakes, lowered the gear and full
flaps and throttled back to flight idle power, the sun
dropped below the horizon and a peaceful mantle of grey
dusk settled on the countryside below. Distant lights blinked
feebly and grew clearer as I lost altitude, heading down
to the runway.

The Delfin needed little assistance. A gentle pull on the
stick and the wheels ran smoothly down the tarmac.

I parked far enough from the hangar to present a small
solitary target. 'I can fly you, baby,' I said. 'Now let's see
if I can fight with you.' I patted the fuselage and checked
that the mechanics placed the red air-intake dust covers
in position and draped the cockpit covers.

I had supper, a couple of drinks, then flopped on my
bed. The mess was quiet and I thought about Gisela,
and wondered if and when I'd see her again, as I drifted
off to sleep. Oil concession deals were slipping through my
mind like numbers in a telephone directory, when an orderly
woke me.

It was 5:00 A.M. and time for me to start looking for the B26.

*

For five weary days, I maintained a constant patrol from dawn to dusk. The B26 was active. Once I heard the flying controller at Makurdi issue a frantic call for assistance. The elusive bomber had plastered the runway, creating several large craters. It was too far south for me to get there in time.

Twice again, during the five days, the B26 struck with impunity against military targets at Onitsha, and Federal positions north of the Biafran capital, Enugu.

Now the rebel pilot was top of the list of those most unloved by the Federal Military Government. They put a price of £20,000 on his head, in addition to the £20,000 promised for destroying the B26.

CHAPTER TEN

T H E mercenaries, operating from Makurdi, joined in the hunt for the elusive B26, dropping their homemade bombs from DC3s on every Biafran hangar they could find. The 'search-and-destroy' missions continued unabated.

Six frustrating days dragged past, finally I decided to position the Delfin at Makurdi to the south and operate from there. It was closer to Biafran-held territory, and a change might bring luck.

At Kaduna, heavy rain, falling in violent gusts, lashed the soaking ground crew as they hauled off the Delfin's cockpit covers and dust shields.

I signalled I was ready to start and checked that a mechanic was positioned at the rear where he could signal that the engine was actually flaming. I hit the ground start button, listening as the engine hissed in spasms, like a car motor running minus a couple of plugs. Then the whine of the turbine increased, and the rpm needle crept towards the 40% mark, and the tailpipe temperature rose suddenly. The needle swept towards the danger red line, paused for a second, and then fell to the normal setting.

I increased revs to 60%, and checked flap and dive brake operation, emergency gear extension pressure, oxygen quantity, and radio systems. Everything was functioning satisfactorily.

I pushed power up to 96% rpm and felt the Delfin strain against the chocks. The mechanics were using their thumbs as ear plugs.

As I flipped the 'Bord Net' switch to check the operation of the auxiliary fuel pump, the rpm dropped characteristically. Finally I checked 100% rpm for a second, then throttled back and signalled I was ready to go. The mechanics pulled the chocks away and I taxied out.

Minutes later I was in a white rain-lashed world. I saw nothing of the ground all the way to Makurdi, watching the Delfin's blue tinted flying instruments roll from side to side as air currents flipped continuously at the ship. I homed in on the beacon, broke through cloud at three thousand feet, and slapped her down in a light drizzle at Makurdi.

'Fill her up,' I told the servicing chief, and left him supervising the refuelling, while I booked in at control. I hurried back and impatiently watched the tedious transfer of a thousand litres of fuel into the Delfin by means of an old-fashioned wobble pump ex drums. However, the delay had its blessings. In the interim the overcast started to lift and I could see odd patches of blue breaking through the grey overcast. The drizzle had stopped.

The runway had been repaired after the recent bombing, the red earth used in the refilling scarring its green. The air was loud with the whirr of insects after the rain. Across the field a woman came out of one of the earthbrown shacks and shouted across to a neighbour. I leaned against the fuselage and soaked up the peacefulness. The past five days had been hard and the strain was beginning to tell. I felt tired and drained. I worked out that I'd averaged eight hours a day searching for the damned B26. The weather, mainly cloudy, had been in his favour. All the reports of his strikes stressed that he had usually appeared out of cloud.

I thought of the £20,000 reward, and the old adrenalin began to surge. Come on Gibson, I told myself. Get that bastard if it takes a month, the pay's good for a month's work.

As the squad finished refuelling, I checked that the oil and filler caps were secure, then wearily lowered my aching carcass into the cramped cockpit. 'Here we go again,' I told myself.

I fired the motor and picked up the mike. 'Makurdi, Delfin Four Zero Two. Taxi clearance for mission area as per flight plan. Request clearance to 16,500 feet.'

'Roger, Four Zero Two. You are cleared to runway one eight and flight level 165. Two DC3s on bombing mission Enugu due here in thirty minutes. Will advise when ETA and flight levels known. Over.'

'Four Zero Two checks.' I shoved the throttle forward. The sun was burning up the overcast, and when I levelled out at 16,500 feet it was clearing fast. I hauled back to 80% rpm and started watching the lush green countryside sliding past beneath the stubby wings. Palm plantations showed as dark smudges against the pale green of the plots of cassava. Dirt roads cut red strips through the jungle, thatched villages sprawled along their sides. Occasionally a great tree flamed russet amongst the prevailing green.

Then I saw the B26!

I'd completed my first leg to the east, when a shadow slipped across a light patch of jungle, and flashed over a river.

Etched clearly against the jungle was the B26.

I'd seen that silhouette too often to mistake it. There was no possibility of confusing it with the returning Dakotas.

Heading north; it was probably making for Kano to pay it another visit, I thought. As I watched, it disappeared beneath a small patch of low-lying stratus.

Gibson, I said, you've £20,000 in that Swiss bank.

I rolled the Delfin fast to port to keep the sun behind us as I closed in. Cutting power to 60%, I flipped the dive brake button on the stick and pointed the Delfin's blue nose straight at the white cloud mass. After the long hours of hunting, the kill had to be right. There must be no crude dive, hauling back on the controls, and blasting off the rockets. The dive curve I'd take would be a pure mathematical abstraction and as beautiful in its truth. The end of my dive curve would level out five hundred yards behind the B26. At two hundred yards, I'd hit the rocket switches simultaneously in pairs. The B26 would disentegrate into one great blossom of flame as they struck.

Gently, lovingly, I moved the switch on to 'Fire' and went into my dive curve. It would be a smooth polished execution. It was a pity, I thought, that the B26 pilot, a professional himself, would never see it. The curve of the dive and classical purity of the attack he would have appreciated. And as a fellow mercenary he'd have appreciated even more the 20,000 nicker in Switzerland!

The clouds hurtled towards me as the jet plummeted earthwards, the airspeed needle indicating Mach .70. Seventy percent of the speed of sound was more than enough to catch the Biafran aircraft. As I hit the cloud layer, severe turbulence rattled the Delfin. I adjusted the radio altimeter selector switch to 700 metres. I'd need all of that to pull out of the dive.

The Delfin broke through the overcast at 1000 metres with a whopping kick that made my shoulders ache against the straps. I retracted the dive brakes, applied 96% rpm and waited for my eyes to adjust from the glare to the dark haze.

Slowly, like a movie coming into focus, the ground took on depth and colour, a brilliant mass of green threaded with glistening probes of rivulets.

And somewhere ahead was the camouflaged B26.

At this low altitude I had barely thirty minutes fuel left in the Delfin. I glimpsed the fuel gauge needle moving ominously towards the EMPTY mark. I had to find the B26 fast.

I rolled the jet steeply from side to side to get a view underneath, then searched left and right, craning my neck, but nothing moved, only the fuel needle, as it fell below the 500-litre mark. At low altitude, the jet Delfin's appetite for kerosene was voracious.

As I cursed the consumption, two small whirring discs momentarily reflected the sunlight and there, as clear as crystal, was the B26, ahead and to port, flying serenely along over a carpet of green and brown forest.

Carefully I dialled the B26's wingspan on the gyro gunsight, adjusted the rocket selector to the Roman numeral II so that they'd fire in pairs, and half rolled into position for a line astern attack as I closed in.

Now I was almost in position, the silhouette of the B26 large and life-like in the gunsight. I flipped the throttle dive brake switch to slow me down, and simultaneously the bastard rolled suddenly in a tight turn to the left. He must have seen me in the rearview mirror above his windshield.

His turn was so tight that I was unable to obtain the correct deflection angle or keep him in the middle of the gunsight. Despite use of dive brakes and wing flap, my speed was still too high, and I began to overtake him.

With machine-guns, I could have sprayed the area ahead of his turn, trusting that he'd fly into the stream of lead. With rockets, it was another matter. It was pointless pumping the only eight I had into fresh air.

As I drew up, the B26 remained locked in the tight turn, his port wingtip clipping the tree tops. This was a pilot who knew all the tricks of the trade. He knew damn well that he could turn tighter and slower than the Delfin, and if he kept it up long enough, I'd have to break off combat for lack of fuel.

I tried another tactic. Applying full flap and 96% power, I zoomed to the right, to the outside of the turn, my thumb on the dive brake switch. It was no go. I still couldn't maintain my position. In a few seconds, I'd have to abandon the turn before the Delfin stalled, flicking into a fatal spin. There could be no recovery at this low altitude. Now I was practically on his wing tip, in a close line-abreast position.

Then he looked up and I saw him, as I hovered on the verge of a stall. The pilot was Tubby Sanders!

It was impossible. I'd have shot him down seconds before if he hadn't taken evasive action. So he'd found his way to Biafra. I might have known.

The Delfin commenced to judder, warning of an impending stall. As I pushed the stick forward and the B26 disappeared to the left, I resumed level flight and there he was, flying towards Biafran territory, waggling his wings, waiting for me to pull up alongside.

He was flying faster now, and I had no trouble maintaining position, using 70% rpm and quarter flap with occasional flicks of the dive brakes. He waved as I levelled up on his wing tip.

I signalled with my hands, spelling out the VHF frequency 123.6 and pointing at my microphone. Tubby nodded and leaned forward to adjust his selector.

'Tubby, you bastard!' I said, 'Why didn't you let me know you were in Biafra? Christ, I nearly shot you down a few minutes ago.'

He grinned, 'I saw you in the nick of time. I didn't know it was you.'

I looked anxiously at my fuel gauge. Four hundred litres left. I calculated we were about seventy-five nautical miles south of Makurdi now. There wasn't much time. 'Take this address, c/o KELLY OIL, ROME. Liaise through that. There's a price on your head of £20,000. Egyptians and East Germans will soon be flying MIG17s; they've got 26- and 40-mm. cannons. You can't last more than a couple of weeks.'

'What do you suggest I do? Surrender?' Tubby's voice crackled sarcastically in my head-set.

'Wait,' I countered. 'Here's a proposition. You put the B26 down on the nearest Biafran airfield. Is there one nearby?'

I saw Tubby nod, 'Yes, north of Nsukka. The Biafrans

hold a strip and I can sit down there. What happens then?'

'I come in and rocket the B26, claim the reward, and we split 50-50. You then fly DC4s or Connies on the arms airlift into Port Harcourt. It's a lot safer.'

As Tubby thought about it I studied my map. There was still sufficient fuel to reach the Nsukka strip, finish off the B26 and just make my base at Makurdi. But it was going to be touch and go and I'd be landing on the smell of the kerosene in the fuel tanks.

'Come on, Tubby,' I said irritably. 'I'm running short of fuel for this primus stove I'm strapped to. If you don't decide now, I'll have to eject somewhere on the way back. You're earning your share of the loot the easy way.'

Tubby changed course abruptly. 'It's a deal. We'll be over Nsukka in ten minutes. Make a good job of it. My excuse for going in will be technical trouble. I don't want anything left of the B26 to enable them to discover I was lying.'

'Roger,' I climbed to the rare air at 16,000 ft to conserve fuel, then levelled out and got back to Tubby on the radio. We arranged to listen out on the frequency we were now using, 123.6, each time we flew. His call sign would be Pussy and mine Tom-Cat. The B26 was a minute green dot below slipping across the dappled forest and I kept one eye riveted on it and the other on the fuel gauge.

'Pussy. This is Tom-Cat. Am going straight in'. The strip appeared, a brown smear against a green backdrop. I was too high to see if any Biafran vehicles were around.

I threw out the dive brakes and spiralled lazily left, watching the strip get bigger. The B26's propellers as it landed created twin brown vortices of red dust that swirled for a moment before drifting languidly off the runway, indicating practically no wind. That would help the accuracy of the rockets.

Now I was down to four thousand feet. I could see the tiny speck that was Tubby emerge from the machine. I couldn't afford the precious fuel required to run in with the sun behind me. I re-adjusted the gunsight for normal ground strafing and commenced a steep dive as Tubby reached the edge of the trees.

Although the sight was harmonized for accurate shooting at 1200 feet, I could only afford the fuel for one pass. Allowing for gravity drop, I put the red centre pipper of the sight 2 inches ahead of the parked B26. I kept the Delfin very steady in that position, and thanked God there was no wind.

At 3000 feet, I squeezed the firing button. Trailing black smoke, the first pair of rockets sped away with a hiss that could be heard in the cockpit. Two brown mushrooms erupted ten feet ahead of the bomber.

I cursed and moved the stick forward gently until the pipper was an inch ahead of the target. The roar of the thundering jet reminded me to be careful of target fixation. Too many pilots had followed their weapons all the way down on to the target.

I squeezed the button again. The B26 swung sideways like an enraged wounded buffalo. Much better, I thought.

Four rockets to go. The next pair struck somewhere behind the wing roots, and the B26 collapsed, pointing its green nose in the air, its back mortally broken.

As the last pair ripped into the wreckage, there was a white hot eruption of flame and smoke. Simultaneously, I saw I was under fire from a score of flaming automatic weapons manned by soldiers around a small, heavily sandbagged control hut.

I banked steeply left, pulling the stick hard towards me, the G-forces pinning me to the seat. My eyesight faded and my legs felt like leaden blocks.

I eased up on the zoom climb as I swept through 5000 feet, and set course for Makurdi. I had less than 200 litres of fuel remaining. The B26 was destroyed, but I had a tight feeling that the Federal Air Force might lose a Delfin. I checked the gauge again.

At 22,000 feet, I placed the Delfin on a slow downhill ride, one that enabled me to fly with greatly reduced power yet still have a fair airspeed. At 22,000 feet the VHF would be within range of Makurdi.

I lifted the microphone. 'Makurdi. Delfin Four Zero Two. Mission accomplished. Rebel Bravo 26 destroyed at Nsukka airstrip, 1123 hours Zulu. Am declaring fuel emergency. Request priority straight in on runway 36 and all other traffic diverted till I have landed. Confirm!'

'Roger, Roger Delfin Four Zero Two.' The underlying excitement of the controller's voice was clearly discernible. 'Copied OK, B26 destroyed. Priority clearance direct approach runway three six approved. Will alert other traffic. What is the nature of the fuel emergency?'

'Chasing the B26 used up more than I expected.'

A red light on the dash blinked momentarily, died, blinked again and stayed on. The 'low fuel' warning light. Ten minutes of kerosene left.

I checked the map. I was 142 kilometres south-west of Makurdi. Cruising at 450 kilometres per hour, the fuel remaining would bring me 52 kilometres short of the airport. I still had 20,000 feet of fresh air between myself and the ground. It would be pretty useful, but was it enough to enable me to glide the rest of the way? I had my doubt about the answer to that one. I hadn't had a chance to study the pilot's manual thoroughly and check on the glide profile of the Delfin.

I looked at my watch. It was less than a minute since the fuel warning light had blinked into life. It seemed like five. The engine purred contentedly, unaware that its life blood was draining away.

I looked around for a suitable stretch of road I could use if necessary. No luck. All the roads I could see twisted and turned like earthworms through the jungle, rising and falling over hilly ground.

I began to sweat. I looked up at the windshield, trying to judge how close my knees would pass by if I had to eject, as I remembered the Russian's briefing. The cockpit seemed smaller than usual and it had been a small cockpit to begin with.

The red warning light stared defiantly at me. No encouragement there. The fuel quantity needle flopped against the empty stop, like a catfish having a swim in an almost dry pond.

Now the terrain below looked very hostile. Yet it had seemed peaceful when the Delfin was fat with gas.

'Delfin Four Zero Two. This is Makurdi. Report your progress, please.'

The call startled me. 'This is Four Zero Two. I have you in sight now. Position approximately thirty nautical miles south west. Am expecting flame-out any second now. Will attempt to glide to runway. Stand by with fire-tender.'

'Roger. All necessary precautions taken. Call again very long final for three six.'

'If I get that far. Will call as instructed.' As I replaced the microphone, the engine died. It didn't cough or splutter, it simply wound itself down. The rpm needle moved languidly towards zero, as if there was no hurry, and it could afford to take its time.

I shut off the fuel selector and trimmed the Delfin for the best possible glide angle. Distance was what I required now, and I needed every available foot.

There was a new sound in the cockpit, one I hadn't heard before. It was the wind hissing over the wings, over the windshield, and along the fuselage to the fin and tail-plane at the rear.

The runway was a blur in the distance. It seemed to take years before it was any closer. I checked the altimeter, 10,000 feet. Still a long way to go. I tightened my harness straps and told Makurdi: 'Four Zero Two. On long final.'

'Call again 2000 feet or short final, whichever is sooner.'

'Roger.'

The Delfin hissed towards the white patch of runway. It was getting turbulent now and I was in much warmer air. This could be both a blessing and an aggravation. Warm air produces updrafts and downdrafts. A sustained updraft would do wonders for me. A sustained downdraft would make my inevitable contact with the terrain a lot sooner.

Gliding steadily, passing through 5000 feet, I told myself that I was definitely going to make it. Then the Delfin sank, the speed decreasing by ten kilometres. I cursed as I was forced to lower the nose, and lose height at a greater rate.

The downdraft was a sustained one. I held on grimly, feeling the controls and hoping until, a mile from the runway, I knew I wasn't going to make it. The runway overshoot threshold was grassy, undulating, with numerous folds and ruts, but seemed free of boulders or tree stumps. My approach speed was 180 kilometres per hour. I could reduce it slightly nearer the ground.

I grabbed the mike.

'Four Zero Two. Crash landing on extended centre line four hundred yards short. Stand by.' I can't remember whether or not the controller replied. I was concentrating too hard.

If I landed wheels up on the undulations, I'd cartwheel. My feet were only a foot or so away from the front of the nose, the rest of me only another 18 inches farther back. If the jet cartwheeled, my chances of survival were remote.

I waited till the ground loomed nearer, then dropped the wheels. I needed those legs to take the first force of impact, to slow up the jet. Anything I hit after that would be at a much reduced speed. I applied full flap and waited.

Holding the Delfin just above the twisting ground, I applied full dive brake, and eased the stick towards me.

With a slight wobble, the Delfin pitched forward on to the main wheels and nose gear. There was a violent crunch from the nose wheel and the Delfin leapt high in the air to alight in a very nose down attitude with a thump that jarred through me.

On the next sharp rise, the nose wheel took a hammering that bent it completely backwards. The main legs folded with a crunch of screaming twisting metal.

The jet took the next crest like a roller coaster. The left wing dug in and the ship spun crazily towards it, churning up an enormous cloud of bright red dust. Suddenly there was silence.

I released the harness, got out and dusted myself off. I was still in one piece, I decided, as I patted myself gingerly.

The Station Commander leaped from the fire tender as it pulled up.

'Are you all right?'

'I think so.'

'Then congratulations, Major Gibson,' he said cheerfully. 'That makes two aircraft you've destroyed today.' He slapped my back. 'We'll celebrate the first one in the mess.' He looked at the wrecked Delfin. 'It was worth it,' he said, 'That B26 would have destroyed a lot more of our aircraft.' He opened the door of the tender. 'Jump in.'

'Just a moment,' I said. I probed in the wreckage of the wings until I found the camera-gun film canister.

The station commander watched me curiously as I dusted it off and slipped it into my overall pocket. 'The camera-gun film. It records when the rockets fire.'

'Ah,' he said brightly. 'You wish to show the film to my men when it's been developed?'

'No, to Headquarters in Lagos. It's proof that I earned £20,000 today!'

He slapped my back again and we drove away from the mangled remains of Delfin Four Zero Two, which, like the Biafran B26, would never fly again.

All in all, from the Federal Government's point of view, it had been a good swop.

CHAPTER ELEVEN

NEXT morning I hitched a lift in a Nigerian Air Force DC3 via Kaduna back to Lagos, and after showing the film, collected a bank draft from Colonel Bello at the Defence Ministry for the £20,000. I had to hand it to the Nigerians; there was no hesitation about settling.

After that, the next few weeks were a dreary span of boredom. I flew various communication flights with the Aero Commander, while daily the mercenaries struck at Ore and Benin City, relentlessly keeping up the pressure against the Biafrans until they'd forced them back five miles east of the city and the vital airfield was in Nigerian hands. Now the short range Delfins could be positioned there to carry out strikes against the Ibo entrenchments around the Onitsha oilfields.

It seemed as if Kelly's prospects were brightening. Retreating, the Biafrans had destroyed the east span of the £6,000,000 bridge over the Niger. It would, I thought, only delay the inevitable end.

The new air of confidence in Lagos was unmistakable. The headlines of the tabloids screamed their message at every street corner, with typical African exuberance,

COWARDLY CRINGING OJUKWU BEGS PEACE.

REBELS RUN HELTER SKELTER ACROSS NIGER.

REBELLION CRUSHED. NO MERCY FOR RULING CLIQUE.

It wouldn't be as straightforward as that. The odds were in favour of the Nigerians with their superior equipment, but the Ibos were not going to be all that easy to take. The Federals were going to get a mauling before this little affair was settled. I hoped Tubby had his escape route organized when the inevitable crash came.

Sprawled out beside the hotel pool, I watched a formation of five MIG17s scream over in a ragged V, flown by Egyptian pilots, recruited after the refusal of the Russians to allow the mercenaries to fly them. The Egyptians, I guessed, must have been amongst those fortunate enough to be on leave during the six-day war. Having survived that, they had no intention of taking any chances. Day after day they flew morale-building sorties over Lagos for the benefit of the local inhabitants, claiming they were necessary as preliminary terrain- and route-familiarization exercises before they sallied forth to destroy the Ibos.

I ordered a Spey Royal and, lying back, admired the blazing colours of the tropical plants. They grew like weeds beneath the tall jacarandas swaying lazily to the breeze. Orange and green lizards darted from bush to bush and the air was loud with the hum of insects. The scene was idyllic but I'd had enough. The reward for destroying Tubby's B26 had been very acceptable, but to date the quest for the oil concessions had been long on danger and short on results, and the vital survey maps were still missing.

I wished Gisela were here. I'd cabled her to check the bank draft had been cleared through my Swiss account and she had confirmed that it had gone through. Next time I saw her I'd tell her to transfer Tubby's share of the reward to his account.

I showered, changed, and went into lunch. The Federal Palace bar was full. Standing at the bar I could feel watchful eyes. Some of the espionage agents, I was certain, could rotate their ears without moving their heads.

As I finished lunch—a fresh bream cooked in butter and washed down with a bottle of Chablis—and settled down on the verandah, a car pulled up. Gobi slammed the door and bounded up the steps. He collapsed in the chair beside me, breathing heavily.

'Scotch?'

He nodded and mopped the back of his neck. 'Thank you. Important information has just come into Headquarters. I came over immediately.'

'The only important information, as far as I'm concerned, is anything that concerns the oil concessions.'

'That's why I'm here.' He paused as the waiter brought the drink. He watched as I added water, then tossed back a generous slug, his Adam's apple bobbing up and down like a decapitated chicken. 'Thanks. I needed that.' He put the glass down delicately and leaned towards me. 'I have discovered the whereabouts of the oil survey maps.'

A little nerve in my cheek began to twitch. Here we go again, I thought wearily. Gobi would never have rushed over in such a state of excitement merely to tell me they had recovered the maps. 'That's great,' I said casually. I swallowed my drink and signalled for another. 'When you get them, please let me have photocopies for Mr Kelly. He'll be pleased to know that he hasn't wasted his money keeping me and his plane in Lagos.'

Gobi twirled his empty glass nervously.

'If you want another drink, let me order you one.' I eyed him carefully.

He released his glass. 'No thank you, Major Gibson. It's not quite that simple, I'm afraid.' He nervously mopped his neck again.

I called the waiter. 'You'd better have another drink. What's the catch this time?'

Gobi produced a folded aeronautical map from his breast pocket and spread it across the table. With the tip of his gold ballpoint he indicated a spot a few miles below Benin City on the west bank of the Niger. 'A rebel gunboat left here this morning. On board were a party of Frenchmen. Oil men, with a contingent of rebel guards. We are told they have the maps. The boat will turn west and proceed

along this tributary of the Niger. It is due to arrive here,'
his pen made a neat circle, 'just north of Burutu, at 6:00
A.M. tomorrow morning.'

I studied the map. Here the Niger Delta consisted of a
twisted mass of blue tributaries interlocking and splitting
as they wound their way to the coast. The area was
choked with massive reed-filled swamps and mangrove
forests.

Gobi continued. 'Here is a French-owned trading concession. There is a small jetty and we know fuel is available. We believe the gunboat will refuel there then head
for Port Harcourt. There are French-registered ships
in the harbour and once they arrive there that's the end of
our hopes of recovering the maps.'

I watched him thoughtfully. 'How reliable is your information?'

He spread out his hands. 'One hundred percent,' he said
simply. The brown bullfrog eyes watched me steadily.

I picked up my glass, took a long pull, and slumped back
in my chair. 'So the shit's really hit the fan. Now what?'

'Please, Mr Gibson,' he held up his hand. 'I am authorized
on behalf of my ministry to give you written confirmation
that, should you assist us to recover these documents,
Mr Kelly will be granted 25% of the unallocated oil areas
and he will be allowed to select the areas he requires. This
I will give you now, in writing.'

'Perhaps you'll tell me how I'm to stop them?'

The bullfrog eyes watched me hopefully. 'It would have
to be an air operation, we cannot get there by road or
river. Maybe you can suggest some plan. I don't know . . .'
His voice trailed off.

I thought it over. There was only one way to mount
this operation. Immobilize the gunboat with the Delfins, fly
troops in with helicopters, capture and search it, then
evacuate before the Biafrans could bring reinforcements
to the scene. It seemed simple but this type of deal, I'd

learned, never works out that way.

I pointed to Gobi's briefcase. 'Any writing paper in there?'

'Sure. Why?'

'I've got an idea, but I'm not talking until I've got your offer down in black and white.' I waited while he unzipped the briefcase and produced a pad. I took it and pulled my chair up to the table. 'Now, let's get everything clear. First, I was sent by Mr Kelly to fly his plane in a strictly civilian capacity. Then, in an attempt to recover these oil maps, you talked me into the Wakki Operation, which turned out to be a floperoo, and, I almost got my arse shot off into the bargain. Secondly, you talked me into the B26 operation. I'm not complaining about that one. I was well paid and that deal is finalized. Thirdly, I'm roped in as a test pilot. I agreed, and I've got no beef about the money. But none of these deals are what I was sent here to do : to get the oil concessions. This attempt, I warn you, will be my last. Now I'm going to draw up an agreement. I want no alterations. You can sign it as it stands or not at all.' I took his pen and started to write.

'I, Yusef Gobi, a member of the Federal Nigerian Government Council of Ministers and duly authorized by them, do hereby agree that should the oil survey maps, at present believed to be on a Rebel gunboat, be recovered due to the efforts of Mr J. Gibson, his employer, Mr A. Kelly of Kelly Oil Associates, will be granted the sole concession to exploit 25% of the unallocated oil areas as shown on the maps, whenever and in whatsoever manner he pleases. Dated November 3rd, 1967 at Lagos. Signed.

I handed the agreement to Gobi and while he studied it, called two waiters across to witness it.

'I'm no lawyer, but this is good enough for Kelly to go to work on. God help you if you try and cross him up on this one. These big oil boys play for keeps. Remember that.'

Gobi read the document in silence. He was suddenly tense.

'My pen please, Mr Gibson.' He signed and the waiters witnessed it, tip-toeing away nervously as soon as they'd signed.

I pocketed the document and leaned back. The muddy brown eyes were watching me steadily.

'What do you suggest, Mr Gibson?'

'I'll check the Aero Commander and have it ready to leave in an hour for Benin City. You and I are boarding it. Signal the Federal Commander at Benin City to place the Delfins and the five ex-Austrian Air Force Westland S55 helicopters on full operational standby.'

Gobi looked at me eagerly. 'How are you planning the operation, Mr Gibson?'

I patted the pocket with the document. 'I'll explain it all at Benin City. I'm going to pack. Pick me up in an hour or as soon as you've got the signal off.' He drove away fast, his wheels churning the gravel.

I wrote a short note to Gisela.

Lagos. 3/11/67

Honey,

It seems there's a good possibility of recovering the oil survey maps. I'm taking off in an hour to go after them. Send the enclosed agreement to Kelly and catch the first available plane to Lagos. The situation here is about to break one way or another and I think you should be out here as Kelly's brain trust. Besides, I want you too,

Love, John.

Gobi picked me up half an hour later and I mailed the letter at the Ikeja airport post office in the internal services reception block. Outside, a faded sign announced W E S T A F R I C A N   A I R W A Y S   C O R P O R A T I O N. I wondered when Nigerian Airways would get around to changing it. The maintenance crew had the Aero Commander ready. We parked in front of the control tower, and took off immediately.

Gobi settled back and slept. I watched the brown inscrutable face and wondered just how far I could trust the bastard. I found my fingers were tightly clenched on the wheel and relaxed them.

To hell with it all. If we retrieved the maps that was great. If not, I was getting to hell out of it. My half share of the £20,000 plus the other money I had, would keep me in sin and idleness until something suitable for my own peculiar talents cropped up. Maybe I'd head for Rhodesia and join up with Tubby's outfit. I wondered how the fat son-of-a-bitch was getting along. Knowing Tubby, I guessed he was doing fine.

I lowered the aircraft's nose. Benin City was fifteen minutes ahead and the game would be on.

I greased the ship on to the runway and a grey Land-Rover drove us to the mess. The two heavily-armed soldiers parked on the front mudguards obscured the driver's view. The risk of a collision was greater than the remote possibility of an Ibo sniper's bullet connecting and added to my general irritation with everything Nigerian.

The mess was an old colonial-style mansion with orange tiles, the grounds crowded with shrubs and trees, blazing with colour. It was the type of mansion that belonged to bygone days. I imagined some stiff moustached old governor reading stale copies of *Tatler* and knocking back the inevitable gimlets before lunch. It was a different world today. Maybe a better or a poorer one. Certainly a lot of the bullshit had been swept away.

The mess was jammed with Federal Army Officers, some in khaki but the majority in jungle camouflage, all drinking heavily and most of them rather glazed about the eyes.

In the corner, Karel and Jerry were closeted with two

Nigerian pilots. I was glad to see they were drinking beer and both appeared to be sober. With Gobi in tow, I moved across and joined them.

Jerry spotted me. 'For Christ's sake. Look what's arrived. The bounty hunter from Lagos.'

Karel grinned. 'Come to look for another B26? You can buy a round with all the money you made. What brings you this close to the war?'

I ordered a round, paid for it, and told them. 'There's a special strike tomorrow and I'm leading it. If it's successful, I'm sure Mr Gobi will recommend a suitable bonus. What do you say, Mr Gobi?'

Gobi nodded unhappily. 'Yes, I think it might be arranged.'

'How much?' Jerry leaned towards Gobi who looked at me enquiringly.

I took a chance. 'I think £500 each would be fair, Mr Gobi.'

He nodded. 'I can get that approved.'

Jerry grinned. 'Now you're talking. What's the deal?'

I glanced at Gobi. 'We'd better get down to details. I need the chief helicopter pilot, and the local Commanding Officer. Can you arrange a room and a meeting right away?'

'Sure,' Gobi went off.

Karel snapped his fingers at the barman. 'There's time for another round on that £20,000 of yours.'

As we finished the new round, Gobi returned with two Nigerian officers, a stout elderly Colonel, and a younger tall lean Lt.-Colonel. He introduced them. 'Colonel Okra, the local Divisional Commander. This is Lt.-Colonel Benjamin Adenku.' The second name rang a bell. Adenku was one of the up-and-coming younger officers. He had had a lot of publicity in the local press, and was said to lead his men from the front.

I felt better. With Adenku participating, the operation's

chances of success increased appreciably.

'Where's the helicopter pilot?' I asked.

'He's coming,' Gobi pointed. A stout balding character in his thirties was pushing his way through the crowd towards us. Gobi introduced him. 'Captain Peré.' His handshake was wet and flabby.

Christ, I thought; that's all I'm short of, a bloody Frenchman. All our security might be blown. Maybe he was a straightforward mercenary. Maybe. I decided to watch him during the briefing.

'Shall we go?'

Gobi led us along the passage to a small lounge marked 'Senior Officers Only'. There was a large circular table and I spread the map.

'Will you gather around please, gentlemen?' I'd worked out the details on the flight up in the Aero Commander and I gave it to them fast. 'At six tomorrow we believe that a rebel gunboat will be here.' I tapped the spot. 'This is the operation. The Delfins will attack it at first light before it has a chance to refuel. We believe it is trying to make for Port Harcourt. The Delfins must not sink it. I will give the reasons later. The engines are at the back of the vessel and that's the target. Once the engine room is hit, firing will cease. The Delfins will then maintain a protective patrol up to the limit of their fuel reserves. I repeat, we do not want the ship sunk, only immobilized. So much for the Delfins.

'Now the helicopters.' I turned to the French pilot. 'Arrange with Colonel Adenku to deliver his men in the five helicopters, arriving over the site at 6:15, fifteen minutes after the Delfin strike. Landing beside the jetty, Colonel Adenku's men must rush the gunboat and capture it. They will search it for certain documents that Mr Gobi requires and which he will describe later to Colonel Adenku. As soon as they are found, destroy the ship and fly back to Benin City. Speed is essential. There are rebel troops nearby and you can expect to come under attack within an hour of landing.'

I grinned at Adenku. 'Can you manage in the time?'

The black eyes, with the yellow muddied whites, watched me like a tiger eyeing a goat. 'Leave it to me. Those rebels won't know what's hit them.'

I stood back. 'That's all there is to it. I'll lead the Delfin strike and it's up to Captain Peré to land the assault force there at 6:15. I'll time my take off to be over the ship at six. The radio frequency will be 118.5 and the rest is up to you.' I glanced at Gobi. 'Any suggestions?'

'None at all. The plan is excellent. I will go with Captain Peré to see the papers are the correct ones.'

'Fair enough.' I left them and, followed by Jerry and Karel, went back to the bar. We had a final drink, then turned in for the night.

I slept badly. All night I twisted on the hot sweaty bed. As soon as the curtains lightened, I padded across the dark room and glanced out. The bush stretched far beyond the perimeter fence, as it had swept for the past few million years, guarding its oil.

'You've had it long enough,' I thought. 'Today I'm going to get those maps and find out where you've got it stashed away. And Kelly's going to come and take it away. And I'm going to screw you personally for a million dollars.' I went back to bed.

I woke to the sound of tropical rain lashing the windows and cursed as I dressed. If ever we needed clear weather for a flight, it was today.

At the mess building, Gobi was waiting on the verandah, puffing nervously on a cigarette, and watching the rhythmic sweep of the waiting Land-Rover's windscreen wipers. A white mist belched from its exhaust and vanished into the heavy downpour.

I shivered as Karel and Jerry arrived. Together with Gobi, we formed a dejected group.

'We're buggered,' I said. 'Any plans of doing a formation strike on the boat are completely washed out. This is a solo affair, and even then, it's going to be a hit-and-miss deal.' They nodded glumly.

'We'll space ourselves thirty minutes apart,' I carried on. 'I go first, Karel second and Jerry number three. The choppers will be listening out on 118.5. They ought to be able to give us the cloud base and general weather conditions in the target area.

'Remember, if you find the boat, don't sink it. Clobber the engine room. The chopper boarding parties *must* get aboard. Any questions?'

Nobody spoke. 'Let's go,' I said.

We drove in morose silence to the airfield. Gobi suddenly spoke to me. 'You know something, Major Gibson? I believe we're going to get away with it.'

'I hope you're right.'

'I'm usually right.' He grinned meaningfully.

I let it ride, whatever he meant. I found myself increasingly disliking Gobi.

The dark green trees were dripping diamond droplets, shaking gently as the heavy drops struck them. I looked enviously at a flock of grounded birds, huddled together for comfort on a massive branch. Their feathers gleamed with an oily gunmetal sheen, matching the glint in their bright alert eyes.

The driver pulled up at the verandah of the small terminal building, and we made a dive for its protection. Peré and his chopper-pilots were waiting.

Gobi turned to me. 'I'll leave with Captain Peré immediately. We'll keep you informed of the weather. You'll get to the target area before us, of course. I'll join the assault force when they board the ship. Keep us informed on VHF what transpires.' He held out his hand. 'Good luck!'

'Thanks,' I said. 'If you get the survey maps, call me

and say "operation successful".'

He paused, then nodded. I watched him hurry away with Peré to the hangar where Adenku's men were waiting.

In the entrance hall, Karel was pouring coffee.

'Coffee?'

'Thanks.' As I sipped the insipid brown liquid I heard the helicopters take off, their blades flapping in a noisy farewell. A flight sergeant came up and halted smartly. 'Your aircraft is ready, sir.'

'Thank you.' I stood up and looked at my watch. 'Thirty minutes after me,' I warned Karel. I ran through the rain and scrambled into the cockpit of my new Delfin four zero six. Five minutes later, I rotated off the glistening runway into the overcast. The base was only a hundred feet. Maybe over the Delta it would have lifted.

I cleared the main layer at 5000 metres. The red sun combined with the black of night to produce the first blue of early dawn. As it rose, it began to pour its heat into the clouds. Enormous cumulo-nimbus thunderheads spread their blue-grey anvil tops as if protecting the weaker overcast below. I skirted cautiously round them, but they weren't really my problem on this operation. The real difficulty lay in the very low cloud base.

Somewhere down there was a ship that I had to find and disable, and this without any form of navigational aid. Even if a full Instrument Landing System could somehow have been laid on by the target ship for my benefit, the cloud base was still well below any airline minima.

I checked the radio altimeter. I could set it to any height above ground level I desired. The radio would then transmit a steady stream of pulses vertically downwards, measure the time it took them to bounce back, and in a microsecond calculate if the aircraft was still above the height selected. If it was, the radio remained silent. When you hit the selected height, the earphones would suddenly screech into life in a series of high-pitched 'peeps'.

This was fine if the terrain below was reasonably flat. It didn't help much if you were heading for a cliff but fortunately the Niger was flat country.

Using the radio altimeter I could, at the appropriate time, lower the landing gear and wing flaps and apply full-dive brakes, maintaining a shallow descent angle with a lot of engine power. I'd drop my speed to just a fraction under 180 kph. Even so, this was still 176 feet per second. If visibility was this distance or less as I broke through the overcast, and there was an obstruction ahead, I'd buy it. It would take more than a second for my motor nerves to signal what I'd seen to my brain, it in turn would then have to trigger an alarm alert to my left hand to apply 100% rpm and my right hand to haul back on the control column.

Twenty minutes later, my overalls clinging wetly to my back, I picked up the microphone. 'Chopper leader, this is Delfin four zero six. Do you read?'

'Loud and clear,' said Peré's professional voice. I'm all right, Jack, it implied. We're below cloud and doing nicely, thank you. 'Go ahead.'

'Roger. What is your present position from the target area and the weather conditions prevailing. I require very accurate cloud base and visibility. Over.'

'Stand by one.' I waited long enough to become irritable.

'Sorry for the delay, Delfin four zero six,' he apologized. 'Cloud base is 150 feet, drizzle, visibility half a mile. We're parked on a clearing sixteen nautical miles east of target area. What are your intentions?'

'I'm coming down for a look-see,' I said. 'Please advise me if you hear my motor, and its direction from yourselves. Stand by.'

'Standing by.'

Wisps of white cloud clutched at the Delfin, bumping it off balance. I marked the helicopter's position on my map and tucked it into a leg side-pocket. I leaned forward and set the radio altimeter on forty metres, the lowest setting available.

The Delfin's turbine died to a gentle sigh as I applied flight-idle rpm, and activated the dive brakes. We sank rapidly into the overcast. I could lose 12,000 feet rapidly before I'd have to worry about commencing a precision let down. I watched the panel as the instrument needles flickered, swept anti-clockwise or remained stationary, depending upon the messages they conveyed.

As the altimeter registered three thousand feet, I reduced the rate of descent by retracting the dive brakes and applying 60% rpm. To avoid telegraphing an advance arrival message to the ship, I circled eight miles east of its forecast position.

The overcast was a gloomy mixture of hissing greyness, irregular bumps that made the Delfin lurch, and white cloud streaks that served to accentuate the depressing opaque void through which I groped my way blindly earthwards.

I re-selected the radio altimeter to four hundred metres and kept the descent constant. My earphones seemed unnaturally quiet, like the interval on a radio station between the last announcement and the commencement of the news.

High-pitched 'peeps' startled me, as the altimeter told me I was not much more than one thousand feet above solid earth.

I eased the Delfin into a near-level position as I applied 70% rpm, then selected two hundred metres on the radio altimeter and headed towards where, on a dead-reckoning basis, the helicopters should be.

'Chopper leader,' I called. 'Delfin four zero six descending dead-reckoning. Advise if engine noise detected.'

'Will do, zero six,' Peré acknowledged.

I concentrated on the descent. I lowered the gear and flaps. The rain increased and horizontal streaks of lightning flashed viciously ahead across the Delfin's blue nose, as if warning of approaching danger, a violent substitute for the marker-beacon position lights that blink into life on an ILS* approach.

Six hundred feet and the 'peeps' in my earphones sounded frantic. Still wrapped in a shroud of impenetrable gloom, partly water and partly moisture, I set one hundred metres and continued the descent. I was conscious of my fingers as they gripped around the throttle and forced myself to relax. My overalls clung to my body like a second skin.

I glanced repeatedly from the panel to the windscreen and back to the panel. My hands were a pair of nervous, highly-strung twins, the movement of one watched and countered by a move from the other as I nursed the Delfin lower.

Again the radio altimeter bleeped in my ears, and my eyes strained to see ahead. I was three hundred feet from the ground vertically below, less if a ridge lay directly in front. Sweat droplets collected on my eyelashes, forming tears of salt that made my eyes smart. I couldn't spare a hand to wipe them away.

I felt I was swimming in a heavy viscous fluid that seemed denser than the overcast above. I watched the instruments as I felt for the radio altimeter selector. I knew without looking where the forty-metre height selector position lay. I heard the creak of the dial as I twirled the knob and set it for forty metres.

A little more power would place me in the flattest approach slot. My thumb on the throttle toggle applied full-speed brake as I increased power. One action would counteract the other, but both would combine to give me the shallowest approach angle at the lowest possible speed which I required.

Again the radio altimeter shrieked its warning as I reached forty metres above ground level. I divested myself of all feeling and became a living computer, all emotions

* ILS. Instrument Landing System.

programmed for the card to punch out the answer, for me to break through into the clear and find the ship.

I merged with the instruments and became part of the Delfin as I dropped those last few feet through the murk. Then, suddenly, the greyness was splashed with green and silver and I'd broken through.

I flicked the dive brakes, held them in the full open position until I felt the thud as they locked. Then I released my thumb.

The Delfin seemed to be sinking towards a world of dense green with flashing mirrors of white. I applied 90% rpm and raised the gear, leaving the wing flaps fully down. There was no point in having a lot of speed when you were barely one hundred feet above ground level with visibility less than a mile.

Veins of silver capillaries threaded their way through masses of mangroves and tropical bush. Each rivulet was capable of carrying a vessel of the size which was our target. I couldn't even guess exactly where I was, give or take ten miles.

I was too low to attempt establishing VHF radio contact with the choppers, unless I was in their immediate vicinity, but I tried anyway.

'Chopper leader, Delfin four zero six, do you read?' Silence.

I studied my map, keeping an eye on the terrain and trying to fit the confusing landscape into something identifiable on the chart. I flicked the microphone switch.

'Chopper leader, from Delfin four zero six. One, two, three, four, five. Do you read me? Come in, please.'

I kept my speed as low as possible, turning in a huge circle. By dead reckoning I was definitely in the area the choppers were supposed to be, and they were sixteen miles from the target area. To the east, the chopper leader had said.

I circled, watching the fuel gauge. In ten minutes I

would have to climb to 5000 metres to make Benin City. I thought of the crash landing at Makurdi, and decided there'd be no repetition of that deal. Ten minutes was my maximum.

Then, banking steeply left, something hit the Delfin's nose with the sound of a jack-hammer drilling into a wall, and I felt the rudder pedals jump with the impact.

I rolled the Delfin level, easing the strain on the wings. I knew I'd been hit by gunfire, and checked the dials. Pressures and temperatures were normal.

Then, as red, orange and black fireballs swam upwards and around me, I saw the vessel directly ahead. It was a large PT bristling with guns, all flaming hostility and manned by desperate men who knew how to handle them.

As I skidded over them, I saw their gun barrels swinging in unison while they tracked me. My heading was one seven zero degrees. I continued for one minute, turned ninety degrees to the left and then banked to the right for a total of two hundred and seventy degrees on to a heading of three fifty degrees, to bring me back to the ship.

I had applied standard airline procedures to this operation, using the ship as a radio beacon. I was now inbound, the target vessel somewhere ahead and one minute away.

I selected the firing buttons in sequence for the pairs of rockets I was about to fire. The flat trajectory was unsatisfactory, but I had no alternative.

I saw the flaming muzzles before I saw the ship. Even at my necessarily low speed, I was closing in on it at an alarming clip. I set the pipper on the engine-room and fired. I watched the first pair of rockets rip off a portion of the steel deck above and to the left of the engine-room. Correcting, I banked right and then left, then fired another pair as I rolled out. I missed, and saw twin eruptions of smoke in the white sand beyond the vessel on a small island. I cursed. I would have to make another pass.

The ship's guns fanned a continuous streak of red and white tracer as I streaked towards it. I instinctively ducked as I headed into a curtain of highly metallized airspace, and felt the Delfin lurch crazily. I heard the noise of the bullets' impact and felt the ailerons go limp and fail to respond to left or right movement of the stick. Out of range, I gingerly tested the controls. The rudders were a poor substitute for banking the aircraft, but a slight pressure on the left pedal initiated a roll to the left. The same to the right.

I could maintain a nose-up or nose-down attitude with the stick. I could bank and turn, very gingerly, with the rudder pedals.

I had four rockets left. Only one of them in the engine-room should be enough to prevent it from sailing.

Using the same airline procedure, I turned back towards the ship lurking somewhere ahead in the drizzle, nursing the Delfin carefully around in a flat wide turn.

Beneath me the mangroves stood in lines like the crosses of Allied war graves, stretching in rows in all directions whatever angle you looked at them. Then, as I came out of the turn, I saw the flashes I was expecting.

I manoeuvred the Delfin's pedals lightly, and checked the deflection on the gunsight. Ignoring the tracers I waited until I was two hundred yards away before I squeezed the rocket-firing button and watched the dark trails of smoke speed towards the engine-room. A gaping hole appeared inwards, then erupted in a holocaust of black and orange as the last pair of rockets also struck home.

I couldn't bank steeply this time, but it didn't really matter. Firing had ceased, and men were running in all directions as I skimmed over the stricken vessel. My fuel was too low to investigate. It was over to Peré now.

I climbed gingerly into the overcast and turned on to a heading for Benin City.

At 500 metres I called the helicopters. 'Chopper One

from Delfin four zero six. Mission accomplished, escape vessel immobilized. It's all yours, boys.'

'Roger dee,' Peré replied. 'What is the position of the ship?'

'Where it's supposed to be. Proceed to its forecasted pinpoint and you'll find it. Good luck.'

'Thank you : taking off now zero six. See you at Benin City.'

'I hope so,' I replied, feeling my lifeless ailerons. 'See you later. Zero six out.'

Half an hour later I slid gingerly out of the overcast on to the runway at Benin City, the ailerons drooping from the wings, as limply as headless chickens.

CHAPTER TWELVE

I taxied to the control tower, clambered wearily out of the cramped cockpit, and inspected the damage. Apart from the burst that had shredded the skin of the port aileron and destroyed an essential bell-crank, it was superficial. The bullets through the nose, fortunately, had not struck any vital hydraulic or electrical equipment. A couple of hours' work, and four zero six would be serviceable enough to be flown to Lagos for permanent repairs.

Pushing through the excited soldiers, I went along the traffic hall and ran up the steps to the control tower. By now the helicopters should have taken off from the operational area, on their return flight to Benin City.

The controller looked at me respectfully. 'It must have been quite an operation, Major Gibson. I hear your Delfin took a hammering.'

'So did the rebel ship. I'd like to call up Captain Peré. Can you tune me in?'

'Certainly.' He selected frequency 118.5, and handed me the microphone. There was a lot of confused talking, some of it in French. The helicopters were airborne.

I thumbed the transmitter. 'Chopper one. Gibson calling from Benin City control tower. Do you read?'

I recognized Peré's voice. 'Hallo Gibson, strength four. Go ahead.'

'What's your news? Over.'

His voice had the slight undertone of tension that you sometimes hear on an aircraft radio when a pilot reports an emergency condition. 'All helicopters airborne and re-returning to base. We lost several soldiers and have wounded. Please warn Benin to have ambulances on standby.'

I acknowledged. 'Will do, chopper one. Is Minister Gobi with you?'

'Affirmative.'

'Was the recovery action successful?'

'Affirmative. We obtained some documents . . .' His voice trailed off.

Cutting across his transmission, I heard Gobi shout, 'Stop, you fool! You have no right to . . .' and the transmission ended.

I depressed the mike switch. 'Chopper one, Benin City. Come in please.' Twice again I called, without result. Only the hiss of static came through the speakers.

Thoughtfully, I laid the mike on the table. 'Thanks,' I told the Controller. 'You'd better notify the hospital to stand by. There are some wounded.' I left him and went down the steps back to the traffic hall, in time to see a Delfin break through the overcast and touch down. I watched it taxi in and Jerry climbed out. I met him as he scrambled down from the cockpit.

'How'd it go?' I asked.

'Dead right. The choppers were already down when I broke through and found the ship. You'd certainly clobbered it. The ground attack was in full swing. There was nothing I could do so I stooged around until they took off, flying protective cover in case any truck-borne troops arrived on the scene. No Biafrans pitched up, so I came home. Karel is about ten minutes behind me. The choppers should be here soon.'

There was the whine of a jet motor and we watched Karel touch down, and taxi in. As he cut his motor and the whistle of the turbine died, I heard the clatter of the choppers' rotors and four specks appeared from the south.

I ran across to Karel as he climbed out. 'Did you see the choppers take off?'

'Sure. I flew cover until they were all airborne.'

'All five of them?'

'That's right. Why? What's the problem?'

I pointed to the south. 'There're only four coming home!'

He shrugged. 'Maybe one of them stopped a bullet, ran short of fuel, and landed somewhere. The others will know what's happened.'

I watched the four helicopters land beside the hangar and begin offloading the wounded into the waiting ambulances. There was no sign of Peré or Gobi, they must be in the missing helicopter. Colonel Adenku, surrounded by his soldiers, moved towards me followed by his pilot, a tall thin Frenchman I'd met in the bar the previous night.

'Where's Peré and Minister Gobi?' I asked the Frenchman casually.

He shrugged. 'Peré was with us when we took off. After maybe ten minutes he called up and said they had decided to proceed direct to Lagos. I suppose the Minister wanted to return in a hurry.'

'Thanks,' I said thoughtfully. Adenku had paused at the entrance of the traffic hall and I walked across to him. 'Congratulations, Colonel.'

'Thank you. Congratulations also on your immobilizing the ship. Your rockets hit the engine-room right on target.'

'I hope Minister Gobi got the papers he wanted,' I probed.

'Yes. He told me on the ship that he had found what he was looking for, and we could take off at once. We wasted no time after that.' He laughed and moved off.

So Gobi had the oil survey maps. But somehow, somewhere, something smelled. Why had Gobi suddenly decided to head direct for Lagos? We'd arranged that we would return there together after the strike.

It had all the appearance of an impending double-cross. Perhaps he wanted time to study the maps before I saw them, or prepare a similar set with a few strategic alterations that would render them valueless. Whatever his motive was, the solution wasn't to be found in Benin City.

I walked across to the Sergeant inspecting the damage on my Delfin. Fortunately, the Aero Commander didn't require refuelling. I tapped his shoulder. 'Sergeant. I've urgent discussions with Minister Gobi in Lagos and must leave at once. Is there any message for the servicing chief there regarding this Delfin?'

He straightened respectfully. 'No, sir. I'll have it safe enough to fly there by tomorrow morning. The rest is up to him. What about your kit, sir? Can I send a Land-Rover for it?'

'Please do.' I patted his arm. 'And make it quick. I'll pre-flight the Aero Commander in the meantime.'

He hurried away and I got busy. I was suspicious and searched the Aero Commander carefully for any signs of unwanted nitro-glycerine pencil bombs or any other forms of sabotage. The way things were developing, I figured that not only the Biafrans would like to read my obituary notice.

As I cleared the runway and climbed through the overcast, I did some mental arithmetic. I calculated that I'd land in Lagos about an hour behind Gobi. Maybe I'd still be in time to prevent any double-cross he was contemplating.

I pushed the revs to a fast 75% power cruising setting and settled down to fly, my thoughts as black and hostile as the angry cumulo-nimbus anvil heads I kept dodging between.

Twenty miles out I called Lagos tower and was cleared for a direct approach on to runway zero one. Taxiing in fast, I saw no sign of Peré's Westland S55 helicopter. I handed the Aero Commander over to the duty mechanic and ran up the steps to Control, taking them two at a time.

'Where's the helicopter with Minister Gobi on board?'

The controller grinned. 'Nice to be a big shot. He was given authority to land directly inside General Gowon's Dodan Barracks Headquarters.'

Now it was useless trying to locate Gobi. There were a dozen places where he could have holed up. I decided to go back to the hotel. From there I'd phone the Ministry. There was a remote possibility that he'd contact me, but I didn't pin much hope on that one.

'Thanks,' I told the controller. 'Be seeing you.' He grinned cheerfully and I left him talking to a BOAC VC10 due to land at Lagos in the next hour.

I grabbed a taxi and headed back to the hotel. At the reception desk, as the clerk handed me my key, and an airmail letter from Italy addressed in Gisela's handwriting, I had my first break. Peré, the Westland pilot, came sauntering up the steps and turned into the bar. Stuffing the letter into my pocket, I followed him in and stood beside him as he lowered his massive buttocks on to a bar-stool.

'Have this on me,' I said. There was nothing suspicious about his reaction.

'Hallo, Major Gibson. You got back quickly. Congratulations on your work this morning.' He held out his hand and his smile seemed genuine.

'Thank you, and congratulations to you, too. I left Benin City an hour after the other choppers landed. The operation seems to have been a success. Did Gobi get the papers he wanted?'

Peré frowned. 'Look here, Major, I'm well paid and I don't want any trouble. When you called me, as I was replying, Gobi pulled the microphone away.'

'I know,' I told him. 'I heard him tell you, "You fool, you've no right to . . ." and then your transmission ended.'

'That's so,' he admitted.

I ordered two whiskies. 'Tell me off the record, did Gobi get the documents he was looking for? That's all I want to know.'

Peré frowned unhappily. 'After Gobi snatched the microphone away he told me that the mission was confidential and under no circumstances was I to discuss the documents with you or any one. He stressed the point.'

I tried again. 'Look Peré, as one mercenary to another, we are both pilots, and one day I may be able to roll a stone out of your path. I swear no one will ever learn that you told me, but it means a lot to me. I'm asking you again, did Gobi get the survey maps?'

Peré glanced uneasily around the empty bar. It seemed to reassure him. He picked up his whisky, splashed in a little water, tossed it back, then ordered a fresh round. He glanced sideways at me. 'Do you have oil business with Minister Gobi?' He grinned slyly.

'I wouldn't say it too loudly, if I were you,' I said. 'If your French SDECE* ever discover that one of their own countrymen—you—played a leading role in assisting the Nigerians to recover a French company's oil survey maps, you're a goner. They'll get you, even though you take a Belsen diet course, have a sex-change operation and wear make-up and a blonde wig.'

Peré nodded his head and three chins. 'You have a point there. OK, I haven't seen you, and I'm leaving now. I'll tell you this. On the way back, Gobi called up the Defence Ministry. He told them we would be landing inside Dodan Barracks, and asked for the Oil Concessions Committee to meet him on arrival.' He put his glass down and, as he turned to go, said over his shoulder: 'Gobi also said the mission had been successful.'

'Thanks, Peré.' I watched him waddle out of the door

* SDECE—French Intelligence.

and head for the street.

The reception clerk tripped into the bar. 'Phone call for you, sir.'

I took the call at his desk. Gisela's voice, warm and exciting, answered.

'John?'

'Gisela! So you made it.'

'Yes, honey. I've just landed. I caught a BOAC VC10 from Rome as soon as I got your cable. I'm at the airport.'

'I'll come and fetch you.'

'Don't bother, John, I'll take a taxi. See you at the hotel in half an hour. 'Bye darling.' There was a click as she rang off.

I reserved her a room, then showered and changed. Pulling a clean shirt out of the drawer, I noticed that it was lying at an angle. I recalled that it had been straight when I'd packed it away. Someone had been going through my belongings during my absence. Whoever it was, the best of Irish or French luck to them. There was nothing of any importance lying around, but I was sharply aware of hostile forces manoeuvring behind the scenes. I checked but nothing appeared to be missing. So I went downstairs to wait for Gisela.

George Dakis beckoned from the bar as I walked past. 'Hallo, John. The clerk told me you were in. I was on the point of phoning you to join me for a drink. What will you have?'

'Scotch, thanks. I'm waiting for Gisela. She's just landed. She'll be here in twenty minutes or so.'

'A nice girl,' he said appraisingly. 'And how are things otherwise?' Shrewd brown eyes swept my face.

I shrugged. 'Fair. How well do you know Gobi?'

Dakis smiled. 'So it's like that, is it?'

'I don't follow you. Like what?'

'By your attitude you don't appear too pleased with Mr

Gobi, and I'm always tuned in to atmosphere, my friend. I have to be, in order to succeed in my line of business. Am I right?'

'Maybe,' I conceded.

'Maybe means yes, John!'

'OK,' I said. 'You're right.'

'So the business involving Mr Kelly is not going well?'

'The business involving Mr Kelly is simply not going at all. Period.'

He watched me over the rim of his glass. 'Perhaps the suggestions I made to you some time ago now appear more attractive?'

I guessed he was referring to his proposal to defect with one of the Delfins to Biafra. 'Let's say that I'm a little more interested.'

He smiled. 'I think we'll still do business, John.'

'Maybe. First I must find Gobi and have a little heart to heart talk with him.'

'And if the talk is not satisfactory?'

'Then we'll shake hands, but yours will be wearing £100,000—for me.'

'It's a deal. Now you're being practical.'

'OK, but first help me locate Gobi.'

He smiled. 'That's not difficult. You'll find him at his villa, 426 Lugard Avenue. Few people know it belongs to him, and it's not registered in his name.'

'How did you know?'

He waved his cigarette airily. 'In order to do business, much of my stock in trade is to know such things. Why don't you go and see him? Tonight! Once you have satisfied yourself that there's no future for Kelly or yourself in dealing with him, we can get down to our own arrangements for our mutual benefit.'

The bastard was right. 'I must first check with Gisela if Kelly has any orders. After that, I'll trot along to see Gobi.'

Dakis nodded slowly. 'I think you're wise. I'll wait here for your return, then we can get down to details. Gobi's villa is nearby. I'll draw a map for you.'

As he completed the map on the back of my cigarette box, Gisela's taxi drew up. I opened the door, she threw her arms round me and kissed me. I was conscious of Dakis beside us, watching approvingly, a slight smile on the dark face. I released Gisela reluctantly. 'You remember Mr Dakis?'

'Of course.' She smiled radiantly at Dakis. He took her hand and brushed the back lightly with his sallow lips. 'You are as beautiful as ever.'

Gisela beamed. You had to hand it to the continentals, I thought.

While I supervised the offloading of the luggage, he whisked Gisela off to the lounge. I made sure her baggage was sent up to her room and joined them.

Dakis stood up as I pulled out a chair. 'I know you must have a lot to discuss. If I may, I'll join you later. I shall be in the bar.' He bowed to Gisela and moved off, a graceful compact man with something almost feline in his walk. He was, I felt, completely untrustworthy, unless his interests coincided with yours. Fortunately at the moment they did.

Gisela took my hand. 'Tell me, darling, all that's been happening.'

So I told her. Finally, I told her of Dakis' defection offer, and that I was going to see Gobi in a last attempt to settle the oil concession. If I drew blank, I would take up Dakis' offer and defect.

'How do you feel about it?' I concluded.

The large brown eyes, watching me, were troubled. 'Let me think about it, John, while you're at Gobi's. Then we can decide.'

I left it at that, and went across to the bar. I told George. 'Gisela knows the score. You can talk openly to her. I'm going to see friend Gobi now, and I should be back within an hour. Perhaps you'd care to entertain Gisela in the meanwhile.'

'That,' said Dakis smoothly, 'will be a pleasure!'

I left them at the table, and went out into the street. Tonight, I decided, was going to see the payoff. One way or another. I pulled out Dakis's map and began to follow his directions. They were straightforward enough and ten minutes later I found Lugard Avenue.

With the blackout of the street lights the moon was a dull lantern, reduced to a pale ghost of its normal self by a broken layer of grey cloud that scudded overhead.

Stars blinked feebly in small clusters through the moving clouds. The air was hot and humid, and there was no wind at ground level. It felt as if the existing air mass would never move on towards the centre of Africa, and Lagos was condemned to sweat forever under its clammy humidity. I wished to God that a moist front would move in from the Atlantic, bringing a stream of cooler fresher air.

I passed an array of ranch-style houses tucked cosily away from the street, amidst shrubs and bushes and tropical flowers that partly revealed the yellow gleam of lighted interiors. No one moved in this quiet street, only crickets and beetles chirped an endless counter-chorus at each other.

I used my lighter to check a house number. The flame flared on the number, 424. The villa I was looking for, number 426, was next door, set well back from the street. The driveway lost itself amongst a dense bloom of shrubs and overhanging trees. A solitary light beamed yellowly from an upstairs window, but the lower half of the villa was in darkness.

My feet crunched loudly on gravel as I approached the front entrance. A large black limousine, almost invisible some thirty feet away, was parked on the edge of the drive. I recognized Gobi's car.

Within four feet of the front door, the upstairs light

died suddenly, leaving me in a deep black void. I tensed. Perhaps Gobi had seen me and was stalling for time. Perhaps.

I rapped on the door, lit a cigarette and waited.

I rapped again, an urgent and far louder tattoo this time. There was only silence.

I listened carefully. Nothing seemed to move in the dark interior as I turned the doorknob slowly and gently. When it reached its full travel, I pushed forward lightly, and the door swung silently inwards. I waited for a long minute, breathing slowly and quietly through my mouth.

Then taking a step inside, I smelled the faintest trace of what could have been cordite fumes. I stiffened and, flattening myself against the wall, called out: 'Gobi! Are you home?' The silence was unbroken as my voice died away, lost in the impenetrable darkness.

I fumbled for my lighter, and flicked it on. The gas flamed and I saw a light switch on the wall to my right. I took four strides towards it and, before my forefinger prodded the switch, I realized with a sick tightening of my stomach muscles that there were steps behind me.

I spun round. The back of my head seemed to split and a wave of scorching molten light engulfed me. I was vaguely conscious that my arms had closed around the torso of a man. I tried to hold on, but there was no strength in my arms.

I looked up and recognized the Frenchman who'd followed me to the Defence Ministry Headquarters months back.

I hardly felt the next savage blow. It was more like a gentle prodding that propelled me into a tunnel of darkness that seemed to have no end.

*

The light was shining in my eyes, and it was a strain to open them. I tried again and groaned. My mouth felt as if somebody had stuck an old fur-lined flying glove in it. I tried opening my eyes again. This time I kept them open long enough to see I was lying on my back next to the wall and under the light-switch.

My head now throbbed painfully. I sat up slowly and then I saw the pistol. I rolled over and studied it. On the bulging muzzle-end was a silencer, the rest looked like a heavy 9-mm Luger. I picked it up, sniffed the barrel and knew it had been fired—very recently.

I checked the magazine, there were five cartridges, including the one in the chamber. I made sure the safety-catch was off, and stepped carefully on the landing, feeling for switches, when my foot collided with something soft. I knew it could only be a human body. I found the switch and snapped it on. A Nigerian servant, in white flowing robes, was sprawled out at my feet. The amount of blood on his robes would have horrified him if he'd been alive to see himself.

I stepped over him. Gobi was the one I was looking for. Maybe the Frenchman killed the servant, because he'd been discovered prowling through the house.

I opened the door of what seemed to be the master bed-room. I fumbled on the wall and plunged the switch. Gobi was stretched on his back on the floor, clutching his glasses as if he'd awake soon and would need them to read the minutes of the Oil Committee.

His head lay in a pool of blood and white bone-splinters protruded through the short dark hair on the left side of his head where the bullets had smashed through his skull.

I stepped over Gobi to examine a wall safe. The door was wide open and it was empty, of course.

Too late, I cursed savagely. Always too late. From the beginning that had been the pattern and this was the ultimate fiasco. Everything I'd done, all the risks I'd taken to get the bloody concessions, had gone up in smoke with Gobi's death.

The double-crossing bastard had had it coming, but it didn't help me. On the contrary.

The alarm bells began to sound off. Western oil interests probably feared that Gobi would channel concessions to the Russians. The Russians expected concessions for supplying the jets and doubtless suspected Gobi was double-crossing them. The French wanted their survey maps Gobi had in his possession, and in the middle of it all was a sucker called Gibson. I was in Gobi's villa, with Gobi and his servant dead—with the murder weapon in my hands. And all Lagos knew I worked for Kelly! Carefully I wiped the gun and threw it down beside Gobi. Bending down I went through his pockets. Maybe I'd find a letter or something. They were empty.

I straightened as I heard the siren of an approaching police car. It skidded into the driveway, churning gravel and crunching to a halt. I looked desperately about me.

A French door led to a small balcony facing north, away from the south entrance to Gobi's villa. I didn't wait to judge the distance from the balcony to the lawn. I opened the door, jumped the railings, and dropped heavily on to the grass some fifteen feet below.

I crawled through a hedge to the garden of the villa next door and waited for my panting to subside. The police pounded noisily on Gobi's door, then swarmed inside, their voices loud as they switched on all the lights. I slipped quietly into the deserted street, then began to walk swiftly down the pavement.

I remember the smell of frangipani was heavy on the air as I headed on a long roundabout way towards the hotel. The breeze I had hoped for earlier rose suddenly, buffeting my hair and making my shirt cling coldly to my body.

Keeping close to hedges, and slipping into every shadow, I heard the noise of police activity recede in the distance. But I didn't fool myself. The Frenchman had found a convenient patsy and had tipped off the police, probably by means of an anonymous phone call. They'd be looking for me pretty soon.

Arriving at the hotel I joined Gisela and Dakis. I'd been away no more than forty minutes, but it seemed like years since I'd last seen them. I slumped into a chair.

Gisela half rose, 'What's the matter, John?'

'Something's happened,' I said, 'but act casually, for Christ's sake. I could use a drink.'

Dakis clicked his fingers. 'Did you find Gobi?'

'Yes. He was dead.'

'What!'

'Murdered in his bedroom. The servant as well. A Frenchman who'd followed me once before slugged me as I went into the house. He got away.' I swallowed the whisky, shuddered, and tried to read George's eyes.

'You didn't stay there very long, John?' the arms dealer said softly.

'There was no point in staying longer. I heard the police coming and beat it. The Frenchman must have tipped them off, or someone who knew Gobi was dead and wanted them to find me there.'

Gisela clutched my arm. I told them how the Frenchman had knocked me out.

'You sure it was the one who followed you?' asked Dakis.

'Yes. Let me finish,' I said irritably. 'I went through the house. The servant was lying dead in the passage. Stabbed or shot. I never checked. Gobi was lying on the floor upstairs, shot in the head. There was a wall safe, the door was open. I remember the keys were still in the lock.'

'You checked the safe?'

'Of course. It was empty.'

Gisela watched me silently, her face pale. 'What are you going to do, John?'

'Take George up on his defection deal and get the hell

out of here as fast as I can.'

'There's a new Delfin ready to be delivered to Benin City,' Dakis said gently. 'It's at the NAF hangar.'

'If you are prepared to give me a cheque for defecting right here and now, I'll fly it across to Uli instead.'

'That,' said George easily, 'I'm prepared to do. Did anyone see you enter or leave the house?'

'Not to my knowledge, but the police arrived there soon enough, didn't they? After the Le Clarry affair, the cops will really suspect I've a motive for the Gobi killing.'

Dakis considered the matter. 'The sooner you get away the better. Tomorrow will be too late. The Delfin is scheduled to take off for Benin City at 7:00. You'll have to leave tonight if you're going. Can you do it?'

'I'll have to,' I said. 'The snag is, I'm liable to be shot down when I arrive over Uli.'

Dakis hesitated. 'I can help you there. I am also concerned with the arms airlift operating in and out of Uli. My company supplies certain material to the Biafrans. Knowing that you might be landing there sometime, I arranged for a copy of the landing codes to be delivered to me. I have them in a safe place nearby.'

'You cunning bastard,' I said bitterly. 'You were pretty sure I was wasting my time with Gobi, weren't you?'

'I was,' Dakis said matter-of-factly. He pointed to my glass. 'There's time for a drink. While you drink your whisky, which will do you good, let me tell you about the oil business, and you'll learn why I keep out of it.'

I watched him roll his cigarette around the corner of his mouth.

'Oil is big business. Too big for you and me, Major Gibson. It is also a business of immense strategic importance. All governments view their oil companies' activities with more than just a tax interest. Many countries already have a stake in oil fields in the Biafran region. Russia, to date, has none. But, she has supplied, through my company, aircraft essential to the Federal Government. Aircraft denied them by their former so-called friends, Britain and America.' Dakis spoke softly, as he tapped the table. 'So, surely, it was only reasonable to expect that they would be given any new concessions. After all, the Reds have supplied twenty MIGs and twelve Delfins. How could your Mr Kelly's single Aero Commander hope to match that consignment?'

He sipped his drink and continued: 'I believe that Gobi intended from the beginning to give the survey maps to the Russians. Perhaps French Intelligence or the Israeli Intelligence outfit or the CIA or MI6 discovered this. Who knows?' He shrugged. 'I don't care! It's none of my business. I sell arms to whoever wants them, from whatever source I can procure them, and keep out of the oil business.'

It made sense. I glanced across at Gisela. 'You'd better return to Rome tomorrow in the Aero Commander. Hire somebody to fly it back on the pretext of having it serviced. I shouldn't like Kelly to have his plane confiscated. Can you arrange a pilot, George?'

'Sure. I'll go and collect the codes. I'll be back in a few minutes . . . Meanwhile you'd better collect what you require from your room.'

'I'll do that. Don't forget the cheque. You can make it payable to Gisela.'

Dakis stood up. 'You must trust Miss Griffin.' He went off.

Gisela grasped my hand. 'Oh, John,' she said unhappily. 'Why not come back to Rome with me. We'll make out somehow. The police may not act all that quickly. Why take the awful risk of going tonight?'

I squeezed her hand firmly. 'Because my computer has worked it out and come up with the answer that the risk is more than offset by £100,000 for delivering the Delfin. And tomorrow may be too late. Listen, darling,

I promise you that in ten days' time we'll celebrate together at the Bibliothèque night club in Rome. We'll drink Pol Roger 57, and watch the dawn break over Rome from the Villa Borghese.' I leaned across and kissed her.

She smiled wanly. 'You're hopeless, John,' she said simply.

'Wait here. I'll nip up and collect my briefcase.' I collected my key and went swiftly up to my room. Leaving my clothes and suitcases I took only my briefcase with maps and my passport and personal papers.

When I returned to Gisela, Dakis was waiting. 'I have the codes, Major.' He handed me an envelope.

'Thanks, George.' I tucked it safely away in the briefcase. I hoped they were up to date and accurate, or I'd never live to spend the cheque. That reminded me. 'The cheque?'

'I have already given it to Miss Griffin.'

Gisela nodded. I grinned at her and kissed her. She didn't smile and her cheek was damp as she turned away abruptly.

Dakis had moved across to the door and was waiting.

I cut the leave-taking brutally short. 'Pay the cheque into your account the moment you hit Rome. Then open an account in Tubby Sanders's name and pay £10,000 into that for his share of the B26 swindle. Send him the deposit slip c/o Airport, Sao Tomé.' I glanced up to see Dakis nod impatiently. 'Dakis is in a hurry, darling, I must go.' I slipped my hand under her arm. Her eyes were bright with unshed tears. 'Remember, the Bibliothèque ten days from now.'

'It's a date,' she said in a low voice, keeping her head down as I ushered her into the plush interior of Dakis's automobile.

'The call-signs,' Dakis said as we purred away. 'The important thing to remember is your call-sign : "Rooster." They've been expecting a defection and Rooster is the call-sign assigned for the purpose.'

'Very clever,' I said sourly. 'A rooster coming home to roost amongst the doves. Let's hope they don't turn out to be vultures. I've met enough.'

He dimmed his lights as a police car sped from the direction of Lugard Avenue. I watched it through the rear window, as it ground to a halt in front of the hotel.

'The cops aren't far behind,' Dakis said cheerfully. 'If you don't make it tonight, you'll never make it.' He swung left and accelerated towards the waterfront. Despite the partial blackout, ships' cranes stood tall against a bleak horizon, swinging lazily like giraffe heads. They swung and dipped.

'You're a great comfort, George. How come you're prepared still to pay me £100,000 for defecting when under the circumstances you know I'd be prepared to do it for nothing?'

His silhouette was still for a long moment. Finally he shrugged, 'I have my reasons,' he said softly. 'There are broader aspects to this unfortunate conflict which my interests compel me to try to prolong as long as possible. I hope you understand.'

Gisela shivered, and I held her closely. The cold-blooded bastard, I thought. 'Feed both sides and keep them going. I thought I was hard. You've given me a cheque that can't be presented for payment in less than three days. I hope I can trust you.'

'You cannot do otherwise, but have no fears, the cheque will be met. And I guarantee you a one-way passage out of Biafra.'

I groped in my briefcase for my passport, Dakis's envelope with the code, flying licences and the necessary maps. I tucked them away into my pockets.

'Drop me here,' I told Dakis. 'I'll catch a cab the rest of the way. There's no point in us being seen together at the airport.'

Dakis braked gently and I kissed Gisela's moist cheek. 'Look after my briefcase, honey. See you in Rome.' She nodded silently. I shook hands with George.

'See you around. Let me know when you've another war on the go.' I stepped out.

The arms dealer nodded. 'Goodbye, Major,' and the limousine sped away.

I caught a glimpse of Gisela's waving hand as the tail lights disappeared down the road. The sixty-four dollar question was, how the hell was I going to hijack the Delfin. I flagged a taxi and was still working it out when it pulled up in front of the Ikeja International Terminal.

CHAPTER THIRTEEN

W E pulled in behind a row of silent cabs, the drivers nodding sleepily. Their only hope of a fare lay in snaring the odd off-duty official, or the occasional drunk. I paid the driver, giving him a healthy £5 tip. Whether he remembered me or not was immaterial. After what I was about to do, he'd be lucky if the police didn't bounce their night-sticks off his skull merely for having driven me to Ikeja. The security guards at the entrance knew me and showed no particular interest as I went by. They waved me through the barriers and I strolled past the dimly lit curio shops towards the bright glittering bar. Four officials, draped across the counter, eyed me glassily.

The barman brightened when he saw me. 'A tall or a short one, Major Gibson?'

'Both.' I leaned confidentially across the bar. 'I'm checking the NAF security tonight,' I told him.

He poured and slid a glass of whisky towards me before reaching down and producing a quart bottle of Amstel beer. 'Shall I open it now?'

'Sure.' I gulped the scotch, and took the beer bottle from him as he opened it. 'Don't bother about a glass, I'll take this with me. I'll be back soon for a refill.'

Gripping the bottle, I headed out towards the tarmac. The glassy-eyed boys stopped propounding their theories to watch my departure, then switched their minds back to their original wavelength. As I walked through the door I was completely forgotten. Waving the beer bottle, I stopped beside the soldier mounting guard on the sandbagged machine-gun nest. He grinned approvingly.

I produced my Defence Ministry pass and waved it beneath his nose.

'I'm checking up tonight. Have you any complaints?'

'No sah.' He came to attention.

'Where's the jet guard?'

'By the hangar, sah. The sergeant was here about an hour ago.'

'Good,' I said. 'Keep your eyes and ears open.'

I heard the click of his heels as I faded into the japonica hedge that ran between the main terminal building and the internal reception wing. Through a large gap loomed the brown hangars of the Nigerian Air Force. As the hangars took shape in the darkness, I paused, clutching the beer bottle grimly. A sentry's heels tapped rhythmically away from me. I slipped through a gap in the hedge and paused again. The heels beat an about tattoo, and the steady clicking grew louder as he headed towards me. I squeezed into the hedge until I was part of it and waited. He was two feet beyond me when I smashed the bottle against the back of his head. The bottle shattered as he slumped silently to the ground.

Bending over him, I grabbed his head with both hands and slammed it hard against the tarmac to make sure he wouldn't come round before I'd got clear, then slipping my hands under his arms, I dragged him behind the hedge. I removed the 9-mm pistol from his holster and tucked it into my belt, picked up his automatic rifle and slid silently along the hedge towards the jet parking lot.

Now I'd burned my boats and there was only one way out—to Uli.

The wind suddenly sifted the clouds, allowing the moon to spill its light through a gap. Ahead, moonbeams reflected on the Delfin, parked two hundred yards away, etching it in a sudden flash of silver purity against the dark background of a hangar. I relaxed and breathed again as the wind sealed off the cloud gap, leaving the darkness relieved only by the reflected light off runway one nine zero one, and the brightly lit control tower.

Silhouetted against the flat concrete parapet below the angled glass control room were two gunners. They sat idly beside a pair of tripod-mounted heavy machine-guns. I knew their orders were to shoot at any unauthorized aircraft attempting a take off or landing by either day or night at Ikeja Airport. I would have to gamble on one fact. With their total lack of flying knowledge, thinking that any aircraft attempting a take-off would have to taxi past them first to reach the runway threshold, they would wait to see what developed, and not open fire when I started up the Delfin. Then I'd play my trump card and take off down the narrow taxi strip. I hoped fervently that by the time they'd registered, and in their excitement, they'd aim directly at the jet's flaming tailpipe and forget to lay off for my speed. I was holding the weakest hand in the pack, but I had to bet on it.

The taxi strip was about six hundred yards in length from the NAF intersection, and ran parallel to runway zero one. Most of the take-offs and landings at Lagos originated from this access point, along the reciprocal of runway one nine.

The normal take-off run of the Delfin was plus-minus eight hundred yards, but offsetting this were two factors in my favour: the comparatively cool night air, which would help the jet get airborne sooner, and the grass over-shoot area. This added another 150 yards. If the Delfin wasn't airborne by then, the laws of aerodynamics would take over and it would wrap itself into a neat package of scrap metal amongst the trees at the end of the runway. Unfortunately, I'd be inside, and the £100,000 would become just a cold book entry in the balance sheet of the estate of the late John Gibson.

Praying that the clouds stayed put, I moved stealthily across to the Delfin, keeping an eye on the sentries on the parapet. So far, so good. I slid under the wing and crouched against the fuselage between the wheels. I could hear my heart pounding in my ears, and my mouth was dry. From the internal services terminal lounge the sounds of drunken laughter drifted across the field. I wondered where the sergeant was on his rounds and my mouth got even dryer. The Delfin was draped with a canvas cockpit cover and I had no knife to speed up removing it. I'd have to battle with the knots. This I hadn't bargained for, I should have known better. Frantically I began to fumble, worrying about the sentry I'd knocked out coming round and raising the alarm. As I untied the knots, there was a stab of pain and I realized I'd broken my left thumbnail. The cool air and moisture had tightened the knots, and my fingers were raw. It was all of ten minutes before I finally loosened the last knot and began to haul the cover off.

As I tugged, I heard army boots slapping the tar and voices getting louder. I leaped on to the wing and fell beside the fuselage in the shadow cast by the control tower lights on the far side. I froze. If they saw the ropes dangling loose, it was all over.

Three soldiers materialized from the darkness. They passed on the other side of the Delfin, too busy talking to notice the loose cords. The sergeant slurred, 'We'll have to mount a permanent guard round the Aero Commander. He may attempt a getaway in it—tonight.'

They moved away and I watched them stroll towards the hangar where the Aero Commander was parked. So they'd been warned about me, and the hunt was on. Someone at Headquarters had remembered the Aero Commander and considered the possibility of my making a dash for it. It was certain that the rest of the airport staff had been alerted. A match flared as the Nigerians settled down beside the hangar. The Delfin was my only hope.

Cautiously I slid off the wing and coaxed the canvas off the cockpit, pulling it toward me inch by inch. I bundled the cover, lowered it gently, and, dropping to my knees, crawled towards the tail, dragging it behind me.

Leaving it there, I crept back to the shelter of the wing. The blast of the jet motor would blow the cover safely clear of the tail plane and rudder controls. I pulled away the chocks in front of the wheels and undid the turbine air-intake protective covers, cursing the conscientious bastard who'd tied the knots. My fingers were one raw throbbing ache as I wrestled with the covers.

Next, I removed the Pitot cover off the tube that fed the readings into the airspeed indicator. All I was short of, I thought, was to forget that one, and go haring off into the dark without an airspeed indicator. Now there was only one cover left, that over the tail pipe. I crawled back, hauled it off and worked my way back to the shelter of the wing. One of the sentries at the Commander hangar lit another cigarette. They seemed relaxed enough. I wondered how long they'd stay that way when I fired up the Delfin's motor and they began to register. They'd been sent to guard the Aero Commander, not the Delfin. Maybe that would give me the break I needed. Maybe? You'll know in a couple of minutes, I told myself. I jumped up the steps, cautiously moved the canopy upwards, and slid into the cockpit.

There was no time to waste engaging the parachute harness and strapping myself in. In the dark, working from memory, I set the trim tabs to their approximate positions, switched on the main fuel tank, and checked that the brakes were locked. Then, taking a deep breath, I flipped the master battery switch on and simultaneously engaged the starter. The turbine whined and as the motor flamed, I watched the rev counter and temperature gauges come to life.

I glanced towards the control tower. The sentries were standing on the parapet staring across the field. The flame from the tail pipe must have been clearly visible. I saw them leap into their sandbagged gun positions. I'd know in the next few seconds if the gamble was going to pay off. Either they'd wait for the Delfin to taxi past, or open fire immediately.

My stomach was a tight knot as I tensed in anticipation of a steady burst. Feverishly, I checked the trim, flaps, speed brakes and gear extension pressures, then poured the kerosene into the motor and switched on the navigation and landing lights. The Delfin might look more innocent with them burning, I hoped, than taxiing with them off. Maybe they'd think it was a mechanic, working overtime doing a check. It was a remote possibility, but might give me the few vital seconds I needed. I turned sharply right on to the beginning of the taxi strip, and as I reached it, headlights on a cluster of vehicles parked outside the terminal building beamed brightly into life. Some sped towards the hangar and others towards the centre of the runway. Behind me, from the right, the sergeant and his guard crew were making a frantic dash towards the Delfin, not sure whether they should open fire.

I whipped the Delfin throttle wide open and took a quick note of the heading on the direction indicator. Now the surprised Nigerians would know that I was taking off, and the fireworks could be expected to start up in full fury.

I switched off the navigation and landing lights. All they were going to get from me as an aiming point was the flaming tail pipe. I held the Delfin dead straight. A swing of a few degrees to the right meant disaster. I'd either hit the fence or run into the storm water drains. I was heading into a dark black all-enveloping shroud, and only the bumping of the wheels told me I was not yet airborne.

The airspeed had risen to 120 kilometres, still thirty short of possible lift off, when the darkness was pierced by a flame-splashed nightmare of incandescent tracer surrounding the Delfin. Red and white balls of fire streaked about me, dying languidly.

A sudden jolt told me that I'd run out of taxi strip and had struck the grass overshoot verge. There remained only 150 yards to get airborne. I punched the full wing flaps button and as the jet ballooned, forced upwards by the sudden surge of lift, I nursed the control yoke gently towards me to coax the Delfin to remain off the ground. I flipped on the landing lights to see where I was heading. The beam knifed a path through the tropical bush ahead. Desperately, I hit the gear retraction button. Slowly, the wallowing jet stabilized as the wheels swung inwards into their wheel bays. Immediately beneath me, the trees waved pale-green beckoning arms as the Delfin brushed mere inches over them. I had better control now and the airspeed increased by a precious twenty kilometres. I doused the landing lights and noticed that the tracer-infested airspace was thinning.

I began to retract the wing flaps in easy stages. Now the jet gathered speed rapidly and started to climb steeply away, the turbine spewing flame at 96% rpm and the airspeed steady on the optimum climb speed of 340 km. I zoomed through a shallow layer of stratus and then burst into clear moonlight. I rolled into a climbing turn on course for Uli.

Above the overcast, the stars were bright speckled diamonds, and the moon hung like a yellow Chinese lantern on the end of my port wing as I took the Delfin up and up. I hit twenty thousand, levelled out, and settled back to fly.

I doubted whether the NAF could get organized swiftly enough to scramble a brace of MIGs from Benin City or Makurdi in an attempt to intercept me. The odds were stacked against them, with their Gyppo pilots heading the world league for poor flying qualities and poorer marksmanship.

Even if they guessed where I was headed for I figured at least an hour would pass before they could possibly thunder off in pursuit and wait for me over Uli. Fuck them, I reflected. Even in the slower Delfin, I'd fly circles around any wog strapped to a MIG.

I thought about Kelly. I'd arrived in Nigeria full of high hopes. Now my dreams of making a million from Kelly had blown away with the red Nigerian dust at Ikeja. I'd given him a fair run for his money but it hadn't worked out. It was all past history. The only problem now was to get this bird down in one piece at Uli. Then I'd get to Rome, collect Gisela, and take that long holiday I'd been promising myself for the past five years.

It had been a long hard night, beginning with finding Gobi murdered. Now, like a shuttle on a loom, the tension was beginning to unwind. All I had to do was find Uli, avoid being shot down by some over-enthusiastic Biafran warrior, and land in one piece. Then I could throw the shuttle away and let the loom unwind. All in all, I thought, I'd earned Dakis's defection bonus.

Suddenly the wind shredded the clouds below and I saw the Niger Delta. The rivers under the moon ran silver between black patches of mangroves and swamp trees, twisting back on themselves for miles and miles to gain one mile forward as they struggled seawards.

Ahead, sheet lightning flashed suddenly and the sky was solid with cloud. I hoped it was only a local storm and would clear before I reached Uli. I pulled on my harness straps and tightened them. Turbulence over Nigeria could be as bad as it came any place. The sheet lightning flickered incessantly, and I could see the mighty rolling masses of cumulo-nimbus stretching up to forty thousand feet as I headed towards them at 450 km an hour. I picked my way through the clouds until they finally wrapped themselves around the Delfin, clutching it in a wet sheath of glimmering drops that shone as the flashing sheets of lightning lit the skies, but the turbulence was relatively slight, and the little jet rode steadily through. At times the cloud broke and we sped through deep sky canyons between great grey-white peaks where the blue lightning fires flickered and flamed. Above the canyons the moon beamed spears of light towards the black earth, where they shattered and were lost in the darkness beneath. Soon the gaps became more frequent, the clouds thinned and finally there was a sudden sharp bump and I flew again into clear moonlight.

I thought about Gisela. If I could hitch a lift with either one of the arms runners operating out of French-directed Libreville or one of World Federation of Churches' operators from the Portuguese island of Sao Tomé, I could be with her in Rome within three or four days.

I watched a pair of satellites become the brightest stars in the sky as they trailed each other along some mysterious predetermined orbit, transmitting their space or terrestial information in a steady stream to some distant coldly efficient computer. They passed overhead and faded to pinpoints, leaving the stars to regain their momentarily eclipsed brightness.

It was time to think about losing height, preparatory to locating Uli and landing. Slowly, I pulled the Delfin up another three hundred feet then dropped the nose like a pendulum completing its swing and let it begin to build up speed for the long convex descent curve towards the Ibo stronghold.

I opened the envelope and studied the Uli approach code Dakis had given me. The code, he'd said, changed every week. The call for Uli tower for this day, Wednesday, was simply 'Tango Quebec'. After midnight it changed to Oscar Papa. The four Cardinal compass headings, North, South, East and West for this week, were Lemon, Cedar, Juniper, and Hazel respectively. Dakis had planned well ahead, I thought sourly. Even the call sign for a defecting aircraft was included : 'Rooster'. The Biafrans would be able to put the Delfin to good use. A few raids on the oil storage tanks at Bonny and Port Harcourt would bring the war a little closer home to the Federal Military Government.

I checked my watch. Another fifteen minutes should bring me over Uli. I switched on the VHF set and selected the frequency, 118.1. My earphones were suddenly alive. Over the next few minutes I identified French, Portuguese, American, South African, British, and Swedish accents. I checked the cryptic calls against the code. A call reading 'Tango Quebec, this is Three Victor Romeo, Request flight level three nine zero' and the Tower's reply, 'Not approved. Proceed flight level 350,' meant, 'Do not land here, proceed Uturu.'

Uturu might have been taken some weeks earlier according to Federal Government claims in Lagos. I looked at the code unhappily. Maybe I'd not read the message correctly. There was only one way to find out. Holding the code open on my lap, I selected transmit. 'Tango Quebec. This is Rooster. Request flight level three nine zero.'

There was a brief pause and then an excited controller came back.

'Roger. Report reaching three nine zero.'

Hastily I checked Dakis's code. He meant the radio beacon was on. I tuned in to the frequency on the code sheet, and watched the radio compass needle sweep over to port.

'Roger, Tango Quebec from Rooster. Check mode three.' Now I was asking him to switch on the runway lights.

'Mode three unserviceable for five minutes. Meanwhile cross Mike Alpha at flight level two nine zero.' I checked again, holding the control column between my knees. This last instruction meant 'switch on your navigation lights.' I flipped the switch.

'Roger Rooster,' Uli called, 'we have you in sight. Maintain Mike Alpha Romeo.' Rapidly, I scanned the code. Now the bastard was telling me to put out my navigation lights.

'Rooster, mode three now serviceable.' He would switch on the runway lights. I saw them blink into life, a twin row, so close together that from the altitude I was flying it seemed that a mini could barely squeeze between them.

'Rooster. Stand by for radar contact, channel zero four approved.'

I checked hurriedly. I was cleared to land on runway three four. I lowered the wheels and flaps and turned in towards the strip, lining up with the narrow line of lights. As I lost altitude, they widened slightly, but it was still like landing on a pencil. I yawed the jet slightly from side to side as I slid down the glide path to stay within its limits. Slowly, it broadened from a tar road into a strip some seventy yards wide where the Biafrans had widened the road. The runway threshold loomed, I flared the Delfin and the nose wheel rose high as the main wheels hit the tar. The runway, although narrow, had plenty of length. I used the brakes sparingly and kept the nose riding high for aero-dynamic braking. My landing lights were shining high and far ahead.

The runway lights died suddenly. I let the nose drop and relied on my landing lights. I saw two aircraft parked on a wide dumb-bell at the end of the runway etched sharply against the blackness of the surrounding bush.

I headed towards them, swinging the nose from side to side to make sure I didn't taxi into some obstacle and write off £100,000 of Delfin. Not at this stage. I pulled up beside a shabby oil-stained DC3 and cut the motor. Under the blaze of the landing lights as I'd taxied towards it, I had noticed the Zambian Airways colours. A white top with a green cheat line and a silver lower section. The official Zambian registration letters could still be clearly seen beneath the thin coat of disguising paint. It was now registered as 439B. So the Zambians were also in on the act!

I scrambled out of the cramped cockpit and jumped down

on to the dim tar. A tall Biafran, wearing the rising sun insignia of Biafra on his shoulder flashes, was waiting. Behind him were several armed men.

'I'm Colonel Christopher,' he introduced himself. 'I understand that this is a Federal Government aircraft and you have defected with it.'

It was hot and I could feel the sweat running between my shoulder blades. 'That's so. I could use a cold beer.'

He nodded. Two of his men moved forward and strong hands gripped my arms.

'I'm afraid not,' the colonel said sharply. 'My orders are to place you under arrest until your arrival has been thoroughly investigated.'

CHAPTER FOURTEEN

I climbed into the jeep beside Christopher as his two soldiers crowded into the narrow rear seat. One of them was a short dark sergeant in muddied jungle camouflage. He watched me with indifferent black opaque eyes. I knew that he would have shot me equally indifferently with the Sten gun he was nursing so carefully. The 9-mm he'd removed from my pants was tucked safely in a side pocket.

The other character was an enormous Ibo well over six foot weighing at least 230 pounds, without an ounce of fat and armed with an old British Army .303. The jeep sagged as he'd stepped in. He worked the bolt and drove a cartridge into the chamber.

I abandoned any ideas of trying to make a break. In any event, there was nowhere to break to. If either of those two had any hopes that I'd make a dash for it, I had news for them. Dakis, I thought hopefully, will sort this little lot out. Be patient, Gibson.

As Christopher pulled away, I asked, 'Where are we going?'

'My orders are to take you to prison. You are to be kept there under military supervision until further notice.'

'I love that phrase "until further notice". Who gave those instructions?'

'You will learn later. Please do not talk to me. My instructions are definite.'

I sat back and watched the heavy bushes making splotches of darkness and shaking their heads at me as the wind blew through the derelict buildings beside the road.

Trees lined the road, some of them supported by roots that rose out of the ground in a grotesque tangle, like a piece of modern sculpture.

I could see that the Benin City-based Delfins and MIGs had been giving Uli a fair working over. Piles of rubble were silhouetted everywhere. I wished that I was back with Karel and Jerry. There was a lot to be said in favour of being a purely mercenary pilot without getting involved in deals on the side.

Overhead, a four-engined aircraft rumbled in a few hundred feet above us as it nosed down to the strip. The wind was shredding the clouds and it flashed momentarily silver in the moonlight. For a trained intruder pilot it would have been a sitting duck.

Now the Federal ring of steel was drawing tighter around the shrunken territory of Biafra, I wondered why the Nigerian Air Force refrained from carrying out night strikes with their jets against Uli. With the MIGs and Delfins now based at the relatively nearby centres of Benin City, Port Harcourt and Calabar, night intruder missions were not only feasible, but logical.

Though capable, the mercenaries would understandably not volunteer, or suggest, such missions.

I wondered where they'd go when this show was over. Africa had enough potential to keep them going for years. It was merely a matter of where and when. Give or take two or three years and the mercenaries would probably be sharpening their teeth on the Chinese-trained Tanzanians. It ought to be interesting. I'd have to get a copy of Comrade Mao's little red book to figure out how they brainwashed the masses.

Despite the breeze I was sweating. I loosened my collar and tried Christopher again. 'You know Mr Dakis?'

'Please. No talking.'

'Suit yourself,' I shrugged. We drove past a small old-fashioned church. The tombstones in the adjoining graveyard shone white. I crossed my fingers while I wondered if it was an omen.

Then we bounced between a small collection of dila-

pidated buildings with corrugated iron roofs. The road
worsened as we jarred over a series of ruts and potholes
into a gravel drive that led to a squat concrete building.
Christopher pulled up. 'Follow me, please.'

The guards flanked me as I followed Christopher up the
steps. A sentry at the door saluted. 'Is Major Azikwe here?'
Christopher snapped.

'Yes, sir,' and he pointed.

I followed Christopher into a small hall. The soldiers
who'd accompanied us from the airstrip returned to the
jeep. Christopher turned left into a passage that led off
from the small entrance hall. The first door on the left
was partly open and without knocking, he pushed it open
and walked in.

A man rose behind the desk in front of the window. Tall
and thin, he wore steel-rimmed glasses. A shabby uniform,
a size too large, hung from his narrow shoulders. It looked
as if he'd slept in it for a week. There was a major's
insignia above the rising sun flash of the Biafran army.
His features were more Arabic than Negroid, the nose
sharp and the lips thin and compressed. Expressionlessly
he watched Christopher walk in.

'I've brought Mr Gibson here as ordered.' Christopher's
tone was curt and abrupt.

Azikwe's bloodshot eyes looked me over indifferently.
'You haven't interrogated the prisoner?'

Christopher's eyes flickered towards me. 'Ask him yourself. I had my orders. I obeyed them.'

Azikwe's mouth turned down. 'I'm sure you did, Colonel,'
he said sourly. He wiped his hands on a dirty khaki handkerchief. 'Thank you, Colonel. I will take responsibility
for the prisoner.'

'Very well.' Christopher walked to the door and paused.
'I'll see you in a few days, Gibson.' He slammed the door
behind him.

Azikwe smiled thinly. 'Sit down please, Mr Gibson.'

I took the comfortable chair nearest him, stretched out my legs, sat back and waited.

'I'd like to ask you a few questions and I want you to answer frankly.'

'Sure.' Now maybe I'd learn what was behind this deal.

He took off his glasses and placed them carefully on the table. 'Our information is that you are the personal pilot of Mr Kelly, an American oil man? Is that so?'

'Yes.'

'Then tell me, Mr Gibson, why did you defect to Biafra with a Nigerian jet bomber? Surely that's not going to advance your employer's prospects of obtaining oil concessions from the Federal Government?'

'I came to the conclusion that there was no hope of his ever obtaining the concessions he'd been promised, so when somebody made me a proposition to bring the Delfin over, I accepted. It's as simple as that.' I spread my hands, leaned back, and smiled. I might as well have smiled at a shark for all the response I got. The thin lips were a straight line slashed across his face.

He fiddled with his glasses while he thought that over, then asked softly. 'Is Mr Dakis a friend of yours?'

'I'd rather say a business acquaintance. Why?'

Azikwe sat up stiffly in his chair. 'Because, Mr Gibson, several weeks ago we received a letter from Mr Dakis. He said that there was a possibility that he would be able to persuade you to defect with one of the Nigerian aircraft. He also made other suggestions as to how we should deal with you.'

I considered his last remark carefully. Somewhere, something was out of place. I picked my words carefully. 'He paid me to defect with the Delfin. I flew it to Uli.'

Azikwe shrugged. 'Maybe that's not the whole story. We are not concerned with the financial arrangements between Mr Dakis and yourself . . .' He replaced his glasses and pressed a bell. 'Your case will be thoroughly investigated and you will be interrogated later. There is a great deal that requires further investigation.' He stood up as two soldiers entered. 'Put him in cell fourteen. That will be all.' He sat down and began dialling the telephone as the soldiers took me away. Sandwiched between them, they took me farther down the passage. At the end was a heavy wooden door, with number 14 painted roughly above it. The front soldier slid the key into the lock, and stepped aside as the door opened. As I stepped in, the door slammed, and I heard the key turn in the lock. Their footsteps faded away down the passage. So this is it, I thought. I'd give ten years off my life to have Dakis with me in that cell for an hour. It occurred to me that maybe I hadn't ten years left to offer.

There was a grimy washbasin in the corner. My hands were hot and dirty, and my shirt clung to my body in the damp heat. I turned on the tap without result. Angrily I sat on the bed and thought about Dakis. I felt a dull ache in my hands, they were tightly clenched and the knuckles were white.

Slowly I released them and forced myself to relax. I'd been in worse jams than this and walked out of them. One day I'd have the chance to settle my account with Dakis. I stretched out on the bed with its single stained blanket and stared at the twenty-watt bulb burning dimly behind its dirty shield in the ceiling.

Later they switched the lights off. Through the bars I watched the moon come up. It slid gently over the distant hill tops, caressing them with its warm yellow light and while I watched, I wondered what deal Dakis had arranged with the Biafrans.

CHAPTER FIFTEEN

T H R E E monotonous dreary days were to drift past before
I saw the prison Governor, Major Azikwe again. I spent
my time watching the hot humid breeze shuffling the
leaves about the courtyard like a pack of cards. At times
it blew them along in long brown lines like streamers of
smoke. At night it wailed like some lost Irish Banshee
around the walls.

On the second night I watched a line of fire that lay
in a gleaming wreath across the top of a distant hill where
the advancing Nigerians had probably fired the grass to
destroy the cover it afforded the Ibos. Each time it rained
the rain changed the colour of the plaster to a dirty grey
and the green mould stains, that splashed the lower sections,
brightened.

Each morning I watched the sun flare up, burning scarlet
through the mist, and wondered how much longer I had
before the Nigerians drove into Uli.

I learned one fact in favour of military prisons: they
were punctual. Meals were brought twice a day at pre-
cisely the same hour. At nine-thirty the warder would produce a bowl of mashy porridge, handing it carefully through
the door while the guard pointed an old-fashioned shot-
gun in my general direction. They'd repeat the process
at four-thirty when my ration consisted of a bowl of
watery soup with a few green leaves washing around. Even
a toilet at the end of the passage seemed to gargle and then
clear its throat at regular intervals.

On the fourth morning there was a clatter of heels. The
key rattled and a soldier threw the door open and stepped
back. Major Azikwe strode in. He was sweating and his
skin shone dark with moisture. He flashed a set of white

glistening teeth. 'Good morning, Major Gibson. You're looking a little pale.'

'I've got the curse.'

'Pardon? I don't understand.'

'Skip it. What can I do for you?'

He looked at me quizzically. 'Isn't it rather what can I do for you. How are they treating you?'

'I've eaten better. One consolation, I don't have to pay for it.'

He grinned sourly. 'I'm sure you could afford to do so. I've been told that you've made a considerable sum of money since your arrival in the Federal Republic.'

I shrugged. 'I fly for an American oil company, they pay pretty well.'

He waved his hand as if to brush the remark aside. 'I'm not here to waste time. We've been checking up on you since you landed. There is a warrant out for your arrest in Lagos on a charge of murdering a Mr Gobi, a senior government official.' He walked to the window, looked out for a minute, then strolled back and stood over me as I sat on the bed. 'Tell me about the other man you killed in your hotel in Lagos.'

I yawned. 'Why bring that up? I came into my room and found him searching through my effects. I tried to grab him and he jumped out of the window. He forgot that my room was on the second floor. The Nigerian police accepted my explanation.'

Azikwe sneered. 'Because it suited them. The man you killed was a French intelligence operative, working on our behalf. You flew Gobi to Wakki and took certain maps from the offices of the French company. The agent, Le Clarry, was an experienced operator. Such men don't jump out of windows, Mr Gibson.'

'Perhaps he was due for a refresher course,' I ventured hopefully. 'Anyway, surely the delivery of one brand new Delfin jet is worth a French spy and a Nigerian politician?'

Azikwe looked at me sourly. 'Maybe. It is not for me to decide. There are the other allegations against you over which my senior officers are concerned.'

'Such as?'

'The destruction of the B26!'

It was inevitable that it would eventually leak out that I had shot the B26. It was common knowledge round the bars in Lagos. To deny the charge would be futile. 'The Federal Government offered a reward of £20,000 for its destruction,' I told him. 'I patrolled the area where it was operating for a week, until one day I saw it landing and shot it up. That's all there is to it.'

Ibo intelligence had briefed Azikwe well. I wondered uneasily what else they'd told him. I didn't have long to wait.

He threw down his trump card. 'The B26 pilot, Captain Sanders, is a friend of yours I'm told?' The dark almost opaque eyes watched me carefully.

I kept my face blank as the bombshell exploded. One slip on my part, and Tubby would get the chop.

'I knew a Captain Sanders in the Congo,' I said casually. 'Is it the same Sanders?'

'Yes,' Azikwe nodded. 'By a strange coincidence it is the same Sanders. Is that why you waited for the plane to land before destroying it? I'd like you to tell me, but I don't suppose you will.'

'Sure I'll tell you,' I said easily. 'I've nothing to hide. I shot the plane up on the ground because I only spotted the B26 as it was coming in to land. I didn't know Sanders was in Biafra. Had I seen the plane in the air, I'd have shot it down then.'

He waved a hand. 'I'll accept your explanation for the time being. Captain Sanders is flying urgent supplies into Uli at present and we still require his services. But we will investigate the matter further. We Ibos have long memories.'

'There is another matter. Last week a Constellation air-craft with a load of Fouga Magister jet wings, was set on fire at Bissau and completely destroyed. The fuselages had already been delivered by the French. A South African mercenary pilot, one of your colleagues, sabotaged the Constellation for $60,000 paid him by the Federal Government. What can you tell us about that?'

I looked at him blankly. 'I don't know who pulled that one, but you can be sure he's out of the country by this time and holed up somewhere. Anyway, it saved the MIGs the trouble of shooting them down. Fougas are unsuitable for this operation. The last time I saw one was in Katanga. It was alleged to have shot down the aircraft flying Dag Hammarskjöld and his UN team to Ndola in Northern Rhodesia. . . .'

He cut me short, 'I'm not interested in your reminiscences. You will also have to account for the attack you led on our patrol boat. Several of our men were killed and your status was technically that of a civilian. Think about it, Major Gibson.'

'I will indeed,' I said politely. My mother had drummed into me that politeness cost nothing. Looking at the angry Azikwe, I agreed. God help any Nigerian he got hold of. The scars of this war were going to take a long time to disappear. I'd have to try and warn Tubby to watch his step. If the Ibos got any confirmation of our deal he'd be out of the top ten in the popularity polls overnight.

Azikwe continued morosely. 'It would save us a lot of trouble if we handed you over to one of our front line units, with instructions to see you fell into Nigerian hands. What do you think of that suggestion, Mr Gibson?'

'I'll be frank with you, Major. It doesn't appeal to me in the least. I'm sure we can find some more suitable solution. One perhaps, to our mutual benefit?' I rubbed my thumb casually against my forefinger. 'I'm not a poor man.'

He pursed his lips. 'Your past record doesn't inspire me with confidence that working with you is likely to produce any mutual benefits. More likely to be the contrary!'

He walked back to the window and draped his arm across the sill. 'One of the objections to shooting you,' he said conversationally, 'is that you are an ex-RAF officer with a good war record. This would create a great deal of unfavourable publicity against the Biafran Government.'

'Very sound reasoning,' I said approvingly. 'I go along with that argument.'

Ignoring me, he continued. 'On the other hand, Mr Dakis, in a letter to my superiors, stated that you and any other pilots defecting, were to be permanently silenced. Let me explain. He has contracted to supply certain equipment to us, and he states that, you know enough about his business with Lagos to make their delivery impossible if you were released.'

What an unscrupulous bastard the arms dealer was. I remember him saying, you have a guaranteed one-way passage out of Biafra. Now I knew he'd meant feet first in a box! He'd also, very significantly, said, '*Good-bye,* Major Gibson' as he'd driven off.

I got up and walked across to Azikwe. 'The only reason that two-timing bastard wants me shot is because he wants this unfortunate conflict prolonged as long as possible. That's all Dakis cares about.'

He nodded slowly. 'And you have his cheque for defecting, Mr Gibson?'

'Do you think I'm stupid! I posted it at Ikeja Airport before I took the Delfin.' There was no point in saying it had been handed to Gisela.

Azikwe sighed. 'You wouldn't care to tell me how much? Purely as a matter of interest.' The tone was too casual.

Dakis would certainly include my £100,000 payment in his claim to the Biafrans for the Delfin, so I'd drop him nicely in the middle and convince them he was trying a little swindle on the side.

'Fifteen thousand pounds, if you must know,' I said reluctantly, and watched the tiny flicker in his eyes as he thought that one over. I threw out a feeler. 'Money's always useful, don't you think, or are you different from us despised, yet sought after, mercenaries?'

The dark eyes watched me thoughtfully as he stood at the door and turned the handle. 'It depends on whether you're alive to enjoy it, I should say.' He paused. 'The Federal Forces have driven our men back twenty miles on the Eastern Front. One of our best divisions has collapsed, and our territory is now cut in two. The roads are blocked with civilians fleeing for their lives. The vultures have never eaten so well.' Abruptly he slammed the door, keys rattled, then I listened to his footsteps fade down the passage.

I sat on the bed. His news left a sour taste in my mouth. I'd seen the arms pouring into Lagos. For Biafra it was only a matter of time, and time was running out fast, as it was for me. My future, when the Nigerians took Uli, was non-existent, and in Biafran hands, little better. I came to the reluctant conclusion that I'd dealt myself a bad hand when I agreed to the defection. It might have been better to have stayed on and argued the toss with the Nigerian police. I'd always been strong on hindsight. Foresight was another matter. I went to the window, stood on tiptoe, and peered out. The sentry was pacing slowly up and down. After the first glance he took no further notice of me. Maybe I could do a deal with him. I waited till he passed near the window, and beckoned. The son of a bitch scowled, unslung his burp gun, and pointed it menacingly at me, then walked off stolidly, continuing his patrol. I got the message. He wanted no part of Mrs Gibson's little boy.

The wind was blowing in from the north-east. To the

north a lone mountain pushed its long pointed snout into the air as if sniffing the ragged clouds as they blew past, hot from their long journey across the Sahara. The wind sighed as it blew over my face and across the bars. Like a requiem for an old pilot, I thought, in a momentary flash of self-pity.

All the rest of that day it blew continuously. In my imagination I saw the north-easter pressing against the backs of the advancing Nigerians, helping them in their drive to the south-east, towards Uli, and to me.

Despondently I told myself, Cheer up Gibson, things might be worse. So I cheered up and sure enough things got worse. I heard the sound of distant gunfire as the Nigerians drove on towards Uli.

CHAPTER SIXTEEN

As Tubby approached the Biafran coast, the white layer of cloud shining silver in the moonlight, that had stretched unbroken from Sao Tomé, broke up. Ahead, the black land-mass of Biafra, dotted with the red specks of innumerable fires, extended limitlessly to the north, to blend into the wastes of the Sahara. He pushed the throttles of the old rattling DC4 up to maximum continuous cruise power, and listened critically to the increased tempo as he synchronized the four motors. Satisfied, Tubby sat back and dropped the nose slightly, to allow the DC4 to build up speed for the dash across enemy territory as it commenced its long slant down to Uli airstrip.

He glanced across at the young Portuguese co-pilot.

'You heard that two jet intruders were supposed to have flown over Uli last night?'

Luiz dos Santos shrugged. 'Probably Egyptians. I couldn't worry.'

Tubby frowned. 'Negative. You won't find Egyptians flying MIGs over Biafra at night. If they were over, they were flown by mercenaries. That's another story. Especially if they're working on a reward basis.' He smiled at Luiz. 'Believe me, I know some of those characters. For a hundred quid they'd shoot their mothers down.'

Luiz straightened and, leaning forward, rubbed the window with a grubby handkerchief. Mercenaries were another matter altogether.

His rubbing didn't help any. Discoloured and scratched, all the cleaning in the world would never bring the windscreens back to standard. Years of tropical sun and dust had left their mark. Behind them, the green soundproofing had fallen away from the duralumin fuselage and hung down in strips, held in position by the criss-cross of the electrical wiring leading to the cockpit. In places there were brown patches where it had fallen away completely, leaving only the bare metal.

The cockpit smelled of hydraulic fluid and mildew. Each aeroplane, thought Tubby, had its own smell. Rather like women. One day, he'd commission a good industrial chemist to concoct a special line of aeroplane perfumes, to match the planes. Then he'd market them. All the veteran and airline pilots would buy them. He'd name the series 'Air Nostalgic'. There'd be 'M O S Q U I T O ', a blend of cordite, wood glue, and real leather. 'B O E I N G 707' would be a composition of synthetic leather, kerosene, and sweating-packed humanity. If it was a success, he'd expand and extend the series to include hair-oil and after shave lotions.

It would be interesting, he mused, to walk down the long bar at the Royal Aero Club and identify the aircraft flown by sniffing the heads of their pilots amongst the assembled drinkers. Provided, of course, the alcohol fumes permitted.

Luiz broke his reverie, pointing to the earphones beside him. He clamped them on in time to hear Uli Control's repeat call.

'Tango Quebec. Do you read?'

He picked up the mike. 'Tango Quebec. This is Zulu Echo. Check mode three and channel zero four.'

The tower came right back. 'Mode three serviceable and channel zero four approved.'

'We're cleared to land on runway three four,' Tubby said to Luiz. 'Keep an eye open for the runway lights. They'll come on any minute.'

He turned to line up with the runway as the lights blinked on, so close together that from six thousand feet they looked like a single line.

Tubby sighed and told Luiz. 'What I do for Biafra. This is my twenty-sixth drop. I reckon my Biafran DFC is long overdue. It's time Ojukwu showed his appreciation. Right, let's have the wheels down, then give me thirty degrees of flap.'

He glanced over the wing instinctively, then settled down on the approach line. Luiz stared at a large bush fire sliding beneath the fuselage. The DC4 was flying through little specks of fire as sparks rose like fireflies through the smoke haze, only to vanish as the prop wash blew them back into obscurity.

Tubby leaned towards him. 'You won't see any intruders down there. This is the time they jump you from up here. Keep looking around. Give me thirty degrees' flap.' Guiltily Luiz depressed the flap handle.

As the flaps bit, the nose dropped into the darkness below the horizon, and the star-spattered sky disappeared above the scratched windscreen, replaced by the yellow runway lights strung out like a string of amber beads as Tubby nosed down for the landing. Turning off well before the end of the runway, he parked between a Super Constellation with French registration and a Portuguese DC3. Farther back, parked deeply in the trees, was a Delfin with Nigerian Air Force markings.

God, he thought, not Gibson. What the hell is going on? Captain Anton, the Biafran Officer commanding Uli airstrip, met Tubby as he came down the steps.

'Good evening, Captain. Have a good trip?'

'No complaints,' Tubby pushed the old baseball cap back on his head. 'What cooks with the Nigerian Air Force Delfin parked back in the trees?' He handed the flight manifest to Anton's adjutant.

Anton glanced around and lowered his voice. 'We've orders not to discuss it, but, confidentially, a mercenary defected with it from Lagos last week.'

'Do you know his name?'

The duty officer hesitated. 'No. Colonel Christopher arrested him immediately. I hear he's in prison.'

'So?' Tubby showed no apparent further interest. 'Where's Colonel Christopher at the moment?'

The duty officer pointed to a DC4 being offloaded a hundred yards away. 'Over there, I think.'

'Thanks. Watch the offloading, Luiz. I'm going to have a chat with Colonel Christopher.' He went off.

As Tubby approached the DC4, Christopher was sitting nearby in his jeep.

He acknowledged the salute with a casual wave of the hand.

'Hello, Captain Sanders. Are they offloading you?"

'Just started.' Tubby waved towards the Delfin. 'I see you've got yourself a new aeroplane.'

Christopher hesitated before replying. 'Yes, Captain,' he said slowly. 'It was flown in by a friend of yours a few days ago. A Major Gibson. I understand that you were in the Congo together.' He watched Tubby intently.

Tubby gulped. 'Good God! I had no idea Gibson was flying for Nigeria.' He watched Christopher warily. 'I thought he was in England.' The palms of his hands were suddenly wet. The words spilled out and were swallowed up in a long silence.

Christopher dropped another bombshell. 'Gibson was the pilot who destroyed the B26 after you landed on the airstrip near Nsukku.'

'What!' Tubby spluttered. 'Gibson! It's incredible.'

Was it imagination or had Christopher stressed the word landed. How much does this bastard know, he wondered. Gibson, he knew, would never have talked voluntarily, but under torture every man had his limits. He registered that Christopher was watching him curiously. 'Why did he defect, Colonel?'

'For money. He also murdered a senior Federal Government official.'

Tubby shook his head in bewilderment. 'Gibson! I can't imagine it.'

'I can,' said Christopher drily. 'Quite easily.' He started up the jeep. 'You'll have to excuse me, Captain Sanders.'

Tubby saluted as he drove off. This, he thought, is the greatest snafu that Gibson has ever perpetrated. A king-sized one! And now it seems they're suspicious about the B26 deal. He pushed his cap on to the back of his head and walked thoughtfully back to the DC4. The sweating, exhausted soldiers finished offloading as Tubby stopped beside the duty officer. 'How's the situation up in the front lines?'

The Ibo captain shrugged. 'I hear it's not good. Thousands of refugees are streaming through and soldiers are beginning to desert from the divisions. God help us if we lose. We'll all be dead. Children and civilians are starving to death. There's heavy fighting around Owerri, and once it falls we have only Uli. If the Feds take Uli that's the end of the war.'

He pointed to the dumb-bell at the end of the runway. 'General Ojukwu's white Constellation parked there is on standby to fly him out of the country. He is still at Owerri, but who knows what will happen next.'

Tubby stared thoughtfully down the field. The position was serious. It would be the end for Gibson if the Nigerians captured him. Also, it seemed the Biafrans had reservations over the B26 affair. He'd think about it on the way back to Sao Tomé. He always thought better when he was flying.

He turned irritably to Luiz. 'Let's get to hell out of here. There's no percentage in hanging around.'

He touched down an hour and a half later at Sao Tomé still trying to work out a solution. How the devil do we get Gibson out of this little jam, he thought worriedly. This one was as bad as they came.

The night was hot and humid on the island and Tubby lay sweating and thinking beneath the mosquito netting. It was almost daybreak before he fell asleep.

He woke tired and bad-tempered. He showered and cursed the tepid water that trickled from the tap. The sky was heating up and the air was still and clammy.

As he walked morosely past the reception desk towards the dining-room, the Portuguese clerk waved. 'A letter for you, Captain Sanders.'

'Thanks.' Tubby looked at the envelope. Bearing Swiss stamps, it was addressed to him in a neat feminine handwriting. Curiously he tore it open. Dated four days previously, it read:

> Apartment 21,
> San Sebastian Building,
> Via Vittorio Veneto,
> Rome

Dear Captain Sanders,

I am the secretary of the Company for which Mr Gibson is flying. I saw him recently in Lagos. He asked me to open an account in your name in a Swiss bank, and pay the sum of £10,000 into it on your behalf. I enclose herewith a bank deposit slip of the Union Bank of Switzerland as proof of payment.

Mr Gibson has left his old job as he couldn't get along with his employer. I was with him the night he gave notice. I hope to see him soon.

> Yours sincerely,
> GISELA GRIFFIN

Breakfasting on a piece of tough garlic-impregnated steak capped with a stale egg, Tubby considered the letter. First, it had been necessary for Gibson to get out of Lagos in a hurry. Hence the hi-jacking of the Delfin. Secondly, he must trust this Griffin girl or he'd never have given her the money. Gibson wasn't the type to hand large sums of money to just anyone.

The fact that she'd deposited his share of the B26 lolly

was proof enough of her honesty, he reasoned, so he'd be justified in cabling her and putting her in the picture.

Tubby chewed the tough steak thoughtfully, then made up his mind. Pushing the plate aside, he walked out of the hotel and headed for the little stucco shack that served as the local post office. On a cable form he carefully printed Gisela's name and address and wrote :

'John held in prison at Uli, Biafra stop Am investigating stop Will inform you any developments stop Thanks your letter and contents. Suggest you bring £10,000.

> C/o World Council of Churches,
> Tubby Sanders,
> Sao Tomé.

He wondered if the Portuguese censor would pass the cable. There was no harm in trying. He decided to spend the morning on the beach. The majority of the flying crews forgathered there, and maybe he'd pick up some information about Gibson. Collecting his costume at the hotel, he thumbed a lift to the beach. All that morning he circulated amongst the crews, but by midday, when the scorching sun drove everyone off the white burning sands, he had learned nothing.

Tubby came to the reluctant conclusion that he'd have to go back to Colonel Christopher and probe a little further. Unfortunately, he wasn't scheduled to take a load in to Uli for another three or four days.

He hoped, for Gibson's sake, the Biafrans would hold out at Owerri. Once the Nigerians took it, Uli would be the next target on their list of priorities. For Gibson, the final ordeal would be unthinkable. He had no doubt that his fate would be, as African states liked to phrase it, to be 'spectacularly punished'.

Tubby realized his hands were shaking as he made for the pub to swallow a much needed double whisky.

CHAPTER SEVENTEEN

S I X days passed before I saw Christopher. I knew, because each day I'd scratched a mark below the window with my thumb nail. From the warders I heard that the Delfin now flown by a Rhodesian mercenary, had carried out a number of strikes at Calabar and Port Harcourt, destroying on the ground a twin jet Ilusyin bomber, two MIG 17s, a DC4 and a DC3. Biafran morale was brutally lowered when a NAF MIG, piloted by a white mercenary, strafed the bushy area surrounding the Uli airstrip. The well-hidden heavily-camouflaged Delfin was hit in the fuel tank by a forty millimetre shell and immediately exploded.

They told me a Swede, Count von Rosen, had supplied a number of Minicon light aircraft fitted with twin rocket pods, but I knew the punch they supplied was feeble in comparison to the jets of the NAF. In any event, they'd arrived too late to have any noticeable effect on the course of the conflict.

It was on the fourth day that I'd heard the big guns again. I was standing by the window watching the afternoon light fade. There had been a shower earlier, and the trees beyond the broken-glass topped wall were dark green and shone where they had been polished by the rain.

Now the sentry no longer tramped enthusiastically up and down beneath my window. For the last couple of days he had sat dejectedly against the gatepost. Hearing the rumble of the guns, he scrambled to his feet, tilting his head as he listened. The wind suddenly veered to the north and the hot air bled into my cell, sweeping the sound of cannon fire clearly along. As I listened, I knew the heavy 122-mm Russian cannon I'd seen offloaded at Lagos, were shelling Owerri. Then the wind dropped and the long sustained rumbling died away, leaving only the silence.

Soon, I thought, there'd be nothing left to justify the bloodshed. Excepting the oil of course, buried thousands of feet beneath the red Nigerian soil, and now guarded by the dead soldiers of both sides who slept peacefully just beneath the surface.

Later the wind rose again but the guns had ceased firing. Tubby must have seen the Delfin some time at Uli. He'd have to be discreet with his enquiries to avoid compromising himself. I knew, somewhere out there, he'd be battling to get me out of this jam. It had better be soon. With the introduction of the 122-mms on the scene, the Biafrans' situation was deteriorating fast. It wouldn't be long before the curtain dropped, on both Gibson and Biafra. Come on, Tubby, I urged, get weaving and get me out of here.

About two hours before sunset I heard footsteps stamp down the passage and stop at the door. The key rattled and a soldier stood aside for Christopher to enter. He kicked the door shut and marched across to where I sat on the bed. The visit was apparently a social one. He waved a bottle of brandy at me as he approached. Judging by the smell, he'd got himself a good headstart.

He sat on the bed and thrust the bottle at me. 'Mr Gibson, have a drink.' He smiled. 'Sorry. No glasses, you'll have to drink out of the bottle.'

'That's no hardship. Thanks.' I tilted my head back and let the equivalent of three good tots pour down my neck before I took the bottle away. Handing it back to Christopher, I clung to the edge of the bed and waited for the pure liquid fire to extinguish itself amongst my gastric juices. I gasped, watching him put the bottle to his mouth and sink about a third of the contents in one long swallow. He calmly placed the bottle on the floor between us, and wiped the back of his hand across his mouth. 'You heard the guns?' he asked conversationally.

'Yes. I saw six 122-mm Russian cannon being unloaded at Lagos a couple of weeks back. Seems they've arrived.'

He nodded glumly. 'Yes. I think it's all over. General Ojukwu left this afternoon in his personal Constellation complete with his white Mercedes. Most of the pilots at Sao Tomé are now refusing to fly into Uli, and the majority of my airport labourers have deserted. I have to use soldiers to get the supplies offloaded. Azikwe tells me that he has received no instructions from the Ministerial Council regarding your release.' He shrugged. 'The Nigerians will be here soon. There's no doubt they will shoot you. If the matter were in my hands I would release you but I have no authority over Azikwe.'

He picked up the bottle and offered it to me politely. 'Would you care for another drink?'

'I sure would.' I sipped nervously and handed it back. Christopher downed another healthy slug and belched loudly.

I resumed the conversation. There was no time for niceties.

'The Nigerians shooting me won't benefit either you or Major Azikwe, I have money in Switzerland. Lots of money. Surely we can work something out? What's your future under a Federal Government? I'll tell you, a Nigerian firing squad.'

He stood up. 'I'll disappear into the bush until it's safe to come back. To hell with Azikwe. It's useless to try and reason with him. He has six soldiers guarding the prison and is a dedicated fanatic. His family were killed by the Hausas in the north. He'll maybe even shoot you himself before he leaves the prison.' Swaying slightly, he saluted. 'I'll leave you the bottle. Sorry there's only a little left, Mr Gibson.'

At the door he paused. 'It doesn't matter now, but did Captain Sanders co-operate with you in the destruction of the B26? Purely as a matter of curiosity, and off the record.'

It was still possible that Tubby might be landing at Uli.

'I had no idea he was flying the plane,' I lied.

'Good-bye, Mr Gibson.' A flash of white teeth and the door slammed.

As his footsteps receded I went to the window and looked out on to the small courtyard. The top of the surrounding wall was studded with broken bottles embedded in the cement. A new sentry, in jungle uniform, patrolled slowly across the yard, then leaned against the gate that opened into the street. Beyond, the corrugated iron roofs of stores and houses shone dull grey in the setting sun.

Three heavy bars spanned the cell window. Putting my feet against the wall, I pulled hard, more as a matter of principle than with much hope of feeling any movement. I might have spared myself the trouble.

I heard the sentry yell at me and looked out. He was a few yards away, his automatic rifle pointed at the window. I gave him the V sign and sat on the bed. The situation could, I thought, be a lot better. It was a pity about Gisela. Maybe we could have worked something out together. If I had paper and a pen I'd write her a letter. Not that she'd ever get it. The Nigerians, on both sides, had been so shot up and obsessed with exterminating one another that, by this stage, nobody would be friendly enough to post a letter for me. I couldn't blame them.

Still, it seemed an awful waste having all Dakis's money over in Switzerland and not being able to spend any of it myself. I hoped Gisela would enjoy it.

*

As the long day bled slowly away, I watched the massed banks of clouds driving in from the Atlantic, coalesce and break up, only to be followed by the never-ending fresh legions behind them. Later they shone golden as the sun dropped into the sea. As the sky darkened a gentle mist was born. Silently, the white dampness built up, in and around the courtyard, the surrounding trees lost their shapes and became strange surrealistic paintings of trees splashed silver by the moon shining through the misty haze.

There was the sound of distant sporadic rifle fire as the Nigerians tested the Biafran defences. It wouldn't be long before they broke through. I was glad that I'd given the money to Gisela, but there'd be no celebration for us at the Bibliothèque night club as we'd planned.

I thought about the good nights we'd spent together in Lagos. Perhaps, with more time together, the inevitable boredom would have set in. Still, I'd have liked to have put it to the test. All in all, I mused, I'd had a good run for my money and there was still a one in a hundred chance that I'd get away with the defection. Then I recalled Gobi as I last saw him, murdered in his villa, and I stepped up the odds to a thousand to one. All I hoped was that the end, when it came, would be quick.

The flight with the Delfin from Lagos to Uli had been good. I saw again the blue lightning flashing and jumping between the great white cloud canyons as I sped between them, and how the moonlight had silvered the moisture-covered wings when I broke through, to fly over the black carpet of land below, speckled with its red roses of flames that was Nigeria at war.

The drumming of an aircraft, the first I'd heard for two days, jerked me back to reality. If flying had restarted, maybe the Ibos had succeeded in pushing the Federal forces back or were at least containing them. The faint spark of hope that I'd thought was extinguished, flickered. This waiting, I told myself, is killing me. I grinned at the irony.

Maybe the plane had flown in from Sao Tomé or Libreville. I listened carefully, trying to distinguish between the high pitched whine of a Constellation dragging itself along in fine pitch towards the runway and the deeper rumble of the DC4s and 6s as they droned into Uli.

I couldn't be sure, but it sounded like a DC4. Stop kidding yourself, I told myself wearily. You've had it and that's all there is to it. I flopped on the bed and listened to the new-born wind rustling the trees in the courtyard as it playfully chased the mist through the trees. Whoever was flying around up there had probably prayed for just such a wind to blow the mist away. The wind strengthened and howled through the bars in a final gust, then died away. The far-off drone of the circling aircraft sounded oddly peaceful. Then the engine sound died and a deep silence wrapped shroud-like round the prison. Once I heard an owl hoot sadly, almost as if in a lament for the fate of the tragic Ibo rearguard. Then suddenly the night exploded. The silence was rent by the angry bark of heavy weapons raining shell after shell on the final strongholds around Uli of the encircled Ibos. The heavy Nigerian artillery was closing in for the kill.

I walked to the window and watched the red glare in the sky as the artillery fired. For the first time in my life I despaired, and I knew there was no longer any percentage in clinging to the vague hope that Tubby would be able to get me out. The time had come to abandon hope and face up to the fact of my inevitable recapture by the Federal forces.

CHAPTER EIGHTEEN

TUBBY eyed the disembarking passengers with a jaundiced eye. A group of OAU delegates, with their status-symbol horned-rimmed glasses and black briefcases were straggling down the steps. They'd probably arrived, he surmised sourly, to ensure that the last minute armaments some governments had despatched to Biafra would not be delivered. Once again, too little too late.

Several women were mingled in the crowd. He wondered which was Gisela. To interest Gibson she'd have to be a looker. He pushed the old baseball cap on the back of his head, mopped his forehead, and thought about the news on the radio that morning. It hadn't been good. The Biafran leader, Colonel Ojukwu, was reported to have fled to Gabon. The Ibos had always sworn they would fight to the end. Maybe he had only left on a temporary visit. Who knew what the hell went on?

He looked at the silent row of obsolete weather-beaten aircraft on the opposite side of the field. The lifeline of the embattled Ibos. A hell of a lifeline he thought. Half the old heaps should have been pensioned and put out to grass ten years ago. Only the skill of their pilots who nursed them along kept them airborne. Encouraged by the money, of course.

If Uli landing strip, now encircled by the Nigerian ring of steel, was cut off, then the Nigerian war was over. At the most, only a few days of last-ditch fighting was possible, and that was going to be a bloody massacre when all the old hates and debts would be paid off.

He looked at his DC4. The three-tonner was pulling away and the refuelling squad were clambering over the wings. The load of medical supplies and food would be his passport if he landed there tonight and found the Nigerians in possession. No arms this trip. Being caught with them on board meant ten years in a Federal prison, unless some victory-crazed Nigerian gave him a hosing down with one of their Russian tommy-guns.

It would have to be tonight if he was to try and get Gibson out. This was almost certain to be his last flight into Uli. God help John, with his record of defection, if the Federal troops caught up with him.

He swung his attention back to the disembarking passengers. They all disappeared into the customs immigration hall and now the polite Portuguese officials, in their clean white tropical uniforms, were processing them and trying at the same time to sort out the one or two inevitable Nigerian agents.

Heels clicked on the cement floor behind him and he swung round. A tall dark girl, in a severely-tailored beige suit was hurrying towards him. She looked tired and drawn. She looked at him anxiously.

'Mr Sanders? They told me that you were out here.'

Tubby rose and took her hand. Her grip, he registered, was almost masculine, firm and brief.

'Yes. Glad to meet you, Gisela. Sit down.' Taking her arm he led her to a nearby table and watched her flop wearily on to a chair.

'Any news of John?'

'None. I'm going in tonight with a Red Cross load. I'll try to get him out. I propositioned the local aerodrome control officer on my last trip. Offered him ten thousand pounds.' Gisela's fists were clenched. The knuckles were white, Tubby observed. This girl, he thought, had quite a thing going for John. The lucky bastard always could find them. Gisela was talking again, as she opened her handbag and began to fumble.

'I've brought the money. Swiss francs.'

'For God's sake. Not here. Give it to me later.'

Her face was strained. 'Time's so short. The paper said last night that Ojukwu has fled. We must get John out tonight.' She was on the verge of breaking down.

He leaned across and took her hand. 'Take it easy. With that money I should be able to buy most of the Ibos in Biafra, especially at this late stage in the game.'

The large hazel eyes watched Tubby hopefully. 'You mean it, you're not saying it to cheer me up?'

Tubby drew a finger across his chest. 'Cross my heart,' he said easily. God help me for being a lying bastard, he thought.

Gisela sighed and relaxed a little. 'Could I come with you tonight?'

Tubby stiffened. 'You crazy? There'll be shooting, looting and a little raping thrown in for good measure around that airport tonight. You'd only be safe as long as the Ibo soldiers were guarding the strip. Once they go it'll be plain hell. I know. I've been through this scene before in the Congo.'

'But perhaps I could appeal to this Biafran official you mentioned. After all, I am a woman.'

'Forget it. You've ten thousand reasons in your handbag. Every one of them is a better reason than any single one you can advance.' He grinned. 'Please don't think I'm not chivalrous.'

A tear shone in the corner of her eyes. 'I still think I might be able to help.'

'Negative. Please believe me.' He took her arm gently. 'There's no accommodation available at the moment, but you can have my room tonight and I'll try and get you fixed up tomorrow. You can help this way. If I'm not back by dawn tomorrow, you wait a day, then get to Lagos and report to the British Consul that Gibson and I are at Uli. He may be able to do something. I doubt it. But at least it will be encouraging to know when we're inside.' He stood up. 'Come on, I'll take you along to the room. Then I have to leave you while I check the plane.'

Gisela nodded wearily. 'Thanks, Tubby. John's lucky to have a friend like you.'

They passed through the traffic hall with the long baggage tables and the porters in the corners curled up and sleeping peacefully into the silent humid night. Across the strip the parked aircraft shone dully metallic in the lights cast from the control tower. The white rotating beacon's light washed regularly across them.

Tubby led Gisela down the long passage to his room.

'No doubt the management will think the worst,' he said as he shut the door.

'I'm too worried to care.' She sat on the foot of Tubby's bed, rummaged in her handbag and produced a small bundle wrapped in white paper. She held it towards him. 'The money. It's in 1,000-franc notes.'

Tubby slipped it into his hip pocket. 'Thanks. I'll leave you now. I'm due to take off in two hours. I'll be at the aircraft. You can stroll down later and have a look if you feel like it.'

Gisela smiled gratefully. The lines of strain vanished and for a moment she was very beautiful. 'Thanks.'

Tubby closed the door quietly behind him. John, the lucky bastard, has got himself a winner there, he thought. That is, if he ever lives to see her again. Morosely he went down the passage and avoided the noisy bar to head across the runway to the DC4. It was an hour and a half later that Gisela heard Tubby's voice as she walked across the strip.

'Why the hell isn't the freight tied down properly? Get hold of the baggage master. I'll kill the bastard. I've warned you before.'

He was standing at the head of the portable stairway. She climbed the steps towards him.

'Hello, Tubby. I came to say good-bye and wish you luck.'

'Thanks.' He was curt. 'I have to report to the tower,

then I'm taking off. The more time I have at Uli tonight the better.'

She was a shape in the darkness. She fumbled in her bag. 'I've a pistol here, a small .25. I thought you might like to borrow it.'

Tubby shuddered. 'That's all I'm short of. If they catch me with any arms, they'll shoot me at once. In any event I'd never take a .25. I'd take a Sten and half a dozen clips of ammo. Your heart's in the right place, honey, but your ideas of warfare are out of date. Tonight I'll go in naked arms-wise, without even the old rusty knuckle dusters I picked up in the Congo.' He chuckled. 'Excuse me, I must go.' He patted her shoulder. 'See you about daybreak.'

He ran down the steps and headed for the control tower. Thoughtfully Gisela watched him go. There was no one in the immediate vicinity. She slipped into the cabin and headed towards the tail section. The toilet door was open. She slid in and locked it behind her.

*

The Portuguese flying controllers eyed Tubby curiously as he walked into the control room of the tower, noisy with the crackle and static from the loudspeakers grouped over the map-strewn operations table. A confused babble of voices filled the room.

The senior three-stripe controller raised his voice, 'Are you serious about taking off for Uli?' He nodded towards the speakers. 'It seems as if all hell has broken loose. The air is full of new call signs tonight. It sounds as if there's another push building up. It will probably be the last. You can't be serious about going, Captain.'

'Yes, I am,' said Tubby irritably. 'Can you raise Uli, on short wave? Is the tower there still in one piece? What's cooking there?'

The Portuguese had difficulty following Tubby's peculiar pilot's English.

'The Council of Churches has phoned, cancelling all their flights as they are unable to contact Uli. Do you still think it's wise to go, Captain?'

'No, it's bloody stupid, but I'm going. I have to bring someone back. Can we try the Uli frequency?'

He watched impatiently as the controller carefully selected the VHF frequency. Uli, he knew, was out of range but there was the possibility that a high flying aircraft trying to contact Uli control would come through. There was only the crackle of static. The usual lively frequency was silent.

Leaving the tower and the sceptical controllers, he walked hurriedly across to the DC4. There was no sign of Gisela. She must, he thought, have returned to the hotel. He ran up the steps to the cabin door. Two of the handling crew were waiting.

'Get the bloody steps away,' he barked.

'What about the co-pilot?'

'I'm not taking one tonight. Get the steps away.'

He watched them drag them away and listened to the usual spasmodic squeaks as the crew pushed heavily. Why the hell don't the lazy bastards grease the wheels, he thought angrily. The damn' thing's been squeaking like that for weeks and they do nothing about it.

He slammed the cabin door and groped his way forward towards the cockpit, now as dark as a dungeon. The thought depressed him and he shivered as he scrambled into the captain's seat and switched on the blue indirect lighting. Tubby hurriedly began to run through the starting-up check list. Without a co-pilot it was a slow process. Methodically he checked each item, then reaching up engaged the no. 3 motor. Ten minutes later he informally called the tower.

'Sao Tower from Three Tango Echo. Ready to roll.'

The correct precise tones of the senior controller came

back disapprovingly. He was, Tubby knew, a stickler for correct radio procedure.

'You are cleared for take off, three Tango Echo. Call again on reaching your assigned operational level.'

Tubby pushed the throttles open. 'Roger,' he said laconically, dropped the mike on to his lap and thundered down the runway. It was an hour and a half to Uli, he thought morosely. It was going to be one of the longest flights he had ever made. An hour and a half to sit and sweat it out.

An hour later he hit the coast. From ten thousand feet the Nigerian countryside was spotted with the glow of hundreds of man-made fires. Ahead, the cloud had broken at the coast and the sky was a blaze of light with the glow of the glittering stars looking down on the funeral pyre of dying Biafra.

For the twentieth time Tubby twirled the tuning knob of the VHF set, tuning it back and forth over the two Uli frequencies. In the past hour there had not been a single call either to or from the tower. It was almost as if the once proud state of Biafra had decided to die in silence.

He eased back on the throttles and the regular roar of the Pratt and Whitneys died to a contented murmur as he dropped the nose just below the black line of the horizon and the DC4 sighed into a steady descent.

He picked up the transmitter. If Uli was already in Nigerian hands he wondered if they'd give him the runway lights. Getting down on the DC4's landing lights only, with no co-pilot to watch the instruments and give him the approach speeds, was going to be tricky.

He knew the Biafran controller's voice, and was sure he'd recognize it. What the hell did it matter anyway. There was only one way to find out if Uli had been captured. Go in and land.

The tenseness left him. Calmly he checked the landing code for the fourth time and gave the call sign for the day.

'Bravo Charlie. Bravo Charlie, Bravo Charlie from Three Tango Echo. Check mode three and channel zero four.'

He knew he was within twenty miles of the runway. He stiffened as he looked out ahead. Dozens of fires were raging, and occasionally there was the white flash of an explosion, erupting in a shower of sparks. He called again : 'Bravo Charlie, from Tango Echo. Come in please.'

The speaker clicked twice then vibrated into life. 'This is Bravo Charlie, Tango Echo. Hallo Tubby. Not advisable to land here. Uli is being shelled and mortared. Return to your base immediately.'

Christ, Tubby thought, the position must be bloody serious. The controller had completely dispensed with the code, operating in the clear.

'Negative. Switch on your runway lights,' Tubby spoke rapidly. 'I'm coming in.'

There was a long silence, then, 'Standby. Tango Echo.'

Angrily Tubby triggered the mike. 'Come on. What's the difference if the runway lights give your position away? You're already under attack.'

Then suddenly, twin rows of lights formed the familiar pattern. Tubby disconnected the auto-pilot hurriedly and the engines popped loudly as he throttled back. Rolling steeply left, he slammed the landing gear lever hard down, hearing the familiar grinding noise as the legs strained against the slipstream into position. Selecting full wing-flaps he spiralled earthwards as if he was once again flying Spitfires. The strip loomed closer, the numerous fires flashing red as if warning him away. To port, tracers scudded across the countryside like thousands of white mice in frantic flight.

'Three Tango Echo, what is your position?' The controller's voice was calm, now he'd accepted the landing. 'On final approach now. Is Colonel Christopher still there?' He mentally crossed his fingers.

'Affirmative. Tango Echo.'

Tubby pressed hard on the left pedal to stay in line with the lights. He selected landing lights and watched the beams cut twin smoke-filled paths through the air. He hauled back on the yoke, the tyres screeched once as they shred rubber and the faithful DC4 settled gently on to the tar.

The runway lamps died as Tubby hit the brakes, maintaining direction on the DC4's landing lights to the dumbbell at the end of the runway. He lined up for an immediate take off, then cut the motors, moved his seat back and switched off the battery master. The lighted dials snapped into darkness like a line of eyelids closing in unison.

Tubby stretched momentarily, then groped his way from the cockpit. At the doorway, he sniffed the air, stopped suddenly and froze. Perfume, Gisela's perfume, his nose told him.

Her shape made a vague form in the darkness. 'Forgive me, Tubby,' she said softly. 'But I just had to tag along.'

Rage swept him. He felt his face flush and there was a throbbing in his temples. 'Forgive you!' he shouted. 'You stupid bitch, do you know what you've done?' He took an angry step towards her. 'Now get back into that bloody toilet and lock yourself in. And hope to Christ the soldiers don't find you and rape you. It would serve you bloody well right.' He watched her dart back into the toilet. Then, squatting on the floor beside the cabin door, he unfolded the aluminium concertina steps and dropped them to the ground. As they touched, Christopher came scrambling up from out of the surrounding darkness.

'Captain Sanders. We were told that there would be no more planes.'

'You're right. There won't be. This is the last.'

There was no time to indulge in a diplomatic approach. Tubby spoke bluntly. 'I came for another reason tonight, apart from flying in the supplies. That was only the cover.'

Christopher turned resignedly to Tubby. 'Whatever it is, it's too late. The Nigerians will be here tomorrow. General Ojukwu has already left so that other senior officers can negotiate with the Federal Government and possibly obtain better terms. Tomorrow is the end of Biafra. Of all of us.'

Tubby took his arm. 'Not all of us. Not of you either, if you listen. The other reason why I flew in tonight is that I want to get Gibson out of jail before the Nigerians get him. I knew him in the Congo. He was a friend of mine, and I don't propose to leave him to the Nigerians. If they get their hands on him they'll cut him into little pieces.'

Christopher stiffened. 'What you ask is treachery.' His hand flashed to the heavy Luger and it pointed steadily at Tubby. 'You have been paid to fly for Biafra, and now you want to try and rescue a man who has bombed and machine-gunned our troops, Who destroyed our B26 bomber on the ground. The bomber flown by you.' He stabbed savagely at Tubby with the Luger. 'I've always wondered about Gibson locating your B26 so conveniently. Now I know. You arranged it between you. I ought to shoot you.'

'You're crazy,' said Tubby easily. 'Gibson's a wealthy man and I reckoned that he'd make it worth my while to get him out.'

'You lie,' said Christopher bitterly. 'With you mercenaries Biafra never had a chance. Vultures tearing at our carcass!' Behind Christopher Tubby watched as a dark shadow moved silently up.

Gisela's voice was steady. 'This is a gun in your back, Colonel. If you shoot, I'll shoot you.'

Christopher froze. Tubby sighed. 'Relax, Colonel. The lady behind you is Gibson's fiancée. She flew out here tonight hoping she could help get him released. Without my knowledge, until I landed,' he concluded.

Christopher took a deep breath and moved slightly.

Gisela's voice was taut. 'Don't move, Colonel. I'm warning you. Your war means nothing to me; but if it will help John Gibson I'll shoot you now.'

Tubby slowly raised his hand. 'Wait a minute before we all get too excited. All this shooting talk is not going to get us anywhere. Let's behave like reasonable people.'

There was a brief silence, then Gisela spoke. 'What do you suggest.'

'That you stop pointing that pistol at Colonel Christopher and he puts his back into the holster where it belongs. The Colonel is hot-headed, but he will listen to what I have to tell him now he's calmed down.'

'And if he doesn't.'

'He will,' Tubby said quietly. 'Now, be a good girl.'

Slowly Christopher slid the Luger back into the holster. Tubby moved to his side, held out his hand to Gisela, and took the pistol gently from her. He offered it butt first to Christopher. 'Take it, if it will make you feel any happier.'

Christopher waved it away. 'Keep it.'

Tubby dropped the small .25 into his pocket. 'Thanks. Now can I try and talk some sense into your excitable head?'

'What do you have to say? What can you say? We have lost.' Christopher's voice was flat and expressionless.

Tubby shook his arm savagely. 'Listen, man. As a senior officer the Nigerians will probably shoot you. In any event there is no future for you in a Nigerian-controlled state. Help me get Gibson out and it's worth £10,000 to you. Gisela brought the money. You can fly back to Sao Tomé with us. Come back to Nigeria when the dust has settled. You really have no alternative. Stay here and you die.'

Christopher spoke slowly. 'Major Azikwe would never agree.'

'For half the ten thousand I say he will agree. I'll throw in a free passage out into the bargain.'

Christopher shook his head. 'He is a fanatic. If I were to make such an offer he would shoot me and Gibson as well. I heard this morning that he wants to shoot all the prisoners.'

Tubby shook Christopher's arm again. 'Get wise. It's Azikwe or yourself. Do I have to spell it out for you?'

'There are guards at the prison,' said Christopher slowly.

'How many?'

'A few, maybe six.' He looked hopefully at Tubby. 'Maybe they have already deserted? Many of my soldiers have.'

'There's only one way to find out. Get your jeep and bring me a burp gun. Tell your soldiers to get the plane unloaded fast. Divide the food up amongst them. It doesn't matter. Quick, man.' He pushed Christopher towards the steps and turned to Gisela, handing her the pistol. 'Get back into the toilet and for Christ's sake lock it and stay there. If you go running around you'll end up by being raped.' He pushed her towards the back of the cabin and ran down the steps. Christopher's soldiers were already pushing the heavy mobile steps towards the door as he passed them and scrambled into Christopher's jeep. 'You got a gun for me?'

'In the back.'

Groping, Tubby reached for it. It was an Israel Uzzi. He knew them from the Congo. Reliable with a high rate of fire. He slid back the cocking handle as Christopher pulled away.

'What are you going to do?'

Tubby leaned forward watching the road ahead, the gun cradled in his arm.

'Shoot every son of a bitch who stops me trying to get Gibson out, and you'll be shooting right along with me. It's as much your party now as mine. We'll either get back to the plane with him or we'll all be dead.'

Christopher changed down and accelerated brutally around a corner at the end of the strip.

'Captain Sanders,' he said, 'you make sense.' He jammed the throttle down savagely against the floor boards and the jeep leaped forward. Fifteen minutes later Christopher skidded to a halt in front of a long grey building. A dim yellow lamp burned over the deserted entrance.

'The prison,' he said, grabbing his pistol with Tubby a pace behind him. Slowly, cautiously, they walked into the building. To the left, in a small room off the passage, a light burned. The door was ajar. Christopher, holding his pistol loosely against his leg, walked in. Major Azikwe was standing at his filing cabinet. The desk was cluttered with files. He looked suspiciously at Christopher.

'What do you mean by coming into my office with that pistol, Colonel?' He looked at Tubby and the Uzzi barrel casually covering him. 'Who is this man? What do you want?'

Tubby pointed to the rack beside the door with its line of keys hanging below the numbers. 'The key, please, of Mr Gibson's cell. We've come to take him away.' He smiled at Azikwe and now the Uzzi no longer pointed casually. It was aimed directly at the major's stomach.

Azikwe took a step towards Christopher. 'You are under arrest. Put that pistol down.' Hand outstretched he moved closer. Slowly, almost regretfully, Christopher brought up the pistol and shot him in the face. He watched impassively as Azikwe fell beside his desk, splattering the files with his brains and blood, standing motionless watching the body.

'What the hell is the number of Gibson's cell?' Tubby's urgent voice jerked him round.

'Fourteen.' Christopher reached across the body and grabbed the key.

'Hurry,' said Tubby. 'The guards may have heard the shot.' Together they ran down the passage.

CHAPTER NINETEEN

I woke to the sharp staccato crack of a pistol shot. It echoed loudly through the prison, followed by the slam of a door and the clatter of heavy boots approaching the cell. I froze as a key rattled in the lock and the door was flung open. Christopher, a .45 Colt in his hand, rushed in. Behind him, clutching a burp gun, was Tubby Sanders.

'Tubby. Thank God.'

He waved the gun. 'Not yet, it's a little soon. I've come to take you home. Let's go.' He made for the door. I was right on his heels with Christopher beside me.

'Did you *have* to cut it so fine? Where does Christopher come in?'

I saw Tubby grin. 'He's on our side. You paid him. No time to talk now.' He grabbed my arm, shoved me forward and we ran down the passage.

In the front office a Biafran officer, the back of his head blown off, lay in a pool of blood beside his desk, his face against the floor. I saw the major's insignia on his shoulders above the rising sun flash of Biafra and knew it was Azikwe, the prison Governor. On a shelf behind him was an FN automatic rifle with a commando type dagger beside it. 'Wait,' I shouted to Tubby. As he paused, I jumped over Azikwe, grabbed the rifle and pushed the knife into the back of my belt. I felt a lot better. I pointed to Azikwe, 'Your work?' I asked Tubby.

'Negative. Our friend here.' He jerked his thumb at Christopher as he ran out the door. I sprinted after him, Christopher was already climbing into a jeep parked across the entrance.

The darkness was momentarily split with the flash of gun fire as a heavy artillery piece again opened up. The crash of the cannon was followed only seconds later by the crump of the exploding shell.

The artillery could not have been more than three or four miles away. The Nigerians had moved them up since I'd heard them earlier that evening.

Tubby leapt into the jeep, started up by Christopher. 'They're shelling the airport. Get in.' Christopher swung the wheel as I jumped into the rear seat. The blood was pounding in my ears as we pulled away.

'Watch it,' said Tubby. 'It's liable to be a little rugged getting back to the airstrip.'

'This kind of ruggedness I can handle.' I pulled back the cocking lever of the FN. 'No one is going to put me back into that cell.'

Christopher gunned the motor and the tyres threw mud and gravel before the treads bit and the jeep shot forward.

I looked back, and saw two soldiers run from behind the building. 'Guards,' I shouted to Tubby. I gave them a short burst and they dived for the ground. I doubted if I'd hit them, but I'd stopped them shooting for the next few precious seconds.

Before they could open fire, Christopher hauled at the wheel. We drifted sideways round a right-angled bend and skidded into the main road. He straightened up and headed towards Uli. I knew it was Uli because the clouds that way were red with the reflected glow of fires.

Several times shadowy figures jumped wildly from the centre of the road for the safety of the verge. I hung on grimly to avoid being flung out, as we tore blindly round the sharp bends.

Tubby twisted round. 'I did a deal with Christopher, to get you out. Gisela came out to Sao Tomé with the money. I've promised to fly him out with us.'

'How much?'

'Ten thousand.'

'I'm cheap at the price.' I saw the flash of his teeth.

'I thought that's how you'd feel about it. Look out!'

An old black pick-up, full of Biafran refugees came charging out of a side street. Before we hit, I yelled, but Christopher was already tugging frantically at the wheel. The front half of the pick-up swung away as the driver tried to avoid us. It was too late. The front near side fender of the jeep struck the pick-up a glancing blow and I braced myself for the crash that would send me through the windscreen into the jungle. I heard screams from the passengers of the pick-up. Then, by some miracle, Christopher scraped past and we were still on the road.

Tubby's frantic bellow: 'Slow down, for Christ's sake,' steadied Christopher.

He eased his foot off the throttle and turned indignantly to Tubby. 'It wasn't my fault,' he protested. 'That bloody fool nearly killed us.'

'Him or the Nigerians, what's the bloody difference? But at least let's get there.'

Tubby slumped back in his seat and stared straight ahead. With the smashed fender we had lost one light. The solitary beam of the offside headlamp shone across the road as we drove on.

Civilians and soldiers were plodding along towards Uli. God knows what they hoped to find there. Some of the soldiers were carrying rough stretchers made of empty sacks, cut down the sides, and bound to roughly cut poles. Most times the arms and legs of the wounded hung down over the end or the sides. I saw one Biafran soldier carrying another along on his back, his head down, trudging unheeding along, silhouetted against the black of the bush by the solitary headlamp. He ignored the jeep, as, hitting a rut, it sprayed a shower of muddy water over him as we hurtled past, leaving him to plod along on his own private Calvary. A Calvary being enacted by innumerable Ibos that night in Biafra over a thousand lonely *Via Dolorosas*, as the Nigerians closed in for the kill.

I leaned forward and shouted at Christopher: 'Where are they heading for? What's the use?'

'They're running for their lives. A man running for his life never gets tired.' He began to slow down as the head-lamp lit up a group of soldiers standing in the centre of the road. They held up their hands for us to stop as the jeep approached.

'Keep going,' Tubby shouted. 'Don't stop.' He grabbed the wheel and swerved past the group as they jumped for the verge of the road. There was a scattered volley of shots as we scraped past. Swinging round I emptied the balance of the magazine of the FN at them, firing in short controlled bursts. The firing stopped.

'Those were Biafrans,' Christopher shouted.

'I don't give a fuck if they were Chinese,' said Tubby. 'We shoot every bastard who tries to stop us.' He slapped Christopher on the back. 'Keep going, Colonel, this is no time for sentiment.'

Ahead the road was bright with the glow of fires as we hurtled towards Uli.

Tubby pointed to the west. 'The dumps are over there. The Biafrans are burning them. The Nigerians will drive in at daybreak when the shelling stops.'

That, I knew, would be the end of Biafra. Without Uli airstrip, and General Ojukwu having fled, the Ibos had had it. Farewell, Biafra. *Bon jour,* Nigeria.

Tubby turned. 'Gisela's waiting at the plane.'

I was stunned. 'What; Gisela here? You must be mad. What the hell? . . .'

He held up his hand. 'She stowed away. I only found her after we'd landed. She thought she could help.'

I sat back. Gisela, I told myself, such a girl happens only once in a lifetime. Ahead the thump of bursting shells was almost continuous as they methodically shelled the airstrip and environs. I saw the flash of the explosions as they bracketed the strip. I thought of the DC4 and

Gisela sweating it out as she waited, and my mouth was dry.

Beside the road the eyes of some small feral animal glowed momentarily red, and hordes of tiny white insects shone white in the beam of the light. Then the road turned and I knew we were on the section of the road that, a few hundred yards on, widened to become the Uli airstrip.

We drove between a line of burning ruined buildings. They must have been storage sheds, because I caught the reek of paraffin and oil fumes. The roofs had collapsed and several bodies lay beside the smouldering embers. Nearby, patches of grass were burning around them. Christopher pulled up just past the smouldering building.

'Where the hell's my guard detail?' he shouted. 'They should be here. I'll take them with us.'

Two figures, rifles at the ready, emerged from behind the building.

'Colonel Christopher,' he shouted at them.

The nearest man raised his rifle. 'Halt,' he shouted. His comrade moved up beside him and they moved warily towards the jeep.

'I'm Colonel Christopher, you bloody fools,' Christopher raged. 'Get down to the plane!'

There was something unnatural about their approach. Tubby also sensed it. I saw him unobtrusively shift his position and slowly bring up his burp gun to cover the nearest man. The other soldier moved up silently beside me. Then I saw their shoulders lacked the Biafran insignia, and remembered I'd emptied the FN at the Biafran roadblock farther back.

'Halt,' said the soldier beside Tubby and began to raise his rifle. Simultaneously Tubby fired the burp gun into him, the muzzle almost touching his body. Cut almost in two he crumpled, fell against the fender and slid into the road.

As the man beside me raised his rifle I smashed the butt of the FN into his face, then dropped it and sprang at him. We fell heavily to the ground with him under me. As he grabbed my throat I reached for the knife at the back of my belt and, as the grip of his fingers tightened, I forced his head back with my left hand and slashed his throat. I felt the blood gush warm on my hands as the knife went in and my hands were sticky and slippery with blood as I scrambled into the jeep. I wiped them on the little seat cushion.

'Go,' Tubby shouted at Christopher, 'and for Christ's sake don't stop again.'

Christopher pulled away and we went slamming down towards the runway.

'Go, man, go!' Tubby shouted.

A scarlet blossom of flame with a black smoke centre suddenly bloomed beside the runway a hundred yards ahead, followed by the deafening 'WHANG' of the explosion.

At the end of the strip, I saw the DC4. It shone with a dull metallic glare under the yellow moonlight. Another shell burst behind us, beside the storage sheds where the Nigerians had tried to hold us up. Now that the Russian 122-mms had found the range, they were methodically shelling the strip and perimeter. Somewhere, someone was spotting the shelling and radioing the results back to the gunners.

Christopher skidded to a stop beside the door of the DC4. Tubby wiped the sweat off his face. 'Looks like we're running out of time. Come and give me a hand with the starting up, I've no co-pilot.'

Gisela was standing in the door as I scrambled up the steps after Tubby. I gave her a brief hug. 'Thanks. We'll still celebrate in Rome.'

Then Christopher was scrambling up the steps and

Tubby was shouting; 'Get a bloody move on! We haven't got all night.'

I ran up to the cockpit and Christopher slammed the doors behind him. Tubby switched on the lights and the old familiar cockpit jumped into view.

We hurriedly applied the boosters, cranking no. 3 engine first, allowing the props to turn through twelve blades before applying the ignition.

Agonizingly, one by one, the engines spluttered and coughed, hesitated, then surged into life.

A shell-burst flamed ahead, but the crack of the explosion was blotted out by the roar of the motors as Tubby rammed the throttles forward up to the stops. Long blue flames jetted from the exhausts as the motors screamed under full power. The DC4 began to gather speed as it moved down the runway. The roar of the four motors boomed back and we passed the ruined shattered buildings that lined the strip. I watched the airspeed indicator needle creep round until it indicated VI, and shouted 'Ninety knots' to Tubby.

There was a thunderous explosion as number three motor beside me blew up, exploding in a shower of red flame and black smoke. We'd either collected a burst from a Nigerian machine-gun or the old over-stressed ill-serviced motor had packed in under the power that Tubby was pulling out of it. The DC4 lurched to starboard.

'Hold it straight,' I screamed. Tubby, his left leg fully extended as he jammed on full port rudder, nodded grimly and twisted the nose gear steering wheel viciously to the left. 'Grab the yoke,' he yelled. 'I can hardly keep the bastard straight.'

I watched the rev counter of the burning motor wind up to 4000 revs as I held on grimly to the crippled ship, trying to coax it off the ground.

'Runaway prop,' Tubby bellowed. 'Now we're in trouble.'

I made a frantic grab for the pitch lever, pulling it hard back into the 'Feather Position', but the overspeeding motor still screamed in the agony of its overrun. The engine oil quantity gauge was moving rapidly towards 'EMPTY.' It would be a matter of a few minues and we'd have a fire to contend with. I wondered when the extinguishers were last checked. Then, with dramatic suddenness, the screaming engine slowed down and the propeller jarred to a halt. Loss of oil had seized the pistons, welding them to the cylinders. Flames poured back over the wing through the cowlings.

Tubby wrestled with the controls, I felt the acceleration drop as the DC4 struggled to get airborne, handicapped by the drag profile of the flat paddle type propeller of the burning engine.

Until the fire from the engine burned through to the fire walls it was useless applying the extinguishers. Their effect would be wasted. The instant the fire burned through to the walls, the alarm bell would sound off, and then would be the moment to hit the extinguishers. I watched the flaming motor with my hand on the extinguisher button, and waited. It was the longest wait of my life. Tubby watched my actions, registering with a brief approving nod. 'Wait for it,' he warned.

Then the alarm bell clanged loudly, and the red fire warning light flashed. I pounded the fire button as the end of the runway came up, and Tubby hauled back on the pole.

As I watched the engine I felt the wheels bump once, lightly, then the flames flickered and died, leaving only a trail of black smoke. The wings bit into the hot humid night air, and Tubby climbed slowly away easing back the throttles to spare the screaming motors. At a thousand feet he levelled out and cautiously reduced the power.

'That,' he said wearily, 'I can do without. I'm getting

too old for all this drama.'

Christopher came forward and stood between us as Tubby slumped back. He looked down at the innumerable small fires burning beneath. 'My country burns tonight,' he said, 'but Biafra will live on in history. Our sacrifices will never be forgotten.'

My eyes were burning and felt full of grit. The tension of the past few days brought on a sharp reaction. I'd had enough of Nigeria, Biafra, and all African wars.

I turned to Christopher. 'Please, go and ask the girl to come up.'

He went back despondently to the cabin.

I pulled down the jump seat as Gisela came up.

I reached across and took her hand, as she sat between us.

'Some time, I'll be able to get around to thanking you, Tubby, and Christopher, for getting me out of there. I never expected to ride out on the last plane from Uli.' I squeezed her hand. 'I'll make up for all the trouble I've caused when we settle down in Rome.'

Tubby leaned across Gisela. 'If you're thinking about setting up house in Rome, how about making it a *ménage à trois,* and including me. Just the three of us, nice and cosy!' He leered at Gisela.

'Negative,' I told him. 'But I'll arrange a *ménage à trois* for you. Dakis, Christopher, and yourself. You can be mister.'

Tubby pursed his lips judicially, then shook his head. 'No thanks, John. Battered old mercenary that I am, I still have my pride.' He sighed and relaxing, sat back, concentrating on the instrument panels as we ploughed steadily through the night to Sao Tomé.

Behind, the fires dwindled to pinpoints, and darkness engulfed the last pitiful remnants of a dying Biafra.

Uli, I thought, would become a lonely ghost-haunted strip, where the sound of aircraft engines overhead at night would no longer be heard, their music diffused and lost in space fading away, plaintive and sad.

Only the little white hot cumulus clouds would look down, as they drifted past on their way to the interior where the hot sun would burn them up and when it rained, the grey mist clouds would weep on Uli as the wind shook the old tattered windsock in a sad salute to the Biafran dead. Then, slowly, like an old forgotten dream, the memories would fade and Nigeria would know peace.